from
I OF THE STORM

• •

I didn't know what to tell them. I knew what I was thinking, but how could I explain it? How could I explain that the hurricane wasn't destroying homes that looked like ours by accident. This hurricane was *looking* for something. And when it didn't find what it searched for, the storm tore everything in its wake to shreds, just like . . .

. . . like a child having a tantrum.

The truth was, Hurricane Zelda wasn't a "Zelda" at all

It was my brother, Jackson.

Also by Neal Shusterman

Novels

Scorpion Shards*
The Eyes of Kid Midas*
Dissidents*
The Shadow Club
Speeding Bullet
What Daddy Did

Story Collections

MINDQUAKES: Stories to Shatter Your Brain*

*Published by Tor Books

MIND STORMS

....

Stories to
BLOW
Your Mind

NEAL SHUSTERMAN

TOR®

A TOM DOHERTY ASSOCIATES BOOK
NEW YORK

This is a work of fiction. All the characters and events portrayed in this book are either fictitious or are used fictitiously.

MINDSTORMS: STORIES TO BLOW YOUR MIND

Copyright © 2002 by Neal Shusterman

Visit Neal Shusterman's Website www.storyman.com

A Tor Book
Published by Tom Doherty Associates, LLC
175 Fifth Avenue
New York, NY 10010

www.tor.com

Tor® is a registered trademark of Tom Doherty Associates, LLC.

ISBN: 0-765-34189-1

First edition: November 1996
First mass market edition: March 2002

Printed in the United States of America

0 9 8 7 6 5 4 3 2

To the Fictionaires,
who are *so* talented it's scary . . .

Acknowledgments

I'd like to thank everyone whose efforts have brought this particular storm to shore.

Many thanks to Terry Black for his invaluable contribution to Midnight Michelangelo; to Veronica Castro, for her tireless hours of work; to Jarrod for a universe of inspiration; and to Jonathan Schmidt, Kathleen Doherty, and everyone at Tor books, who are the wings above my wind.

CONTENTS

· ·

PACIFIC
RIM

• •

YOUR ESCAPE BEGINS HERE.

The sign on the door of the travel agency screams out the words in bold purple letters. I want to believe it, because escape is something I desperately need. So does Mom. Ever since Dad left, Mom's been going on and on about taking a real vacation. Europe maybe, or an African safari.

"I want to do something on the edge," Mom keeps saying, "something special."

I'm all for it. After all, I've lived my whole life in Phoenix, and the farthest away I've ever been was a vacation in Disneyland, which wasn't too adventurous, if you know what I mean. So anything that involves passports and places where they don't speak English would be the best thing as far as I'm concerned.

So Mom and I walk into the travel agency, all wide-eyed and gawking, ready to see the world. The place makes me feel like we're already on vacation. Colorful balloons are suspended everywhere, and loud Caribbean music fills the air with such a contagious beat that I feel like doing the limbo. The staff are all wearing bright Hawaiian shirts, and the walls are plastered with exotic destinations so beautiful that I want to visit every single one of them.

A woman with perfect hair, perfect teeth, and earrings much too big steps up to greet us. "Welcome to Lifetime Travel," she purrs. "How can I help you?"

"We want a vacation," my mom says. "Something *different*."

The travel agent snaps open a drawer and pulls out one brochure after another. "How many will be traveling?"

My mom tries to hide the pain the question brings, but her pursed lips and sorrowful eyes tell all. "Just me and my son, right, Alex?"

I force a weak smile, and the woman looks away. She can't know all the things that happened between Mom and Dad before he left, but she knows enough not to ask any more questions. I suppose she dealt with shattered families like ours before, trying to find a vacation that will somehow, magically, fix everything.

The travel agent fans out the brochures like they're an oversized deck of cards, babbling on about prices and meal plans—but I can tell Mom's not listening. Something's caught her eye. There on the corner of the desk, a brochure sticks out—something the woman didn't seem anxious to show us. There's enough of it visible to show the bow of a boat. Mom pulls it out from beneath the pile. On the cover is a cruise ship, tall and wide, with a least a dozen decks. It's a magnificent thing, with a shiny white hull and ocean-green portholes.

Bright letters across the top of the brochure read pacific rim cruises. The name of the ship is the *Heavenward*. The pages of the brochure are filled with happy people swimming and dancing and eating, in a kind of splendor I can barely even imagine.

The travel agent eyes us warily. "Oh, you don't want that," she says, waving it off. "It's . . . uh . . . out of your price range."

My mother snaps her eyes up. "How would *you* know what our price range is?"

"Well . . . uh . . . I mean, I just don't *recommend* it." She quickly digs into another drawer. "If it's cruises you want, I can book you on dozens of others."

But Mom holds her ground. "Tell us about this one."

The woman looks to Mom, then to me, then reluctantly begins to speak as Mom and I leaf through the brochure.

"The *Heavenward* is a new ship," says the woman, "from a new and inexperienced cruise line. . . ."

I raise my eyebrows. "Says here it's the largest cruise ship ever built."

"A hundred and twenty tons," says the woman. "But—"

"And where does it cruise to?" asks Mom, cutting her off.

"Nowhere yet. Its maiden voyage isn't until next month."

I can tell that Mom's frustrated by the way this woman doesn't quite answer her question, so we find the answer in the brochure ourselves. Mom's eyes widen happily.

"A cruise to the Orient!" Mom says.

"Yes—to the Far East," says the travel agent, as if there's a difference.

According to the brochure, the *Heavenward* will depart from Honolulu and sail west across the Pacific, bound for Japan, China, and Thailand. A three-week cruise with ten ports of call!

I look up from the brochure and catch Mom's eyes.

They are the same eyes she had when she saw that painting in the art gallery. The one that cost way too much . . . and then two days later ended up in our living room.

The travel agent must see that look in my mom's eyes, too.

"I should explain something about Pacific Rim Cruises," says the travel agent in a calm, calculated voice, as if she's trying to talk someone in from the edge of a building. "They've built a magnificent ship . . . but they *don't know much about world travel*. This cruise that they're doing . . . it's going a little *too* far . . ."

"Nothing's too far for me," says Mom. "The farther the better."

The woman pales a bit, and I realize that she isn't trying to be rude. She's trying to warn us of something . . . something she wouldn't dare speak aloud . . .

But Mom doesn't care much for warnings. So she pulls out a wad of credit cards the size of a bar of soap. "We're taking that maiden voyage," Mom says. "Best room available. Money is no object."

And so the travel agent has no choice but to give us what we want.

It begins on July fourth. A flight to Honolulu, a taxi ride to the port, and there we are—staring at the *Heavenward*—a majestic white giant, impossibly huge. The ship fills up my whole mind when I look at it, leaving no room for other thoughts.

Everything on board is perfect, from our stateroom filled with luxurious wood and polished brass, to the nine-story atrium in the middle of the ship, where four glass elevators ride up and down. It's hard to believe this is all on a ship! There's even an entire kid deck filled with video games, pizza places, and just about anything else a kid could dream of. I now know why they named the ship the *Heavenward*, because as far as I'm concerned, it's like I've died and gone to heaven.

It's during that first evening at the midnight buffet that I see the strange old man.

He's in the kitchen—I catch glimpses of him every few moments through the swinging kitchen door. He's not a passenger, but a member of the crew. I don't think he's a cook, because he's not dressed like the rest of the kitchen workers. He wears a rumpled Hawaiian shirt that has seen better days, and his face is covered with beard stubble so dense that even the sharpest of razors would shy away from it. He seems out of place here, with a way about him too dark and brooding for a fun-filled cruise like this.

I can't get his face out of my mind, and even though I pile my plate high with food, I begin to lose my appetite. The old man's eyes seem worn and worried, and for some strange reason, I get the very clear sense that I should be worried, too.

Two days out of Hawaii, with wild parties raging on every deck, I get tired of the all-you-can-eat ice cream parlor, the free video games, and the dance-till-you-drop teen club. There's only so much pleasure a person can stand. So after dinner, I decide to explore.

Ships are great for secret exploration. They're like mazes filled with hallways and dim corners, and everywhere on the great ship you can hear the eerie rumble of the huge engine somewhere down below.

Finding the engine room is my goal. Sure, I could take the engine room tour, but it's much more fun to find it myself and be there when I'm not allowed.

On the lowest passenger deck I come to a door with a sign that reads no admittance, and I admit myself. Suddenly the luxurious beauty of the ship gives way to a dull beige corridor lined with the crew's quarters. I push far-

ther and find a set of stairs leading down. I take it deck after deck after deck, deep into the bowels of the ship, wan-
dering aimlessly through narrow access-ways until I
finally stumble upon the engine room.

You'd think the engine room of a great ship like the
Heavenward would have a huge crew of engineers—but a
ship as sophisticated as this must practically run itself.
There's only one man on shift. A man I recognize.

It's the old man from the kitchen the night before.

He turns his weary eyes to me. He has an intense gaze,
and now that I get a better look at him, I can tell that he's
an educated man by he way he carries himself—as if the
crushing weight of some secret knowledge hunches his
shoulders, like Atlas holding up the world. The shadows
are deep here, and in those shadows his face seems
cragged and cracked, like the Grand Canyon seen from an
airplane. I can see that he's not so much old as he is worn.
Worn and tired.

"You don't belong here, boy," he says. "Go back up.
Party while you can." His words give me a shiver that
rises up my spine, but I force it back down.

Around us the engine roars, and through an iron cat-
walk I can see the silver cylinder of a propeller shaft leading to the stern. Beneath that, the two sides of the hull
come together, like an attic turned upside down. It reminds me that no matter how huge this thing is, it's just a
boat, with miles of ocean beneath it. The thought unset-
tles me, and suddenly I want to be anywhere but the engine room.

"Uh . . . sorry," I say, "I took a wrong turn." I spin and
hurry off, fully prepared to spend the rest of my cruise
playing free video games, swimming, and eating myself
into blimpdom.

But the old engineer calls out to me.

"Hold on there, Alex!" he says.

The ship lurches beneath me, making my stomach feel queasy. Or maybe it's just the fact that the old man knows my name. I can't figure how he'd know it.

I turn, and he grins mysteriously. "The name's Riley," he says. "Third engineer. C'mon, I'll take you back to the passenger decks."

Soon the roar of the engines is far away once again. We wind down the narrow corridors and up flights of stairs, until reaching a doorway. Beyond the door I can hear the sound of distant partying; thousands of people drinking in a lifetime's worth of good times. As if there's no tomorrow.

It's then that I realize that I'm wearing my Little League shirt, with my name plastered right across the back. *Idiot!* I think. That's how he knew my name. All at once, that sick feeling twisting through my gut goes away. I feel normal again, until Engineer Riley puts his hand on the doorknob and turns to me. "Is this your first cruise?" he asks.

"Yes . . ."

He shakes his head. "I'm so sorry for you." Then he swings the door wide into the bright lights of the Aloha Deck.

The next morning we're still at sea, somewhere between Hawaii and Japan . . . or so the map in our brochure says. The ocean stretches out around us, featureless and flat, and although there are a hundred things for me to do today, I can't get Riley's face out of my mind. I can't forget the sorrowful way he looked at me when he opened that door . . . and what he said.

It takes me half the morning searching the ship, but finally I find him. Once again, I'm in a place I'm not supposed to be: the crew's recreation deck. It's a large space at the back of the ship, with a ceiling so low it feels like

I'm being crushed between two decks. The large U-shaped room has wide portholes open to the sea, beyond which the white trail of the ship's wake disappears toward the horizon.

Riley's sitting alone, drinking his coffee steaming black. He doesn't seem surprised to see me; he just nods a weary greeting.

"That was a lousy thing to say to me yesterday," I tell him.

He knows exactly what I'm talking about. "You think that now, but you won't tomorrow," he answers.

"What's that supposed to mean?"

He takes a long time to answer. "How much have you traveled?" he asks.

"A lot," I lie. "I've been all over the world."

"Ever known a pilot, or the captain of a ship, boy?"

I shake my head, and he leans in closer to me and whispers, *"There's things they know . . . that regular people aren't supposed to know."*

"Like what?" I dare to ask.

Instead of answering me, he stands up and goes to one of the huge portholes. I follow him.

"What do you see when you look out there?" he asks.

"Nothing. Just the horizon."

"And what does the horizon look like to you?"

I shrug. "A line," I tell him. "A straight line."

He nods. "That's exactly right—and why is that?"

I begin to get annoyed. It's as if he's giving me a test. As if he thinks I don't know the answer, which I do.

"The curvature of the Earth," I tell him. "The Earth slopes off, and you can't see past the horizon."

Then he looks at me with those yellow, weary eyes.

"That's what they want you to believe," he says.

His words strike me like a blast of radiation. I can tell I've been hit by something major . . . but I don't feel it just yet. But I know I will. Somehow I sense that his words have created some immense damage in me, that will soon get much, much worse.

"Soon everything you know," he explains, "everything you believe in will crumble away."

I feel panic looming inside me like a storm. What he is trying to tell me begins to dawn on me.

I suddenly think of a silly drawing I once saw in history class: the world was a flat disk on the back of a giant tortoise. It was an example of an ignorant belief of people a thousand years ago. People who didn't know any better.

"You're . . . you're joking, right?" I ask him.

Riley says nothing, and I begin to get mad. "I suppose now you're going to tell me that we're all on the back of a turtle, and every time the turtle moves there's an earthquake."

Riley ponders it. I can't believe it—he actually takes me seriously! "I don't know about a turtle," he says finally. "But anything's possible."

As I look out over the flat immensity of the ocean, I become furious—because no matter how impossible what he's saying sounds, there's a part of me that might actually believe him. Not the rational, sensible part of me, but the part that knows no logic. The same part that makes me check under my bed every night, even though I haven't believed in monsters since I was five. I fight to keep down the breakfast that still stuffs my stomach.

"But if the world's not round . . . then how do you get to Japan and the Far East?" I ask.

He looks out toward the straight line of the horizon, worry coming back to his face. "Not the way we're going," he answers.

He breaks his gaze away from the porthole, as if unable to look at the ocean anymore, and moves away. I have to admit I feel the same. In my mind, the horizon, as calm as it is, seems razor sharp, and filled with terrifying un-knowns.

Riley takes a big gulp of his cooling coffee.

"Sailors are a secretive bunch," he says. "We keep the nature of the world to ourselves—and you'd be amazed how easy it is to keep a secret when most everyone in the world already believes it. . . ." Then he sighs. "But some-times the secret is kept too well . . . and every once in a while the wrong people build ships . . . like the people who run Pacific Rim Cruises. This is their first ship . . . and they just don't know . . ."

And then he grabs me by the shoulder, forcing me to look into his eyes. Forcing me to listen.

"When the time comes," he says, *"go to the back of the ship, no matter what they tell you."*

He downs the rest of his coffee, then abruptly tells me I should leave—but before I leave I have to ask him some-thing.

"Riley," I ask, "if we're not headed toward Japan, where *are* we headed?"

He looks down at his empty cup, refusing to look me in the eye. "You don't want to know."

For the rest of that day, I weave in and out of the happy crowds of vacationers, but can't feel like one of them. They are already ghosts.

As the sun begins to cast long shadows across the deck, I find my mother stretched out in a lounge chair, reeking of suntan lotion and sipping an exotic drink the color of antifreeze.

When she sees me, she smiles and says lazily, "Let's never go back. Let's just float out here forever."

Although I know she's kidding, her words bring my last meal swimming toward high tide.

"Mom," I tell her, "I don't think this trip was a good idea."

She looks at me as if I've doused her with ice water. "Aren't you having a good time, Alex? There's so much to do—so many kids your age!"

I look toward the pool to see dozens of kids laughing and swimming and flying down the winding slide. I wish I could join in the fun, but the old man's crazy words strangle all hopes of enjoying myself.

"Just wait until we get to Japan," Mom reassures me. "I promise you, this trip will be something to remember!"

It happens that night.

During dinner, the seas become rough—the ship rolling and pitching so violently that Mom's lobster flies right into her lap.

I figure we must be in a terrible storm, but when I look out the window at the twilight sky, there are no clouds. Still the waves crash angrily against the ship with all the furious power the ocean can muster.

It's as if something is trying to make us turn back, I think, but I swallow the thought with my dinner roll.

I go to my cabin early, trying to sleep off my worry, but it's no use. All I can think about is the old engineer.

What Riley had said is impossible. More than impossible, it's inconceivable—it would mean a conspiracy too immense to be imagined. All the pilots, all the astronomers, all the astronauts—anyone who ever had the chance to truly study the Earth would know. Why would all those people keep it from the rest of the world?

Yet even as I think about it, I know the answer.

Because everything would fall apart.

The whole world would become a bottomless pit of fear and confusion if we suddenly realized we knew *noth-*

ing about the true nature of the universe. We would be lost and helpless if, after all we thought we knew . . . we suddenly discovered . . . that the Earth was flat.

BAM! CRRRUNCH!

I'm suddenly thrown out of bed by the ship's violent lurch. There's no mistaking the meaning of that tearing, metallic sound, and I can already see in my mind the huge gash torn in the side of the ship.

Torn by what? I think. *We're out in the middle of the ocean. It can't be an iceberg—we're too far south.*

The ship's alarms clang in my ears so violently that every thought is blasted from my mind. I can hear my mother screaming, tumbling out of her bunk and banging her shin against the dresser.

Then another jolt throws us to the floor as a second hole is ripped in the hull.

We burst out into a hallway already packed with terrified passengers, and I remember Riley's words.

Go to the back of the ship.

All around us, people push toward the front of the ship, toward their muster stations, because that's what they were told in the lifeboat drill when we first came on board. That's where the closest staircase is.

But I grab Mom's hand and pull her against the crowd, until we join the people heading toward the stairwell at the back of the great ship.

We stumble our way up three flights of stairs to the promenade deck, and only now, as we are pushed against the railing, do we see the nature of the ship's ruin.

The *Heavenward* is wedged between giant crags of rock, massive gray granite slabs that jut up around us on either side. I know that these rocks aren't supposed to be here. We're out in the middle of nowhere, a thousand miles from Japan! I'm pretty certain that there's no map in the world that shows this granite reef.

Caught between the rocks, the back half of the ship is rocked violently by powerful waves . . . but the front end of the ship has a very different problem.

I watch in helpless terror as passengers cram into a forward lifeboat. As the lifeboat is lowered into the water I hear them scream . . . *because there is no water at the front of the ship*. There is no ocean. The crowded lifeboat tumbles into an emptiness as deep as the sky is high.

We have reached the edge of the earth.

I instantly realize what's about to happen. I'd done enough exploring to know that two of the ship's three main stairwells are toward the bow—and only one toward the stern. That means that at least two-thirds of the passengers are flooding the front half of the ship!

It only takes a minute for the weight of the ship to shift forward, off its delicate balance. I feel the ship tilting over the edge, and I scream. Then a hand firmly pushes me from behind. The railing before me gives way and I fall, but instead of landing in the ocean . . . I land in the shell of a lifeboat. People pile on top of me. My mother, and dozens of others.

We are lowered to the water. When I look up, I don't see the side of the ship, but instead see a propeller four times my height, churning the air uselessly.

"Hold on!" a voice shouts. A familiar voice. I turn back to see the weathered face of the third engineer. Riley releases the lifeboat from the crane, and it drops five feet to the surface of the roiling ocean. We narrowly miss being shredded by another propeller coming up through the water as the ship continues to tilt forward.

"We're all going to drown!" shouts my mother, out of her mind with panic—but even in the rough waters of the great Pacific Rim, the small lifeboat manages to stay afloat.

Riley starts the engine and maneuvers us toward the

granite reef that holds the ocean back. A wave deposits us on the shore.

"We'll climb to that ledge," Riley says, pointing to a rock plateau about ten feet above us. "The sea will be calm by morning."

Soaked and terrified, we all climb to the plateau, but I don't stop. I keep climbing, even though Riley tries to call me back. I climb as high as I can, until I come to the top of the ridge and can see everything.

They say you're not supposed to look at awful sights— that you should turn your eyes from things that shouldn't be seen. But no one has ever accused me of doing the right thing. I have to watch it happen.

From where I am, the sight is more incredible than anything I've ever seen, or ever will see again. The great granite reef of the Pacific Rim stretches as far as the eye can see in every direction. For the most part it holds back the sea, but it's filled with many cracks, through which the ocean pours like massive waterfalls spilling off the world into infinity.

The *Heavenward* is wedged in the throat of one of those waterfalls.

I stare in numb silence as the largest cruise ship ever built teeters forward like a seesaw and finally flips off the edge of the earth.

I keep my eyes locked on the ship as it tumbles end over end, down into a darkness speckled with stars. Soon I have to squint to see it. It seems no larger than a toothpick spinning in the void. And then a tiny point of light getting harder and harder to see.

When I turn, I see Riley standing behind me, and I pound his chest with my fists, almost slipping off the edge and into oblivion. "Why?" I scream. "Why didn't you stop the ship? Why didn't you turn us back?"

Riley grabs my flailing hands and looks me in the eye.

"Because I didn't know if I believed it myself . . . until I really saw it."

He turns and looks out over the edge, squinting his eyes into the dark sky below, but the *Heavenward* is gone, with no sign that it ever existed at all. "Maybe it *needs* to happen every now and again," says Riley. "Maybe it needs to happen so that we never completely forget. . . ."

Far to the east, the dim light of the coming dawn paints the horizon a rich shade of blue, as the handful of us wait to be rescued. Below us, our lifeboat has long since been smashed to driftwood, but Riley is certain we'll be rescued—and sure enough, as day arrives, I can see the specks of rescue ships in the distance.

Perhaps it's just shock, but as I huddle with my mom to keep warm, the terror of what I witnessed slowly begins to turn to amazement. I can't help but wonder what the people on board the *Heavenward* saw as they fell from the world . . . but I suppose some secrets will never be known.

I look at the survivors around me and realize that we have all become inheritors of the secret. I know none of these people will ever tell, just as surely as I know that I never will—for if we did, the world would see us locked up as lunatics rather than ever consider the possibility that what we say is true.

How long has this been going on? I wonder. How many generations, and how many shipwrecks ago? But I doubt even Riley knows those answers.

"Are there other things?" I ask Riley. "More mysteries that people don't know?"

He smiles broadly and says, "Have you ever been to Nepal?"

I smile back at him, realizing exactly what he means— because I know my geography.

As I wait for the rescue ships to arrive, I think about my next great excursion. Not a trip of escape, but one of exploration. It may not be next year, or the year after that, but I know that someday I'll travel to Nepal—the gateway to the Himalayas—and Mount Everest, the highest mountain in the world.

There are people who call that place "the Roof of the World."

We'll see about that. . . .

I OF THE
STORM

•••••••••••••••••••••••••••••••••••

A late afternoon wind ushered in the sudden down-
pour. I could see the courtyard of the museum beginning to flood, while up above, lightning volleyed
angrily across the clouds.

"Rainy season," Mom said. "It rains for an hour or two
most afternoons this time of year."

"It's a good thing," Dad added. "It cleans up some of
the smog."

I watched through a fogging window as the dark cumu-
lus clouds slid past one another—and it seemed to me that
they were closer than the storm clouds back home in
Florida. I asked my parents about it.

"Of course they're closer," Dad said in his best know-
it-all voice. "Mexico City's a mile and a half above sea
level—that much closer to the clouds."

A wind swooped down and rattled the plate-glass window. I backed away, and Dad chuckled. "Ashley, this mu-

seum's stood through countless earthquakes. You don't have to worry about a little wind."

He turned and glanced at the gallery behind us. Giant Olmec heads with no bodies sat on pedestals beside sandstone sun wheels and weathered Aztec statues. It must have been what all the ancient civilizations did: carve these statues—because the museum was filled with gallery after giant gallery of massive carved stones.

"Where's your brother?" Dad asked me. "Weren't you keeping an eye on him?"

I heard my brother Jackson's giggle and the pattering of feet somewhere deep in the gallery.

"Don't play games, you two," Mom said, as if I was an accomplice to Jackson's mischief. "We have to get through the whole museum before five." Dad took a last look over the room to see if there was anything he'd missed, then he and Mom went on to the next gallery. Our tour schedule only allowed us three hours at Mexico City's Museum of Anthropology. And my parents were slaves to schedules.

Unfortunately, my life had been ruled by a very different clock lately. One that measured time in tantrums. It was a sugar-powered clock named Jackson.

Three years old, and about as disagreeable as a human can be, my brother Jackson lived by no schedule but his own, and right now, following Mom and Dad was not part of his agenda. He was nowhere in sight.

"Jackson?"

I heard him giggle again—farther away this time.

"Jackson, c'mon. Mom and Dad already left."

"Come and get me!" His voice echoed around the stones, and I couldn't tell where it came from.

"Fine. I'm leaving," I threatened, and turned, pretending to head off toward the next gallery. But I couldn't re-

ally leave him because Mom and Dad would be furious
with me—as if it was my job to take care of Jackson.

"Ashley, take Jackson to the park."

"Ashley, put Jackson to bed."

"Ashley, make sure Jackson doesn't get hurt."

And when his endless tantrums drove them up the wall,
I would always be the one who had to stop him from
screaming, and kicking, and fighting, because I was the
only one who could calm him down.

Not that he's like that all the time. There are times
when Jackson is so sweet and so loving that he makes you
forget how unreasonable he was just five minutes before.
And then there are the times he just makes you pull your
hair out!

"Jackson, you'd better come out now, or I swear I'll—"

"You're not playing right," said Jackson. "You gotta
play right. You gotta look for me."

Outside, lightning struck, bathing the solemn stone
heads around me with a cold light that cast their eyes
deep in shadow. We were the only ones in the gallery
now. All the other tourists had moved on.

"Come fine me, Ashley. You have to!"

"You better hope I don't!" I shouted.

I ducked past a statue of a plumed serpent, around the
chiseled face of a Mayan god. Finally I found Jackson
standing on a worn stone altar behind a sign that said, do
not stand on altar in both Spanish and English. His fists
were at his waist like the Jolly Green Giant.

"Look at me!" he said. "I'm a Mexican statue!"

"Mom already told you not to climb!" I looked at the
Aztec altar and glanced at the placard explaining it. I
shivered in spite of myself. "You stand up there, some
Aztec might come and cut out your heart—that's what
they used it for!"

Jackson paled at the thought. "Did not! You're lying!"

"It says right here. Now let's go!" I pulled him off the altar, and he struggled against my grip.

"No, I wanna stay here. I wanna play hide-and-seek," he said. "And I'm hungry, too. I want a corn dog."

"You can't have one!" I shouted. "You're in Mexico. They don't have corn dogs here."

"You're lying. You're just being mean!" Jackson screamed back at me. He was beyond reason, and I was beyond patience. Mom and Dad were probably halfway through the museum now, and I was getting a headache from Jackson's voice and the city's thin air. So I grabbed him and carried him off, kicking and screaming.

"No! I won't go!" he wailed. "I won't, I won't, I won't!" He bit me on the arm, I dropped him, and he ran—

—right into a dark stone slab.

Jackson bounced off it and fell to the ground. "You did that on purpose!" he insisted. "You pushed me!"

The leash on my temper was fraying, but I held onto it, figuring that maybe now he'd come along calmly. He turned to the figure carved into the stone slab; a young warrior with angry eyes.

"You stink," he told it, still holding the spot on his forehead that had rammed the slab.

"I wouldn't say that to him. Says here that this is Tezcatlipoca—the god of the night wind. It says he could become an angry wind that sweeps unwary travelers away. I wouldn't mess with a guy like that!"

I looked around and noticed that this slab wasn't on a pedestal. In fact, it was right in the middle of an aisle. No wonder Jackson ran into it. I tried to remember if we saw it when we first entered the huge gallery, but for the life of me I could not remember seeing that face before.

"Is he a bad-guy?" asked Jackson.

Lightning struck somewhere far away. The light played off Tezcatlipoca's carved lips. I couldn't tell whether he was smiling, or grimacing.

"No," I told Jackson. "He's just a piece of rock."

"If he's supposed to be so mean," said Jackson, "then how come he winked at me?"

"Don't be silly," I said, and pulled him away.

There are mistakes we make that seem tiny and unimportant at the time—but turn into monster regrets. The kind of regrets that shred your dreams into nightmares over and over again.

What happened next, well, that's *my* monster regret, and no one else's.

I headed out with Jackson to find Mom and Dad, but they weren't in the next gallery, or the one after that. I guess even they got overloaded on the wall-to-wall rocks. We weaved quickly through the maze of dead civilizations: Aztec, Olmec, Toltec, and Mayan. And somewhere along the way, I let go of Jackson's hand.

Finally I rounded a corner to find Mom and Dad studying the features of a fertility statue.

"There you are!" said Mom, not even realizing how far behind we had been. "Where's Jackson?"

"Right here . . ." I said, but when I turned, he wasn't there. "Oh, great!"

"You were supposed to keep an eye on him," chided Dad.

I just boiled at Jackson's continual ability to get me in trouble.

"Jackson, c'mon!" I called. "No hide-and-seek!" I felt dizzy, and a bit off balance. I thought I was light-headed from the altitude, but an instant later I realized the ground was moving.

We were having an earthquake.

It wasn't what I expected an earthquake to feel like. It didn't grind and make lots of noise. Instead, it kind of just sloshed back and forth, like we were standing on Jell-O.

It wasn't big. It didn't last long. And somewhere far away, I heard a deep, heavy *boom!* as something fell.

"Jackson?" called Mom, her worry slowly building.

The tremor was over, and I glanced outside. It was darker, and although the rain had stopped, a night wind blew a flock of twisted papers through the museum's courtyard.

"Jackson, this is not funny!" said Dad in his sternest voice.

Jackson didn't answer.

And suddenly, I knew where he must have gone. He went to take one more look at the stone face of Tezcatlipoca—to see if it really had winked at him.

"Oh no!" I raced back through the winding corridors. Whatever had fallen, it was back that way, and I kept trying to tell myself that Jackson was nowhere near it. We'd find him, Dad would scold him, and we'd go back to our hotel and finish up our vacation.

But we couldn't find him.

Instead, we found a two-ton granite slab that had fallen facedown in the aisle.

The image of Tezcatlipoca.

"Jackson!" screamed Mom. She seemed uncertain whether to be angry or to panic. We all kept believing that he'd leap out from behind some other statue. But he didn't. We had security search the museum for hours, but no Jackson.

Finally, long after closing, they brought a winch to raise the massive stone. We huddled together, Mom, Dad, and I, not wanting to look but knowing we had to. Inch by inch, they raised the slab, until the museum lights lit the space beneath.

And nothing was there.

Nothing but the chiseled face of the slab, and the smiling, scowling image of the god of the night wind.

It's easy to rebuild a house. I know because we had to do it after a hurricane once. But rebuilding a *home*—well, that's something different. Because how can you hope to make a home again, when one of the most important parts is missing?

We never found Jackson. Mom and I stayed in Mexico for weeks, and Dad stayed for months, working with the authorities and chasing blind leads until there was nothing for him to do but come back to Florida and go on with life.

Although my parents never blamed me, I knew it was my fault, and that weight pressed on me like a thousand stone slabs. There were times I would look out from our beach house, across the Gulf of Mexico. I would imagine I could see Jackson still there, hiding behind a giant, fat-cheeked Olmec head. Waiting for us to find him.

We limped along, day to day, for almost a year . . . until the storm.

The news report called it a tropical depression—a slow swirling storm that was riding up the Yucatán Peninsula. Mom and Dad watched the TV with mild disinterest . . . which was the way they looked at everything these days. They had become way too quiet over the months, and surf pounding on the beach sounded almost deafening when we sat together.

"Do you think it'll come this way?" I asked Dad.

"What?"

"You know, the storm." I pointed at the screen, but the weather map was already gone.

I would have forgotten about it . . . but the next day that tropical depression was upgraded to a tropical storm, and the day after that it was a full-fledged hurricane.

Florida has always been like a magnet for hurricanes, so the storm was on everyone's mind at school and throughout the neighborhood. We watched the Weather Channel for days, soaking in the reports, as Hurricane Zelda pummeled Galveston, Texas and continued hugging the Gulf Coast.

"It probably won't come this way," Mom said. But hurricanes don't follow any set path. They wander over ocean and shore until they finally die. No telling where they'll head.

It was the morning after Zelda hit Galveston, that I got my first hint of strange events yet to come. Dad was sitting at the breakfast table, the morning news spread out in front of him like a mask hiding his face from the world. The front page faced me—a full-color picture of the hurricane's devastation.

"Wow!" I said as I studied the picture. "Looks like Zelda shows no mercy." There was nothing left of a beach house but a pile of wet rubble. I'd seen storm damage like that before, but it's still hard to comprehend.

"The news is making too big a deal of it," Dad said. "Actually only a few homes were destroyed." Then he showed me a picture on the page he was reading— the same ruined house, viewed from a distance. There were homes still standing on either side of the wreckage. Sure, they had broken windows and all, but had taken nowhere near the damage that the house in the middle had.

"Probably had termites to begin with," Dad suggested. "A storm can do lots of damage when the wood's weak."

I glanced at the color picture on the front again and this time noticed something curious I hadn't seen before.

The wood of the ruined house was a pale blue, and a gray flap of shredded fabric hung from what used to be a window.

"That house was blue, with gray awnings!" I told my parents. "Just like ours!"

"It's a popular color scheme," explained Mom. And although I wanted to talk more about it, Dad had already turned the page to the sports section.

With winds peaking at 150 miles per hour, Zelda wasted New Orleans.

We watched in numb disbelief as the news showed communities devastated by the raging winds and rain. With the hurricane growing in strength, more homes were washed away by the storm's power. A reporter stood in the ruins of one of the worst piles of wreckage—and although they say seeing is believing, I wasn't ready to believe anything just yet . . . but I was getting close.

"Blue wood and gray awnings," I pointed out to my parents. They had no comment this time. From the look of this waterfront Louisiana community, it seemed to have taken a hard slam from this angry storm. But this blue house seemed to have taken it worse than any other.

"Spooky," I said as I stared at the screen. "Jackson would have said that Zelda's favorite color is blue."

Dad left the room at the mention of Jackson's name, and Mom slipped out afterward . . . but I couldn't leave. I suddenly found my mind fixed on those damage reports, awed by the power of winds that could raise oceans and hurl boats half a mile inland.

There was one boat wedged in the side of a truck. The image made me smile in spite of the destruction, because it reminded me of Jackson and the way he loved to play demolition derby. Especially with trains.

It wasn't until I saw the next report that I began to get a funny feeling inside. Like the kind you get about a minute before you have to throw up.

Three derailed trains.

They were miles inland, but a stray edge of the hurricane seemed to have lashed out and whipped them off their tracks.

My brain told me that it was all coincidence—it had to be. But intuition was filling my arms with gooseflesh and making my heart just about explode out of my chest. *Jackson didn't just disappear,* my inner voice shouted to my disbelieving brain. *He disappeared into thin air. . . . He disappeared into the wind.*

It was a thought I simply couldn't push away. Instead, it built inside of me, like a hurricane in my own head, until I began to believe it . . . more than believe—I *knew.* I knew exactly what had happened to my brother so many months before—and exactly what was happening now!

My parents were already asleep, but I shook them awake. My breathing was shallow, and my eyes must have been panicked because they sat up right away and asked what was wrong.

I didn't know what to tell them. I knew what I was thinking, but how could I explain it? How could I explain that the hurricane wasn't destroying homes that looked like ours by accident. This hurricane was *looking* for something, and when it didn't find what it searched for, the storm tore everything to shreds, like . . .

. . . like a child having a tantrum.

The truth was, Hurricane Zelda wasn't a "Zelda" at all. It was a "Jackson."

"The hurricane," I told my parents. "I think it's heading this way." We turned the news back on, and the weatherman confirmed what I already knew in my heart. The hurricane had abandoned Louisiana and was cutting a fast, furious path across the gulf, toward the Florida coast.

By dawn, the sea was already climbing the old grass-covered dunes, just behind our back porch. An hour later, they gave the order to evacuate.

No one was ready—no one expected the storm to pick up speed and change its course the way it had. Neighbors frantically nailed plywood over their windows as police urged everyone to leave their homes.

Mom and Dad packed our car with whatever it would hold, and we drove inland toward a Red Cross shelter. I looked out the back window of the car at the dark, angry sky looming over the horizon, wondering what the storm would do, and where it would go when it found our house empty.

That's when I realized it *couldn't* find our house empty.

With the wind already whipping the trees around us, we got caught in an evacuation traffic jam. If I was going to do it, I had to do it now. Around me random things were thrown that my parents chose to save. Memories, mostly. One memory poked out of a box beside me—the tattered ear of a gnawed teddy bear. It was Jackson's Nighty Bear. It was missing a leg and oozed white fluff from a dozen moth holes—still, Jackson would never sleep without it.

I grabbed Nighty Bear and opened my door.

"Ashley? Ashley, what are you doing?"

But I didn't answer. Instead I ran into the wind, and toward the approaching storm.

The ocean had already begun to swallow our neighborhood by the time I arrived. Waves washed through streets and alleys, while up above, roofs were shredded by the relentless wind. The hurricane had hit with its full, blind fury, ravaging the town.

I fought the rampage of the winds and waters. Cold and shivering, I held on to Jackson's waterlogged bear. I knew my parents must have been coming after me, but I wouldn't look back, for fear that I might get caught and be pulled away to safety.

With the ocean waist deep around me, an undercurrent pulled my feet out and I went down. I gulped a heavy dose of salty sea before a wave carried me back to the surface, and *bam!* I found myself coughing up water on a tilted porch. A blue porch. I was home!

The house was shifting horribly, and it shuddered every time a wave crashed against it. It had already been washed off its foundation, and it would soon go down completely. Before a wave could wash me away, I climbed in through a broken window and fell to the flooded floor.

The TV and living room furniture were floating, like shipwrecks, half submerged around the crooked room. Another wave came crashing through the kitchen window.

I knew what I was thinking was crazy. I knew that I would probably die—but I had to go through with this. I climbed the crooked stairs toward my brother's room.

Jackson's room had been kept in perfect condition. His cartoon bedspread smooth and neat, his fingerpaints tacked up on the wall. But now the wind and rain poured through his broken window, and the floorboards were beginnning to buckle from the strain on the shifting house.

Okay, I'm here, I told myself. *Now what?*

There was a great gnashing noise, and the roof peeled off like the lid of a can, tumbling upward, until it had shredded to smithereens. Now the only thing above me was a screaming tantrum of violent skies. With both hands, I took the ruined bear and held it high above my head, toward the dark clouds.

"Jackson!" I screamed. I couldn't hear my own voice above the wailing wind. "Jackson, it's Ashley!" The wind ripped Nighty Bear from my hands, and it tumbled straight up until it disappeared. "Jackson, you stop this!" I demanded of the storm. "You come down here now!" The wind changed its pitch; now it sounded like a voice, a frightened, angry voice.

I didn't pretend to understand a force that could turn a child into the wind. I could never understand that kind of power.

But I have some power of my own—because I was the only one who could calm Jackson down. I held out my hands to the sky, swallowing my fear. "I'm here, Jackson!" I called out, and I imagined my voice carrying over the winds and out into the ocean, my words reaching the far edge of the storm. "I'm here . . . and you're home!"

The wind tore at me so strongly that I could barely see. I could feel the clouds collapsing, compressing, squeezing between my outstretched arms until the sound of the storm had changed into the screams and sobs of a child.

What had once been wind tearing at me were now struggling arms and legs—kicking and fighting as I held him in my arms . . . as I held my brother. Soon his struggling weakened, and his screams turned to sobs, and then to whimpers as he clutched me tightly around the neck, gripping his Nighty Bear in his cold hand.

"It's okay, Jackson," I told him softly. "It'll be okay." He dug his face into my shoulder and closed his eyes, relaxing at last. And that is how my parents found me—holding my lost brother and gently rocking him to sleep, to the sound of flood waters washing back to join the sea, in a roofless house, beneath a clear, cloudless sky.

I know there will be lots of questions. Many will be left

unanswered, and even more left unasked. But that's all right. And even though we stand in the shattered debris of our house, I am not sad at all. Because now that Jackson's back, our home is once again whole. And a house can always be rebuilt.

OPABINIA

Darren wouldn't have believed it if he hadn't seen it with his own two eyes—a man, appearing out of nowhere in his room, in the dead of night, stuck halfway into the wall.

It was Darren Strongwater's first mysterious visitor, but not the last.

His father would have called it a dream, and his grandfather would have called it a vision, but Darren knew that it was real—he was awake, and completely alert.

This first night visitor was in a great deal of pain—so much pain that he couldn't even scream. The reason clearly had to do with the way he had materialized, halfway into the wall, his head and shoulders hanging out through the wallpaper like a weird trophy head.

Darren couldn't scream either—the shock of seeing a man, or at least half a man, appear in his room was too much for him. His throat closed up in terror, and he could only watch as the man struggled uselessly to pull himself free. Darren couldn't begin to imagine how incredible the pain must have been—to suddenly have the molecules of your body invaded by the plaster and wood of the wall, and the dense copper plumbing behind it. Even now, Darren could hear the pipes creaking and straining as they tried to share the same space as the man in the wall.

Darren wanted to turn away, but the desperation in the visitor's eyes was more powerful than his own fear. Darren felt drawn toward the dying man, and before he realized what he was doing, Darren's feet were crossing the cold wooden floor toward him.

"B . . . B . . . Bu . . ."

The visitor was trying to say something, but his lungs, invaded by the plasterboard wall, couldn't push out enough air for him to speak. Darren watched in the dim moonlight, close enough to hear, but not close enough to be grabbed by the desperately struggling hands.

Then the visitor locked his eyes on Darren, forced his shallow breath a bit deeper, and hissed out a word.

"B . . . Bu . . . Burgess . . ." he said. "Burgessssss . . ."

And with his last moment of life, the visitor pressed the button on a calculator he was carrying. Suddenly he vanished just as quickly as he had appeared . . . and every pipe in the wall burst.

When the Strongwaters purchased the home, they knew the plumbing was old, but never suspected it would be explosive.

"Never seen anything like this," said the plumber examining the hole. "What did you do, flush some dynamite?"

Of course Darren didn't tell anyone what really happened. His father made it very clear that strange occurrences were not discussed in the Strongwater household.

The last time Darren had tried to talk to them about strange happenings, it blew up in his face with more force than the exploding pipes.

It had to do with the voices.

Lately there had been people talking in Darren's head when he least expected it—but in a world where the only voices in one's head usually come from a Walkman, the announcement didn't go over very well.

"Voices? What do you mean voices?" his father had said. "You don't hear voices!" It was as if proclaiming they didn't exist would make the voices go away. But they didn't. They only got louder, sometimes waking Darren out of a deep sleep. He never understood what they said, but he knew they were talking to him. Him and no one else. It made him feel important. It made him feel special.

It made everyone else think he was crazy.

"He's doing it for attention," his father had concluded.

"It's the stress of moving to the city," Mom had decided.

"The boy's a shaman," Grandfather announced, and that killed any hope of discussion—because if there was anything Darren's father despised, it was the traditions that Grandfather held so dear.

So they did the proper, modern thing and sent the boy to a psychologist, who did nothing but listen, which was useless, since Darren refused to talk to her.

And so Darren knew better than to tell his family about last night's visitor, and he didn't need a psychologist to tell him that seeing the visitor pushed things to a new level. Either he was very, very sick, or someone really was trying to communicate with him.

The hole in the wall proved to Darren that he wasn't crazy after all. He just had to figure out who this "Burgess" was.

*   *   *

The second visitor suffered a fate even crueler than the first. Darren's walk to school through the city streets of Providence took him past a trendy block lined with coffeehouses, cafés, and a microbrewery that manufactured its own brand of beer. Through the plate-glass window, you could see the vats of brewing hops and barley, and every afternoon the place turned into a pub, packed with the business crowd.

At eight in the morning, however, the brewery was quiet as Darren passed by—until a sudden pounding came from inside one of the vats. The one closest to where Darren was passing.

"There's . . . there's someone in there!" shouted a worker, and a few minutes later they pulled a limp woman out of the brew. The vat had been sealed—there was no way she could have gotten in. Still, she was there.

Later that day, the news confirmed what Darren had already suspected. No one could identify the dead woman—and the only thing she had with her was a calculator that had shorted out.

That night, after his parents had gone to sleep, Darren went into his grandfather's room and told him about the woman. The old man listened patiently as Darren recounted the story.

"I have the strongest feeling that she came from somewhere else," Darren told his grandfather. "That she came to speak to *me*—but she failed."

He thought his grandfather might come up with some powerful words of ancient wisdom to explain the cruelness of this woman's fate, and her mystical appearance. But instead the old man just looked away wearily and said, "I think, maybe, your parents are right. And maybe it's best if you tell this to your psychologist friend."

After that, Darren decided he had to ignore the voices and the visitors if he was ever going to lead a normal life. He would deny their existence; choose not to see or hear them.

But as it turned out, he had little choice in the matter.

"Don't be afraid."

The third visitor didn't appear in the wall, or in a vat of beer. Instead he appeared at the mall, sitting across from Darren in the food court.

A few feet away, a little girl in a ketchup-stained dress tugged at her mother's sleeve, pointing to the man who had just appeared out of midair, but other than that, no one noticed the sudden appearance they were too involved in conversations and shoveling down lunch.

Darren wanted to scream long and loud, until mall security arrived to take this invader away, but he didn't. Who would believe him? This visitor seemed just like anyone else in the mall, from his jeans to the backpack he carried. So instead of screaming, Darren filled his mouth with his frozen yogurt until the urge to scream had been numbed.

"I don't want to frighten you," the visitor began. "I don't want to hurt you . . . but we need your help."

Darren studied the man's face. He had a strange tan, and features that seemed to be an exotic mix of many backgrounds. Darren knew about that. Although his father was Manahonset Indian, his mother was half Irish, half Polish—so Darren ended up looking like a red-headed, pale-skinned Manahonset. But this dark-skinned, light-haired man seemed even more a mix than himself. Even his eyes were a speckled hazel—not blue, green, or brown. Darren forced himself to look into the visitor's eyes, hoping to find something—proof of his intentions, maybe. Proof that he was honest, or proof that he was lying, but nothing about the visitor's eyes gave anything away. Darren didn't know whether he was safe or in grave, grave danger.

"My grandfather believes that ancient spirits can visit us," said Darren. "But I'm not sure I do."

"It doesn't matter either way," said the man. "Because I'm not an ancient spirit." He brushed some crumbs off the table in front of him, as if the very presence of dirt offended him. "My name is Rance," he said. "I come from the distant future—a time called the Age of Understanding. We've been trying to contact you for quite a while—you've heard us, no doubt."

Darren nodded. "Seen you, too." He curled his toes in his shoes, determined not to show his fear. "So if you're from the Age of Understanding," asked Darren, "how come the people you send, appear in walls, and get themselves drowned? Sounds like you don't understand much about time travel."

Rance stiffened just a bit at the mention of it. "If you understood the nature of time as well as we do, then you'd know that time travel is imperfect," he answered. "Time is constantly moving—slithering, like a snake with its head and tail gripping the end of infinity."

"Really," said Darren with a grin. "I always thought time was like a snake swallowing its own tail."

Rance was not amused.

"Time travel is not something to be taken lightly," he said. "In fact, we've come to understand that time travel should be avoided at all costs."

"Then why are you here?" Darren dared to ask. "And why are you bothering me?"

Rance smiled, showing his perfect teeth, white as polished ivory. "Because, young man, we need you for a mission of great importance. You, and no one else."

Darren's heart, as fast as it pounded, picked up the

pace. "You need me to come into the future?" Darren asked, not knowing whether he was more excited or frightened.

"No," answered Rance. "Not quite." Rance leaned in closer and lowered his voice to a whisper. "Have you ever heard of the Burgess Shale?"

Darren shook his head. "No."

Then Rance pulled out a small white stone from his pocket and dropped it into Darren's hand. As Darren examined it closely, he realized it wasn't a stone at all, but a tooth. A sharp, barbed tooth.

"The Burgess Shale," repeated Rance. "I suggest you learn about it." Then he vanished as quickly as he had come, and at the next table, the ketchup-stained girl tugged on her mother's sleeve again.

Burgess Shale, the encyclopedia entry read. *Only ten feet high, and a city block long, the Burgess Shale is one of the most important discoveries of prehistoric fossils ever unearthed.*

Aside from his collection of plastic dinosaurs, Darren knew painfully little about the distant past. Until now, he had never realized it could be of any importance to him. Apparently the Burgess Shale was discovered nearly a hundred years ago somewhere up in Canada. It held no dinosaur bones, however—these fossils came from a time millions of years before the dinosaurs, when life teemed in hot seas that covered most of the globe. Three hundred and fifty million years ago, to be exact.

Caught in a massive prehistoric mudslide, the fossils of the Burgess Shale are almost perfectly preserved, continued the encyclopedia, *and give us a clear view of the late Cambrian period.*

Darren turned the page to see the bizarre collection of creatures unearthed in the shale; the anomalocaris—a frightening beast with a round, tooth-filled mouth. The hallucigenia—a tiny multilegged thing that seemed so strange to the man who discovered it that he was convinced he was hallucinating.

But nothing could have prepared him for the sight of the opabinia!

It was spectacular, and like nothing Darren had ever imagined. Only three inches long, the unearthly creature had rows of gills running down the sides of its body, a single clawed arm growing from its head, and five eyes that gave it sight in every direction at once. It was weird, and wonderful.

No creature found in the Burgess Shale survives today. In fact, there is nothing even related to these creatures anywhere in the world. The end of the Cambrian period is marked by their mysterious extinction.

Extinction. Now *that* was something Darren knew about. He only had to look in his grandfather's fading eyes to see the extinction of his tribe. His grandfather would tell stories of the Manahonset Indians, and their proud heritage, but fewer and fewer Manahonset remained each year. Like Darren's father, they moved away and abandoned their culture. And so, while other Native American nations thrived, the Manahonset died a little more each day.

In recent years, we've come to realize that these creatures are unique, and unlike anything else that ever lived.

Darren reached into his pocket and pulled out the strange hooked tooth Rance had given him. Instinctively he knew that this was the tooth from the garbage-disposal mouth of anomalocaris!

The great extinction uncovered in the Burgess Shale changed forever the course of evolution, in ways impossible to comprehend.

Darren gripped the tooth tightly in his hand, wondering what all this had to do with him.

* * *

The time traveler next appeared in a phone booth as Darren walked to school the next day. They took the long way, speaking of things wonderfully complex and incomprehensible. Rance bragged about his great knowledge and dazzled Darren with talk of temporal fractals, dimensional loops, and quantum-multiplistic theory.

"We have come to understand that there are eighteen distinct focal points in Earth's history," explained Rance. "Some of them are prehistoric and others more recent—but put together, these eighteen events have determined the course of life, and of mankind."

"What are they?" asked Darren, hungry to know the great answers of the universe, uncovered in the Age of Understanding.

But Rance shook his head. "Not for you to know. . . . But I can tell you this—the event that created the Burgess Shale 350 million years ago is one of the most important events of all. It's also different."

"What makes it so different?"

"Because unlike any other prehistoric event," explained Rance, "our sub-molecular analysis of the Burgess Shale indicates that there was conspicuous human intervention."

Darren wrinkled his brow in confusion. "What do you mean?"

"I mean that at the time of the great Cambrian extinction . . . *people were there*. Two people, to be exact."

"People? But . . . but how?" asked Darren. "People weren't around for millions of years. . . ."

Rance produced a small calculator from his backpack—just like the one the first two unlucky time travellers had carried. "This is how."

Darren looked at it closely to see that the calculator had a glowing green button, dead center.

"It has taken hundreds of years to generate enough energy to power a 350-million-year time-transport."

"To the Cambrian period!" Darren shouted. "To see what really happened!"

"You're catching on!" said Rance, placing the time-calculator-thingy in Darren's hands. "This is yours. I have my own."

"Wait—You mean—"

"I mean that *you* are to accompany me to the distant past. You will be witness to one of the most important events in prehistory."

Darren held the device as if it were a tiny nuclear bomb. "Why me?" he asked.

Rance laughed as if the question was stupid and the answer obvious.

"Because in our infinite understanding," explained the arrogant time traveler, "we have concluded that of all the humans who have ever lived, *you* are the one who must go."

Darren let his words echo deep within his soul. He had always felt he was meant for something special in the great design of things. Perhaps his destiny truly was a great one! But still, there was a part of him that wanted to know more—*needed* to know more. And he was afraid.

"Wh—what if I don't want to go?"

Rance smiled in that superior way of his. "Oh, you'll go," he said. "History shows that you *did* go, and if there's one thing we know, it's that history doesn't change."

"But—"

Rance dismissed Darren's questioning with a wave of his hand. It made Darren furious. Just because he was from the Age of Understanding didn't give Rance the right to treat Darren this way.

"Whether it's today, or whether it's tomorrow, you're

going to hit that button," Rance proclaimed. "And when
you do, I'll be waiting for you there, at the edge of the
prehistoric sea."

Rance did not come again. Not that night, nor the next
day, nor the day after that. Darren wanted Rance to return
and plead with Darren to press the button. How could
Rance be so arrogant—so sure that Darren would go. But
Darren knew the answer.

Because I've already gone.

Somehow, they know the past. They *understand* the
past, and if it already happened, Rance is right—Darren
would press that button someday and transport to that impossibly distant point in history, when the opabinia, the
anomalocaris, and many other strange creatures swam the
seas.

What made it worse was that Darren really *did* want to
go. It was a grand destiny indeed to be chosen to witness
one of the most important events since the beginning of
time—but what good was such a destiny if he had no
choice in it? Being chosen can only be special when you
have the choice to refuse. Without that choice, he was
merely a tiny gear in the machinery of the universe. Machinery he could never change.

So he refused to push the button.

He refused for a whole month. He barely ate, he barely
spoke. His parents, more worried than ever, sent him on
extra visits to the psychologist.

Then came the dream. It came on a night when the
wind howled and sounded alive with mournful wails. In
his dream Darren was trapped in the Burgess Shale,
buried beneath tons of mud that had hardened into rock
over millions of years. And in the stone around him, a
million creatures called out his name. *"Darren . . . Darren,"* they cried. *"Come to us . . . join us,"* they wailed.

"You can't change what has already been. . . ." A school of one-clawed opabinia swarmed around him, moving through the stone, their five unblinking eyes staring at him. He tried to scream, but his mouth was filled with stone. He had no flesh—only bone. *He* was the fossil now . . . but he wasn't the only one. Beside him was his father, and then his grandfather, and then his great-grandfather. The shale was filled with the bones of the Manahonset, their ancient voices silenced by the stone.

Darren awoke in a cold sweat, gasping for breath, still feeling the heavy pressure of the shale all around him.

Finally the dream faded away, but the images remained in his mind. And that's when he knew he had to go.

He had to see the opabinia—because he understood what it meant to be lost when the world changed. As he lay there in bed, Darren could hear his grandfather snoring weakly in the next room. His grandfather no longer told the old stories like he used to, and when he died, he would take with him a history that should have been Darren's. That was an end just as final as the opabinia's.

So he finally took the time-calculator and punched the button. Not because Rance said he would, but because the opabinia deserved the dignity of a witness. Someone to affirm its life and tell its tale. Someone to make it matter.

The moment he pressed the button, an intense pain shot through him. It was like being turned inside out, while being fired from a cannon, while boiling in acid. He saw time peel away before him, the days spinning like a strobe light until the sun and moon were streaks in the sky. But he wasn't only moving through time, he was moving through space as well, rocketing through solid mountains, moving north, toward the great Burgess Shale.

It seemed to last an eternity, and yet it was over before Darren drew a single breath—and when he did, the air was hot and thick with sulfur, like the smell of a million rotten eggs. The sky was red instead of blue and the air so humid he felt he could almost swim in it.

"There you are," he heard a familiar voice next to him say.

"Waiting long?" Darren sneered.

"Six minutes," said Rance. "Your machine was programmed to bring you here five minutes after I arrived—but, as I said, time travel is imperfect."

Darren looked out over the vista in front of him, and if there had been any anger, any frustration in him, it was washed away by the magnificent sight of Cambrian Earth.

Before him was a great inland sea, surrounded by cliffs hundreds of feet high. It was near sunset, and in the fading light, creatures left phosphorescent trails like underwater fireworks stretching as far as the eye could see.

Darren could only stare in amazement.

"I know," said Rance. "No one has ever seen such splendor, nor will anyone ever see it again."

"Can I get closer?"

Rance nodded. "You can, and you must," was all he said.

Darren approached the water's edge, and there, wallowing in a tide pool, he saw them for the first time. Opabinia. They were only a few inches long, but breathtaking all the same.

Darren scooped one up, and it wriggled in his hand. Its exoskeleton was not a dull gray armor, but a smooth multi-colored shell, reflecting every color of the rainbow. Its five eyes were not empty and cold, but innocent and warm. The claw that grew from its head was not spiny and rough, but soft and velvety.

The creature was not a monster, but a wonder.

"Take a good look," said Rance. "*Your* scientists don't know it—but this is the last place in Cambrian Earth that these creatures still exist." Then he pointed to the enormous cliff that overhung the great inland sea. "In half an hour, that mountainside will come crashing down, clogging this sea with poisonous mud. Everything in it will die."

Darren gaped at Rance as he finally realized why this moment in time was so important. The mudslide that created the Burgess Shale didn't just capture a sample of these strange creatures—*it snuffed out their very existence!* In half an hour, the opabinia, and countless other creatures, would become extinct!

Darren petted the back of the tiny opabinia. *How unfair,* he thought, *that something so wondrous had to die off.*

He was still thinking of the doomed opabinia when Rance grabbed his hand. By the time Darren heard the clink of metal, it was too late. He looked down to see his arm handcuffed to a chain and the chain locked to a steel spike that was embedded in the stone beneath them.

"Wh—what's this?" Darren asked lamely.

"History in the making," answered Rance, just as calmly as could be. "Do you remember that tooth I gave you? That tooth belonged to quite a large anomalocaris. While your scientists were only able to take the fossil and reconstruct what the creature looked like, we, in the Age of Understanding, were able to uncover its entire genetic structure . . . and do you know what we found?"

Darren tugged at his chain. It clanked in the thick sulfuric air, but held him tight.

"We found two very distinct chains of DNA," continued Rance. "One belonged to the anomalocaris itself, and the other belonged to *the last thing the anomalocaris ate.*"

Even in the hot air of the Cambrian dusk, Darren felt a chill rocket up his highly evolved spine. "Me?"

"You," answered Rance. "No one else in the universe has your exact DNA. It took us many years to track you down, and many months trying to contact you, but ultimately we knew we would."

Darren screamed in furious terror: *"You brought me here to be eaten?"*

"Be proud," said Rance calmly. "Very few people know their purpose in the universe."

There was a sound in the sea behind him, like a groan coming up from deep in the shimmering water. The clanking of his chains had drawn the attention of something beneath the waters.

"No!" screamed Darren. "I won't let it happen!"

"No sense fighting it," said Rance. "It already did happen. It's just a matter of letting the event play through to its natural conclusion."

Still, Darren tugged on his chains. To die was bad enough; to be eaten was even worse. But to be eaten by something that would itself die in half an hour—Darren could not imagine a more meaningless end.

"So the only reason you came here was to feed me to this . . . to this *thing*?"

"No," said Rance. "I also came to detonate this." He reached into his backpack—the one he always carried— and pulled out a bulky device with wires and a clock. Even in the Age of Understanding, a bomb looked like a bomb.

All at once Darren realized the full extent of Rance's mission. "You're going to start the mudslide that kills off all of these creatures, aren't you!"

"That is *my* purpose," answered Rance, "to prune the tree of evolution, and make sure that these creatures die, paving the way for life as we know it."

With his free hand, Darren reached for his time-travel device and punched the button. But nothing happened. In fact, the dim digital readout died completely.

"Your transporter only had enough power for a one-way trip," explained Rance. "We, in the Age of Understanding, believe in conserving energy when we can."

And with that, Rance turned and headed up toward the cliff with his bomb of extinction.

The water began to ripple around Darren's feet, and the school of opabinia wallowing in the tide pool flung themselves back into the sea, in a race to escape what was approaching.

A pearly white glow rose to the surface.

"No!" screamed Darren *"No!"*

The anomalocaris launched itself out of the water and into the tide pool. It was only two feet long, but as deadly as something ten times its size, with sharp, gleaming pincers. It came at Darren, its circular, tooth-filled mouth ready to eat this newfound futuristic delight. Darren kicked it away with his foot, but it slithered back toward him again in the shallow water. Then a second one surfaced and launched toward him. And then a third.

"I will not die this way!" Darren insisted. He knew his will to live flew in the face of history, but still he fought his destiny with everything he had.

Over and over the prehistoric beasts attacked—but they had not evolved intelligence—they couldn't learn from their mistakes. Each time the beasts launched the exact same attack, and each time, Darren was able to kick them away with his foot . . . but one slip and Darren's foot would be caught in one of their deadly mouths, and that would be his end.

If he could break free from his chain, he could still run away. He could make it out of the ravine before Rance detonated his bomb of extinction. Even if history said he didn't escape, he had to try.

When the next anomalocaris attacked, Darren plunged his hand deep into its mouth, gagging it, and then pulled his hand out quickly. The dumb beast bit down, missing his hand, but caught the chain—

—and the force of its bite split the chain in two!

Darren kicked it away for the last time, scrambled out of the tide pool, and raced up the steep slope, following the footprints of Rance . . . while behind him the three anomalocari slipped back into the sea, in search of other prey.

Rance had been so sure of himself. They thought they had all the answers in the Age of Understanding—but they didn't, did they? For Darren had changed his own destiny. He had altered the course of history and would not end up in the bellies of the doomed beasts. His DNA would never end up on that tooth! Even as he climbed the mountain he could feel the change radiating forward from this moment, toward infinity—the great serpent of time writhing in agony as all of eternity adjusted itself. It was a feeling of enormous power.

At the top of the ridge Darren came across Rance, kneeling over his bomb. He wasn't expecting to see Darren again, and when he did, the color drained from his face. It was wonderful to see the Man of Understanding at a loss for words.

"But . . . but you can't be here! It's impossible."

"Sorry," said Darren, "but we, in the Age of Video, don't believe anything's impossible."

Darren ran forward and kicked the bomb away from Rance.

"No!" Rance screamed, "you don't know what you're doing. This bomb *must* go off! The mudslide won't happen without it!"

Now Darren was the one who could afford to be smug. "Maybe it's just me, but I don't believe in killing off endangered species—even ones that lived 350 million years before I was born!"

Darren grinned and tore the wires from the bomb. It had no backup triggers because the Wise Ones hadn't expected anyone would tamper with it. And so when Darren pulled its wires, its timer stopped dead.

Rance, his eyes wide in disbelief, backed away from Darren in terror. "It *will* go off!" Rance screamed. "It has to go off! You can't change what's already happened. You can't ch—"

And then the time traveler took one step too far, lost his balance, and tumbled off the prehistoric cliff.

Darren leapt forward, trying to catch him, but it was too late. He could only watch as the Man of Understanding tumbled a thousand feet into the great inland sea. There was a thrashing of white water, and his body was gone—devoured by a school of anomalocari—perhaps the same ones that were meant to eat Darren.

Feeling weak from the thinness of the oxygen and the terror of the moment, Darren fell to his knees and found himself staring at the defused bomb. But that didn't interest him. What interested him was the small calculator-like device beside it. Rance had dropped his time-transporter, and *this* one had the power for a return trip!

Darren took the defused bomb and hurled it off the cliff, so it could do no harm. Then he programmed a date and time into the calculator and punched the green button.

Intense pain turned him inside out as he shot forward to the distant future, and home.

His parents found him lying on the bathroom floor, his hand gripping his gut in pain. The trip home had been far worse than his trip to the Cambrian sea. It was as if his body had been shredded, reformed, and shredded again. He could barely move. But at least he hadn't materialized in a solid wall.

"Darren! Darren, honey," wailed his mom. "Are you all right?"

Darren took a deep breath, and another, and another. The pain was quickly subsiding. "It was a dream," he told them. "Just a bad dream." Although he knew it was real.

His grandfather went to get him a drink, and his father helped him up. "C'mon, Darren, it's only a dream. Everyone has nightmares."

They helped him back to bed, and once everyone had left his room, Darren tried to replay what he had seen—what he had lived through—but the images were already getting lost in confusion. He couldn't even remember what Rance looked like.

Rance had been so afraid of Darren's changing a key event in history—but after all his worries, had anything really changed? For an instant Darren thought something might be different, but the feeling washed away with the memory of Rance's face. No, the time traveler had been wrong. Nothing had changed. Everything seemed fine. Everything seemed normal.

And that was good.

Darren fell asleep thinking of the great prehistoric sea. What an amazing sight it was! He wouldn't have believed it if he hadn't seen it with his own five eyes.

DAWN
TERMINATOR

●●●●●●●●●●●●●●●●●●●●●●●●●●●●●●●●●●

We lost contact with Denver at 4:00 A.M.

That's what the newswoman says on TV. Her hair's a ragged mess, and her hands fidget in desperation—the kind of desperation news anchors aren't supposed to show.

I'm cold and frightened. Terrified of the night outside the huge airport windows and terrified of the noisy crowds moving in that darkness. I hate the dark—I hate the night. I've always been a day person—but that doesn't mean much anymore, according to the woman on the news.

In the crowded airport lounge, people stare blankly at the TV screen. A man curses beneath his breath, even as he rocks his baby in his arms. A woman gapes at the screen as she picks nervously at her peeling cuticles. None of these people can stretch their mind around what's happening. I can't either. It's too big—too awful.

So instead of thinking about it, I take a pencil and my

sketch pad from my shoulder bag, figuring I'll find something to draw. The man with the baby. The woman tearing at her own fingertips. I always get an intense craving to draw when things around me get too rough to handle. Funny, the things you feel like doing when everything's coming down around you.

Mom reaches over and gently restrains my hand before I can lay pencil to paper.

"No, Lauren, not now."

Dad grabs my younger brother tightly. "We can't stay here, we have to move," Dad says. I look out of the lounge; a heavy current of panicked people flows by, heading toward the gates. I try to see their faces, but they wash by too quickly for me to get an image I can hold. They won't slow down, because they know time is ticking away, and time has become everyone's worst enemy.

My family, like many other people, has stopped in the terminal lounge to rest and catch their breath, but wasting any more time here will be a mistake. There are a thousand—maybe a million other people crammed into the gates and hallways of San Francisco International Airport. We don't have any plane tickets, but then no one does.

"We'll get on a plane," Dad promises as we prepare to force our way into the moving crowd. "We'll make it." Dad's the kind of guy who always manages to get his way, but this is the only time it really matters.

"What will happen when the sun rises?" my brother, Kenny, asks.

"You don't have to worry about that," answers Mom. "We're never going to see the sun rise."

I look at my watch. Forty-three minutes and twenty seconds until dawn. I guess we've all memorized the exact time morning will show its blinding face today. I start to imagine what will happen the moment the sun rises, but my mind shuts off like a circuit breaker—as if just imagining it will burn my mind to a cinder.

No one believed it could happen.

The scientists said it wouldn't—they swore that the warning signs were false and that only lunatics and crackpots would suggest such a thing. The truth is, they didn't want to believe that the Sun could go nova.

But two minutes before midnight, it did.

At 11:58 P.M., Pacific standard time, the sun detonated with a force too immense to calculate—just like the crackpots said it would. Six minutes later, Europe, Asia, Africa—everything east of the Atlantic was gone. There was no one left to tell this half of the world what was waiting for us at dawn . . . but we knew.

We knew because of the way transatlantic phone calls suddenly went dead.

We knew because of how brightly the moon suddenly shone in the sky—so bright you couldn't even look at it.

But for our family, it was the honking of horns that woke us up to the truth. Thousands of blaring car horns, all blending together into a panicked siren, loud enough to wake the dead. Every road, every freeway was instantly jammed. We quickly joined in that honking madness, riding over sidewalks and yards, because the roads themselves were already clotted with abandoned cars. I made Dad drive with the dome light on, so Kenny and I wouldn't have to sit in that awfully dark backseat—which seemed worse than any dark I could remember.

In our race to the airport, we passed hordes of people looking heavenward, praying in the streets. I prayed, too. Prayed that we would all be saved—that the Earth would stop spinning and that the line of dawn would stop burning its way across the world.

The Terminator—that's what they call the line that divides the night from the day. It stretches from pole to pole, and never stops moving as the earth spins.

But it doesn't *quite* stretch from pole to pole. Far to the north, there are places where the northern lights dance, and the night lasts for months on end. Places beyond the Arctic Circle. It's late November now—that means the sun won't rise there for at least three months. That's where we must go to escape the killing breath of the sun.

And we have forty-one minutes left to fly from the dawn.

As we try to force our way out of the lounge, more people press in. I see a kid I recognize, but he doesn't spare a thought for me—he's trying too hard to catch his breath. In front of us, the mob races past like a rain-swollen river. You can drown in a current like that. I imagine myself pulled down and suffocated beneath the feet of the moving mass. There are so many bodies that they block the fluorescent light from above—it must be pitch black down by the scuffling feet of the crowd. That's a darkness worth being afraid of.

Mom and Dad hold Kenny's and my hands tightly, and we leap into the dangerous crowd.

Instantly we are pulled into the current. I'm whipped in the face by the red-painted nails of a passing hand. A fat man's belt buckle scratches across my side. My bag slips from my shoulder, and although I reach back for it, Mom tugs me along.

"Forget it," she says. "It doesn't matter."

My bag is trampled, and swallowed, disappearing into the darkness. My sketch pad, with all my drawings, is lost—it was the only thing I had wanted to take with me. The faces I had drawn.

Then my hand slips from my mother's.

"Lauren? Lauren!" I hear her call but can't see her.

"Lauren!" Her cries seem farther away, and all I can see are the dark textures of heavy clothes moving all around me. I'm surrounded by people, and yet alone in the crushing crowd. Although I want to scream, I know that giving in to panic will be even more dangerous than being separated from my family. So I bite my fear back and give my will over to the will of the moving mob. Pressed between the crying old woman to my right and the angry bearded man on my left, I let the mob carry me down the endless airport corridor, toward unseen gates of departure.

Gates 44, 45, 46. I see the signs pass by above me—but each gate is mobbed with people—I can't even see if there are planes at the ends of the jetways. Suddenly there's a burst of cold air, as the human river bursts out through an emergency exit. My feet stumble down a set of metal steps, until I set foot on hard asphalt.

The airport tarmac is a huge expanse of concrete covered with airplanes all facing at strange angles. Not normal airport order. I wonder if anyone is even in the air-traffic tower.

There are people everywhere, racing in random directions. A woman with a raging knot of tangled hair uses her suitcase as a battering ram to get past, and she bounces me to the ground.

And there, through the forests of legs, I see a pair of cartoon-character Nikes I recognize—and they're moving away.

But in the last few minutes I've learned some tricks of survival. I force myself forward, slamming my shoulders into legs around me, hitting people, tripping people—everything short of biting them to get them out of my way—until I finally reach out and grab that small foot with both hands.

Kenny screams and looks down.

"It's Lauren!" he cries. "I found Lauren!"

Dad pulls me into his arms. "Thank god! We thought we lost you!"

He and Mom hug me tightly, but only for an instant. There will be time for hugs later, if there's any time at all. I dare to look at my watch. Thirty-four minutes.

The crowds around us are thickest near the planes, where roll-away staircases are blocked by armed security guards. I guess airport security has taken it upon themselves to pick and choose who gets to go on the planes, and it makes me angry—what gives *them* the right to make the choice?

Dad pulls us toward a plane where a guard who couldn't be any older than eighteen bars the way, letting no one up to the hatch. He scans the crowd with wide, anxious eyes as if searching for someone.

We force our way forward until reaching the guard.

"Back off!" yells the guard. "This plane is full." He aims his weapon at my father's chest. Dad ignores the gun.

"I don't think you want to shoot me," Dad warns the guard. "I'm a pilot."

The guard's eyes light up with relief. "From the airline?" he asks.

"Does it matter?" my father answers.

The fact is, my father once flew fighter jets in the air force, and although he hasn't flown for ten years, he's the best hope for this plane. It's now I realize that there aren't enough pilots to fly all these planes.

"Only you can come," the guard tells my father sternly. "No room for the others."

But Dad stands his ground. "Let my family on, or fly the plane yourself."

"There'll be other pilots," the guard insists.

Dad glances at his watch. "Maybe, maybe not," he

says. "All I know is that sunrise is less than a half an hour away."

The guard doesn't need any more coaxing. He nods, and we clatter up the stairs toward the plane. The guard follows right behind us.

At the top of the stairs, I turn to see the mob forcing its way up the stairs. Their pleading cries rise above the rest of the crowd.

"Out of the way!" bellows the guard. He pushes me into the DC-10 and swings the heavy door closed behind us.

Hands pound on the door outside, and through the tiny window in the door I see a man, his face pressed up against the glass by the mob pushing behind him.

I turn away, but Mom gently touches my shoulder.

"No," she says. "Look at them. Study their faces. *Memorize* their faces."

I look at her, confused. "Why?"

"Because your memory of them is all they have left."

And so I do as she says. I make my way through the crowded aisles, force my way to a window seat. Then I peer out the window, at the faces outside.

There are people on the wing now, and more climbing up the engine, to the wing. They pound on the hull until it sounds like a hailstorm. Men, women, children. They pull at the wing flaps in a mad frenzy. I study their faces. I give them names. Mr. Smith. Mrs. Josephs. Bobby, Angela, JJ.

I hear the engines start, and we begin to move forward.

The crowd moves away from the plane—even the maddened people on the wings jump down. Maybe they know that our hope is more important than their desperation.

Then, as we turn to get in line behind a dozen other jets waiting for takeoff, I see the first trace of the coming dawn.

The eastern edge of the sky doesn't shine a faint blue—

instead it burns a searing, lethal white, fading into the darkness of the night cover still protecting us. It's just a hint of the dawn soon to come. A warning.

"We have to take off!" people around me shout. "We have to leave now."

I squirm out into the aisle and over a dozen people until reaching the cockpit where my father mans the controls. He has no co-pilot—only Kenny sits there, kicking his feet. Mom sits in the navigator's seat, trying to make sense of the navigational charts.

I watch the planes before us, taking off one right behind another.

"C'mon, c'mon," my father says, gripping the controls with white knuckles as the eastern sky begins to burn a brighter white.

At last the plane before us accelerates down the runway, and Dad instantly powers our engines to full throttle, right on the other jet's tail—a dangerous but necessary move. I hold on tight as we pick up speed. I feel the front wheels leave the ground, and then the rear. We are airborne!

Dad instantly banks away from the plane just ahead of us, and soon we are heading northwest. I can feel our airspeed as it increases.

We're airborne, but I don't know how safe we are. The minutes fly by much too quickly, and twelve minutes after takeoff we punch through the highest layer of clouds. I dare to look out a side window as we take a sharp bank to avoid another plane.

That's when I see it happen.

The first true rays of sun assault the horizon . . . and the clouds boil away before it, until they are gone.

Far away, at the edge of the horizon, the towers of San Francisco burst into flames—and I swear I see the Golden Gate bridge melt into the bay.

The tiny dots of planes just minutes behind us turn into fireballs, and Mom gently puts a hand to my face, guiding my eyes away from the window.

"Now's the time to stop looking," says Mom.

I wonder how long it will be until we become like those ill-fated people, disintegrating into the new day. Surely our plane was built to withstand extreme heat and cold. But I don't think its designers had this particular trip in mind.

Inside the cabin, the air temperature keeps rising, but Dad banks us due west and somehow finds even greater airspeed. I turn to him. "Can we make it?" I ask. "Can we outrun the dawn?"

"This is a fast jet," he answers. "We'll see."

In less than a minute that glimmer of sun is gone as we surpass the speed of the spinning earth. The sun seems to set behind us while we keep our eyes locked forward into the trailing edge of night.

12:00 noon. At least that's what my watch says, but time doesn't mean much anymore. It's still dark. We've been spiraling to the north for seven hours, and although the Dawn Terminator is still on the horizon behind us, just as white hot as ever, it's slipping to the south, instead of east. We have already crossed into the Arctic Circle, and Dad banks the plane to the right. Soon we will cross directly over the North Pole ice pack, heading toward a place where the sun won't rise for months.

"What if we can't find a place to land?" Kenny asks, but no one answers him. There's no room anymore for "what ifs."

I leave Dad to worry about that and try to soothe myself by drawing on the back of American Airlines cocktail napkins. I've finished about five of them now and start on a new one.

"What are you drawing?" Mom asks. I show her the napkin I just finished. They say I have a talent for portraits, and now I have a real reason to draw them.

"Who is it?" Mom asks.

"A woman I saw in the crowd," I tell her. Then I hand her the stack of finished ones. "They're all people I saw in the crowd before we took off."

Mom looks at me with surprise and wonder, and hands me better paper.

"I think we've arrived," says Dad, almost an hour later.

We are over the northern tip of Greenland—Cape Morris Jessup, to be exact. It's the northernmost piece of land on the globe. The glow from the fiery Terminator is far away now. That distant white glow will circle around the North Pole, threatening the horizon for months, until it finally engulfs the entire Arctic Circle. Then this icy land will pay dearly for its many months of darkness—for in the summer months, the midnight sun will burn, and this place will not see night until the fall.

"If the sun won't rise for three months," asks Kenny, "what happens *after* three months?"

Mom and Dad look at each other, unsure how to answer. But I know what the answer is. "We have three months to figure that out," I tell him.

He nods. "That's a long time," he says. I suppose to him it is.

"It'll be long enough," I answer.

My father seems to sit up straighter as he hears me say it. "Yes . . . yes, I think it will be." I can almost see his faith in our survival growing with each second—my mother's, too, as if my hope was a seed for theirs to grow on.

The blue glow of a blinding bright moon paints a landscape of ice beneath us. I'd call it uninviting, but here and now, there's no place on earth I'd rather be. It's bright enough to land on—and bright enough to see a hundred other planes dotting the endless expanse of ice. We weren't the only ones who made it—although we are probably among the last.

Then I feel the plane begin its final descent. With that descent, I can hear voices in the cabin chiming forth offerings of hope.

"I'm a thermal engineer," calls out one man. "I can design heat shields, like the ones they use on the space shuttle."

"Hey," shouts one woman, "what if we fly by night to the South Pole in the summer?"

"Hey," shouts another, "what if we find caverns to give us shelter in the spring and fall?"

"Yeah—we can cultivate crops that grow in darkness. Mushrooms, maybe!"

On and on, until the world we've lost doesn't seem to matter anymore—all that matters is tomorrow, and the next day, and the next.

As I think of it, all at once I feel a rush of heated emotions rising in me with more power than the nova we once called the sun. I feel everything all at once. Anger, fear, sorrow, but also an incredible comfort, and intense joy. Now I realize that this great and awesome cosmic event is not an ending—but it's not really a beginning either; it's a link between what was and what will be. *We* are that link. Mom, Dad, Kenny, and me, and everyone on every plane that made it this far. What a wonderful destiny to be a bridge to the future.

Tears cloud my eyes, and Mom puts an arm around me. "It'll be all right," she says. "You'll see." She thinks my tears are tears of sadness, but they're not—not anymore. Because now I know we'll survive just as surely as I know the sun won't rise. With time finally on our side, we *will* find those safe caverns. We *will* build those heat shields. And when the angry sun does find us after the long night, it will find us ready.

We will adapt. I will adapt.

Our wheels touch the surface of the great expanse of ice, and as I look out the window, I have to smile through my tears. I've already learned to love the night.

MIDNIGHT
MICHELANGELO

••••••••••••••••••••••••••••••••••••

With the sounds of traffic far below and the dark sky above, fourteen-year-old Mickey Blake hung suspended between the sky and the angry city. He didn't think about how high he was; he thought only about the task at hand: his masterpiece.

Silver paint hissed out the tip of a spray can, leaving a dazzling streak glistening on the metal surface. *Just a few minutes more,* Mickey told himself. *Just a few minutes more and I'll be done.* He had to remind himself not to look down, or he might lose his balance and fall in front of the cars that shot down the freeway. His work on the overpass was almost done . . . just a few finishing touches.

"Mickey!" shouted a voice from below. "Mickey, we've gotta get out of here!" It was Wendy. He could hear the panic in her voice, but figured it was probably nothing major. She simply wasn't used to this sort of thing. But an instant later, Mickey heard the sirens.

"Mickey, hurry!" Wendy shouted. "They're coming!"

"One sec!" he shouted back. "Just one second more." He couldn't stop when he was this close. He had to risk it. Blue and red lights began to play off the colorful work of art in front of him. He clipped the can of silver spray paint onto his mountain-climbing harness and grabbed the blue paint can. Quickly he filled in the blue iris of an eye that was two feet high. Below him he heard the slamming of a car door.

"That's enough, Picasso!" came the voice of a policeman, bellowing through a bullhorn. "Get down here!"

But Mickey wasn't about to be caught. Not tonight. He rappelled from the steel face of the freeway overpass and swung in a wide arc to the right. He stopped at the edge of his great painting and sprayed the initials "M.M." in bright red. It was a tag that was getting to be known around the city, as great masterpieces of spray-paint art appeared overnight.

Nobody knew who M.M. really was. But everyone knew what it stood for: Midnight Michelangelo.

Two policemen climbed the girder of the overpass to get him. He rappelled once more, his mountain harness holding him tight as he swung over to the left, like a human pendulum. Then he unhooked himself and scurried down a fence to freedom. Wendy was waiting for him. The police were confounded, trying in vain to pursue the boy but unable to catch up to him.

"Are you nuts, Mickey?" said Wendy. "Were those initials worth getting arrested for?" But Mickey only smiled. His head was pounding. The fumes from the spray paint gave him his headaches, he was sure, but his art was worth any amount of pain.

They were many blocks away when dawn began to break, and Mickey had to turn back and look at his creation. The sun told a truth about his talent that the stark streetlights could not.

His work was a high-tech futurescape, filled with swooping monorails, bottomless steel canyons, glass skyscrapers reaching beyond the heavens, and sleek, silvery robotic faces. It covered the metal span of the overpass, looking down at the dull, urban sprawl around it. "It's incredible, Mickey," said Wendy. "*You're* incredible."

"It's my best yet," Mickey proudly told Wendy. As the sun grew brighter, the streaks of silver paint turned to gold.

"Every color has a voice, every texture a soul. . . ."

The next morning at school Mickey sat at his desk half asleep and tried to listen to Miss Clarkson spout forth her philosophy of art. But few kids in class were listening to their ninth-grade art teacher, and the ones that were really had no clue anyway. Paintbrush in hand, Mickey dozed off. He was startled awake by Miss Clarkson's tapping him roughly on the shoulder. She pointed to his blank canvas. "Working in white today?" she asked.

"Uh . . . I'm waiting for inspiration," answered Mickey.

Miss Clarkson smirked. "Inspiration requires consciousness, Mr. Blake."

Snickers erupted around the room, then a voice behind him whispered, "Guess you can't paint unless someone's filling out an arrest warrant, huh, Mickey?" It was Brody Harkin, of course. To Mickey, Brody was everything bad about the world. He was tall, handsome, arrogant, and brainless. He was also Wendy's boyfriend. Sure, Wendy might love Mickey's artwork, but it was Brody who had her attentions in every other way. Somewhere along the line, Wendy let it slip to Brody that Mickey was the Midnight Michelangelo. Ever since then, Brody taunted Mickey with the information—always threatening to announce it to the world. It was just one more frustration in a life that was anything but a picnic—but Mickey had learned to live with it. After all, lots of artists lived tortured lives, and Brody Harkin certainly qualified as torture.

Mickey tried to slip out quietly when the bell rang, but Miss Clarkson caught him and insisted he stay after class. He heard Brody snicker as he left the room, with his beefy arm slung over Wendy's shoulder.

"Someone oughta spray-paint *loser* on his forehead," Brody said.

Wendy threw Mickey an apologetic look, as if it was her job to apologize for Brody, and then she got lost in the crowd of students filing out of the room. Mickey continually wondered how Wendy could like a kid like Brody—but then Mickey figured it was that same poor judgment that made her hang around with *him* as well.

When everyone was gone, Mickey turned to Miss Clarkson. "I can explain about sleeping in class," he said. He was prepared to make up any and every excuse, except the truth, but Miss Clarkson would have none of it.

"I'm sure you can explain," she said. "You have a great imagination. Have you ever thought of putting it to good use?"

Mickey shrugged. "I have been."

"Yes," Miss Clarkson said with a frown, "but you can't make a living breaking the law . . . Michelangelo."

Hearing her say that name sent a high-tension chill weaving through his spine. Wendy knew about who he was, and so did Brody. There were other kids in school who suspected, but for a teacher to know—that meant trouble. The dull ache in his head began to pound with the fury of a jackhammer.

"Listen, Miss Clarkson, I've got a headache. I really have to go." He tried to slip out of the room, but Miss Clarkson stood in his way.

"Your work is great, Mickey," she told him. "I can spot it anywhere. I especially like the robot ninjas on the side of the unemployment office." Mickey thought she would make a move to get the principal, but she didn't. Could it be that she genuinely liked his work?

"You mean you won't tell?"

"I'm not the art police," she answered. "But I hate to see talent like yours going to waste."

That hurt. "Thousands of people see my stuff," Mickey said proudly.

"But they condemn it as trash," insisted Miss Clarkson. "*That's* the difference, Mickey—no one ever sandblasted the Sistine Chapel's ceiling."

Mickey looked down at his paint-stained shoes. "So?"

"So your work should be shown in galleries, winning awards. You should earn respect, not handcuffs."

Mickey scoffed and looked away, pretending he was bored, pretending he didn't care. But in truth, he was savoring every word she said. He closed his eyes and let the compliments sink in, hoping that maybe they'd drive his headache away.

"Your work has a soul, Mickey," she said. "It has a life of its own."

And neither of them knew how very true that was.

That afternoon, Mickey met Wendy at the Martians. It had gotten to be a habit, meeting in secret, because neither of them wanted Brody to know. "The Martians" was one of Mickey's best works. Red faces and bright, luminous eyes stretched the entire length of the wall. But today these martians would die.

"I tried to stop them, Mickey, but they wouldn't listen. They won't even admit it's art!" Wendy said to him as he arrived. "I'm sorry, Mickey. There was nothing I could do. They had already started when I got here. . . ."

"Started what?" Mickey rounded the corner to see workmen with paint rollers covering Mickey's martian masterpiece with dull gray paint; the same color as the rest of the city. His heart sank. What had taken him days in preparation and planning to create was thoughtlessly being destroyed in a matter of minutes. He winced at the sight. It felt as if they were painting the walls of his stomach. He could feel the pain in his head swell with his anger . . .

. . . and that's when he heard them. It was hollow and distant, but he heard them just the same.

The martians.

He could hear their muffled, wailing cries as they died, suffocated by the thick, greasy paint. But there was something more—for as he took another look at the martian faces, he could swear he saw them scowling darkly. He hadn't painted them like that. Their expressions had been glorious, not sinister.

"I . . . I didn't paint this," Mickey said.

"What? What do you mean?" said Wendy.

"These faces, they're all wrong." He moved closer to one of the twisted faces of the martians, and in the shadows of the painting he saw a hulking shape. It was dark, painted in deep burnt umber. The shadow had strange, serpentine coils and eyes like smoldering embers.

"What *is* that?" mumbled Mickey. But before he could have a better look, a workman painted it out of existence.

Mickey's mom wasn't an artist. Nor was she an art collector. Unless of course, you counted all the Elvis paintings she had bought from the Home Shopping Network. She was a single mom working two jobs, which didn't leave her much time for things like art. As for Mickey's dad, he had a new family in the suburbs and only came to visit Mickey around Christmastime—more to make himself feel better than out of any love for his skinny, brooding son. "Tis the season to feel guilty," Mickey had sung to his father when he picked him up last Christmas Day. Dear old Dad had not been amused by the truth.

But Mickey had his art—and *that* was something he could always count on. And so while Mom dozed in front of the TV each night, Mickey sat in his room, lovingly sketching the early drafts of the next great paintings he planned. Tonight's sketch was another alien landscape, this one full of tall, graceful creatures with silky, gossamer wings. They swooped and soared around crystalline towers. But tonight, Mickey couldn't keep his focus. Maybe it was the voices of the martians and the strangeness of their faces. It had to be his imagination, he decided—sleep deprivation can do weird things to the mind. Still, he couldn't stop thinking about it.

Even in the privacy of his room, there was something that didn't quite feel right. He kept imagining that some hideous, tentacled beast was just behind him, ready to grab him. But when he turned, there was nothing there but his rappelling harness hanging on his closet door. He tried to ignore the feeling, but he knew it was there, just like he knew he had seen a creature in his painting of the martians.

Four A.M. The brick wall of the building turned blood red and pale blue, then blood red again.

"Mickey, it's the police!" shouted Wendy.

The flashing light from the squad car painted the entire night red and blue. Mickey quickly hooked his spray cans onto his harness, ready to make a quick exit—but something was different tonight. His hand was shaking, but not from fear. It was trembling in a way he couldn't control. Wendy, standing on the fire escape beside him, reached out to him. "Come on, Mickey," she said desperately. He reached out to her, puzzled by his trembling hand. Why had his hand started shaking like that? And why now? He pulled the emergency release of his harness. But in his confusion, he pulled too soon. Mickey slipped out of Wendy's hand and fell three stories into a pile of trash bags, and into the arms of the Los Angeles Police Department.

He wouldn't call his mother—she didn't need this kind of trouble. Instead, he gambled and called the one person he felt he could trust. Luckily she showed up. Somehow, he knew he could count on the support of another artist. Miss Clarkson arrived at the police station less than half an hour after Mickey called.

"Are you the mother?" asked the cop on duty.

"His parents couldn't make it," said Miss Clarkson. "I'm his teacher."

The cop rolled his eyeballs.

"What is he supposed to have done?" demanded Miss Clarkson.

The cop crossed his arms. "You might say he painted the town red." Then he threw a nasty glance at Mickey. "Do you know how long we've been trying to catch this 'Midnight Michelangelo'?"

Miss Clarkson was too smart to ID Mickey to the police. "Are you kidding me?" she said.

"It's no joke," said the cop. "He's defaced half the city."

Miss Clarkson laughed. "Officer, you've seen those murals. Do you really think that a fourteen-year-old boy could do that?"

The cop, who a moment before seemed so sure of himself, began to stutter just a bit.

"Well, we caught him at the scene of the crime with a spray can."

Miss Clarkson shook her head and looked at the cop as if he was an idiot. "You caught him tagging, Officer. That's all."

Tagging? Mickey bristled at the suggestion. "I'm not a tagger," he said, insulted. But Miss Clarkson threw him a warning glance, and he shut up.

She turned back to the officer. "I think you've sufficiently traumatized this boy for a first offense. You can rest assured that his initials will go nowhere but on his homework from now on." Still the cop seemed unconvinced, until Miss Clarkson laughed again. "The Midnight Michelangelo! Are the police so desperate to find this guy that they have to pin it on a little kid?"

That did it.

"All right," conceded the officer. "Considering the kid's age, we're willing to cut him some slack. But I don't want to see him here again." Miss Clarkson grabbed Mickey and escorted him out.

They talked a lot on the drive home: about his talent, his troubles, his potential. But there was one thing Miss Clarkson asked that seemed to ring in his aching mind even after she had dropped him off at home. She had asked him how often he painted.

"Whenever the inspiration hits me," Mickey had told her.

Miss Clarkson had frowned. "I think your inspiration is your own worst enemy."

The next morning, Mickey noticed the vein.

He had woken up to another horrible headache—the way he had almost every day for the past month. He doused his face with cold water. Then, dragging a brush through his matted hair, he saw it. On his temple. A single vein. And as he looked at it, it seemed to spread, as if it was growing, pulsing, thick and purple. He gasped and slammed his eyes shut. Then, when he dared to open his eyes and confront his reflection, it was gone.

It's my stressed-out imagination, he told himself, *like the creature in the martians.* Playing it safe, he brushed his hair over his forehead where the spot had been. *It'll be all right,* Mickey told himself.

And everything *was* all right, until he approached the front steps of school. That's when he was confronted by a smiling Brody Harkin and his entourage of varsity lettermen and other assorted goons. "Mickey, I'm glad to see you're here," Brody said in a falsely concerned voice.

"Why wouldn't I be here?" muttered Mickey.

"After last night, I thought you might be in reform school or something," said Brody, loud enough to get the attention of just about every kid who was within shouting distance. They all turned to stare at Mickey.

"I don't know what you're talking about," mumbled Mickey. He tried to edge around Brody, but Brody's goons kept him from going anywhere.

"Sure you know what I'm talking about," said Brody. "Wendy told me all about it. I'm just glad you didn't get *her* arrested as an accomplice." There was a circle around them now. The same circle of kids that always seems to arrive before a fight.

"Excuse me, I've got class."

"Obviously not much," snorted Brody. The few kids around them who got the joke laughed out loud. Mickey could feel his head beginning to throb. He could feel that thick vein pulsing and wondered if everyone could see it.

"You don't want to mess with me today, Brody," Mickey warned.

Brody chuckled. "All right, tough guy," he said.

Mickey's headache continued to pound. "Listen, just

get out of my face. Why don't you go and smash some more cans on your forehead, or whatever you do for intellectual stimulation."

"You know why Wendy hangs out with you, don't you?" Brody said with a nasty hiss in his voice. "*Wendy feels sorry for you,* just like the rest of us."

Meltdown. Mickey lost it. He pounced on Brody, like a rabid, snarling dog. Brody clearly wasn't expecting it and was knocked down by the force of Mickey's pounce. They both crashed to the pavement. Mickey wasn't much for fighting, but few people had ever gotten him this angry. He windmilled his fists as hard and fast as he could, smashing them into Brody over and over again. And then, from the corner of his eye, he saw it. A tentacle suddenly appeared and coiled around Brody's neck. It squeezed tighter. Brody's face turned red. He was gasping. Far away, as if through a thousand layers of cotton, Mickey heard a voice.

"Mickey, stop it!" It was Wendy. He turned to look at her. She was standing next to him, screaming down at him, but he could barely hear her voice. "I said, stop it!"

When Mickey turned back to Brody, it wasn't a tentacle but his own hand that was squeezing Brody's throat. Shocked, Mickey pushed himself off Brody.

"Are you crazy?" screamed Wendy. "Are you out of your mind?"

Brody staggered to his feet, clutching his throat and gasping for air.

"Your charity case just turned into a basket case," he said in a hacking, wheezing tone.

Wendy went over to Brody to make sure he was okay. She put her arms around him, then kissed him. Mickey couldn't stand the sight of the two of them together.

Brody was right—Wendy just hung out with Mickey because she felt sorry for him, and now even *she* couldn't be trusted. After all, she must have been the one who had told Brody everything about last night.

"You two deserve each other!" Mickey shouted. Then he ran off. He was cutting school, but he didn't care. What did it matter now?

"Mickey, wait!" Wendy called to him, running. Finally she caught up with him, and he turned on her.

"Why don't you just write it all over the walls, Wendy? 'Mickey Blake just got arrested.' Here, I'll lend you a spray can."

"It wasn't like that," insisted Wendy. "Brody's dad's a lawyer. I told Brody because I thought he might help."

"What makes you think I need help?" shouted Mickey.

"Well, just look at you. It's not just what happened last night. You—you don't look right, Mickey. You've been acting weird." She grabbed him by the shoulder, forcing him to look her in the eye. "Something's wrong, isn't it?"

Almost as an afterthought he reached to touch the vein on his forehead, but it was gone.

"Mickey," she said. "Tell me what's wrong."

There was genuine concern in her voice. But the fact was, he didn't know what the problem was, or how deep it went.

Then Mickey's world grew one shade darker.

There was a commotion ahead of them. Crowds of people were huddled in front of a record store. They were all looking up at an outside wall—the same wall Mickey had started working on the night before . . . before he was taken away by the cops.

"That is, like, *so* cool," someone said.

Mickey looked up and had to grab a lamppost to keep himself from falling. *It was impossible.* There, before his eyes, was an immense horrorscape that covered the entire six-story brick wall. What was supposed to be beautiful birds had morphed into cruelly misshapen predators with steel fangs and flesh-shredding claws. Instead of a metropolis of delicate crystal spires, the raptors flew over a blighted ruin of a city. And there, even larger than before, a tentacled creature lurked in the shadows of the painting.

A policeman spoke with the shop owner.

"Don't worry," said the policeman. "We'll catch him sooner or later."

The shop owner laughed. "Catch him? I want to hire him. You can't buy this kind of promotion. This will sell a million CDs."

"Who do you think this guy is?" someone asked.

"I don't know," the shop owner shouted to the crowd, "but anyone who brings me this Midnight Michelangelo gets a free CD."

Mickey stood there feeling his eyes begin to glaze over. Wendy nudged him.

"Why don't you tell him? Maybe he'll pay you to do another one."

"But that's not what I painted," shouted Mickey. Then, Wendy turned to the crowd. "Hey! He's here. It's the Midnight Michelangelo!" Suddenly, Mickey was the center of attention, and the owner of the record store stormed through the crowd.

"You? You're gonna tell me this kid did *that* painting?"

Mickey shook his head. "No, no, it's a mistake. I didn't do it!"

"He goes out every night," explained Wendy. "He did the martians at the bus depot and the robots by the river— I was with him when he did it. Are you going to hire him like you said?"

Mickey turned to Wendy. "You were with me," he said. "You saw what I was painting, and it wasn't *that*!"

Wendy looked at the mural and shrugged. "I was up close. I couldn't see the whole thing."

Mickey began to panic. There *had* to be a way to prove

what his painting was supposed to be. Then he realized he *did* have proof. He had his original sketch! He reached into his backpack, pulled it out, and unfolded it, showing it for everyone to see. "See! This is what I was painting last night, you see?" The crowd pressed forward to look at it and murmured in admiration. Some people applauded.

"I'll hire you for another one," said the record shop owner. "We'll work out the details later." Wendy looked at the crumpled piece of paper stretched between Mickey's shaking hands and gave him a half-grimace, half-smile.

"It certainly is . . . impressive," she said, "in a twisted sort of way."

Confused, Mickey turned to look at the paper himself. His hands, as badly as they were shaking, began trembling even more violently.

Because his sketch reflected the same bleak and awful mural in front of him.

"That is *so* cool, man," said someone behind him. Even the cop was getting into it.

"You know, some of us don't really want to catch you," the cop whispered into Mickey's ear. "To be honest, I kind of like those werewolves on the federal building."

"Werewolves?" said Mickey. "What werewolves?"

He walked home alone, but by the time he reached his block, he realized he was running. When he got to his room, he took every last sketch off his wall and out of every drawer and threw them away. Then he took every spray can he could find and tossed them into the trash. He wasn't satisfied until the trash was dumped down the garbage shoot, bound for his apartment building's incinerator.

All the while, he could hear the sounds in his aching

head. A mocking laughter, the screech of far-off predators, and the wet, slithery sound of a tentacled creature
moving closer.

The next morning, there was a mural on the lockers at
school. Not just one locker, but spread across the entire
hallway. It would have been bad enough if the mysterious mural was just your typical nightmare. But this one
had a very special guest star: Brody Harkin.

In this mural, Brody was being mauled by a horrible
clawed monster—half lobster, half human—but that
wasn't the worst part, because in the mural's background
a multi-tentacled beast looked on, eating popcorn. The
creature, painted more clearly than before, looked like a
cross between an octopus . . . and a human brain.

Wendy glared at the mural, and then at Mickey with an
anger and disgust she had never shown him before.
"Mickey, what is *wrong* with you? This is sick!"

"I had nothing to do with it!" screamed Mickey. "It
wasn't me." But there in the corner were the initials, just
like there always were. M.M. Midnight Michelangelo.

Brody stood before the perfect likeness of himself, and,
amazingly, held his temper. Brody's friends quickly gath-
ered in front of the mural, yelling, "Hey man, kick his
butt!" And more kids arrived on the scene, joining in on
the group rage, just wanting to see a fight. But Brody
shook his head.

"What a wonderful 'work of art,' " Brody said with a
bitter smile. "I want the principal to see this. I want the
cops to see it." Then his million-dollar smile widened.
"Thanks, Mickey," he said. "I couldn't have done a better
job of getting you expelled."

Ignoring Brody, Mickey turned to Wendy, pleading. "I
swear I didn't do it. I threw all my paint away yesterday.
See! There's none left." He zipped open his backpack to

prove it—but as he turned his pack upside-down, paint cans clattered out. Seven of them. Every color of the rainbow. Wendy turned and stormed away, leaving Mickey alone with his paint and his awful, awful mural.

Wendy didn't stick up for him. Miss Clarkson didn't stick up for him. Mickey was on his own this time, as he faced the principal.

"Young man, you have really asked for it. You trespassed after school hours, defaced school property . . . And look at the disruption you've caused your schoolmates. We have zero tolerance at this school—it's one strike and you're out. Do you know what that means, Mr. Blake?"

Mickey knew what it meant. "It means I'm expelled." Mickey held his throbbing head. It felt as if it would blow apart any second.

"You and your mother will meet with the school board, and we'll go from there. . . ."

Suddenly Mickey closed his eyes against the searing pain in his brain. He could feel the vein throbbing in his head. It felt as if something in his skull was trying to bang itself out. When Mickey opened his eyes, there was a tentacle rising over the chair behind the principal. He wanted to warn the man, but Mickey was frozen. He began to breathe in deep, sharp gasps.

"Are you all right, son? What's wrong?"

Tentacles loomed behind Principal Crenshaw, and one of them reached over, grabbed a pencil, and drew a ghoulish caricature of the principal on his own desk blotter. The tentacle signed it, "M.M.," and the beast let loose a deep, wet, slithery laugh.

But the principal heard nothing—saw nothing. Even when he turned and looked straight at the awful gray tentacle, he didn't see it.

Mickey got his breathing under control as the tentacle slithered away and disappeared. He knew what he had to do now—everything had suddenly become very clear. The principal turned away to call his mother, and the second he turned, Mickey slipped out the door and into the hallway.

A line of silver spray paint trailed down the empty school hall, and Mickey followed it. He tracked it to a doorway and down a creaky set of stairs, into the dank basement of the ancient school. It was a place littered with broken-down desks, battered shelves, and mildewed textbooks. Down here, every surface, every wall, every square inch, was covered with graffiti. Mickey heard the laughter again—the laughter of the beast.

"Where are you?" Mickey screamed. "Come out so I can see you." Something touched his face. He whirled to catch it, but there was nothing there. Nothing but a wet trail of slime on his cheek.

Mickey found a fire ax. It was mounted on brackets behind a glass barrier labeled emergency use only. Well, he thought, this certainly was an emergency. Mickey kicked the glass until it shattered, reached in, and took the ax in both hands.

"Hey, slimeball!" he shouted, "I've got something for you!" In the dark recess he could hear the tantalizing hiss of a spray can. He inched forward, looking from side to side, searching for the beast that had grown in the shadow-painted corners of his own head.

"Come out, come out, wherever you are!" he shouted. Mickey laughed at his own ridiculousness. The furnace came on and shuddered violently, then let out a deep rumble.

Something moved! Mickey turned and swung, knocking over a pyramid of paint cans. They spilled a rainbow of colors across the floor. Again, he heard the laughter.

"Missed me, missed me! Now you gotta kiss me!" it chanted in its throaty, gurgling voice. It only made Mickey angrier. Too angry to hold back his fury. He swung the ax in every direction, splintering a desk, cleaving a filing cabinet in two, smashing an old chalkboard until finally he found the monster standing against the round tank of the rusty boiler.

It was awful. A gray mass of throbbing brain tissue, and from it grew thick tentacles—nerve endings that thrashed and flailed like snakes. But worst of all were its eyes. Two pinpoints of red light in a cloud of gray matter.

"Don't do it, Mickey," the creature taunted. Mickey raised his ax. *"You'll be sorry!"* said the creature. But Mickey couldn't stop himself. He swung the blade in a high arc and brought the ax down with all his might.

He heard a scream. A girl's scream. The blade embedded in the boiler with a hollow clang and a blast of white steam—right next to the face of . . .

. . . Brody Harkin!

The creature had tricked him, and the blade of the axe had missed Brody by less than an inch. Behind him Wendy screamed again, as Brody scrambled away in terror.

"Stop him!" screamed Wendy. "Somebody stop him!"

What little sanity Mickey held onto was gone. The mocking laughter in his head was now unbearable. He pulled the blade from the boiler.

"You missed me!" the creature screamed in his head. *"Accept it, Mickey, you'll never kill me!"* He saw it there again, in the shadows, and he raised his ax to strike it . . . but then he had a better idea. He threw his ax down, opened his backpack, and pulled out a spray can for each hand.

"Oh, you're going to paint me?" taunted the creature. *"Be sure to get my good side."* The creature turned to show its profile and smiled that slimy brain smile.

"Hold that pose," said Mickey. Then he let loose from both spray cans, dousing the creature in a blue-black fog. It laughed again, unbothered by the paint dripping down into the crevices of its cortex—not caring about the jumble of smashed paint cans and spilt enamel that it stood in. But Mickey continued spraying. He sprayed a line of paint from the monster to the hot furnace, like a fuse, and as soon as the wet paint touched the furnace, it caught fire.

The creature realized the danger too late. *"No!!!"*

The flame raced down the paint-fuse toward the puddle of flammable enamel, and instantly the creature burst into flames. It let out an awful, dying wail as it burned, and finally it dissolved into the swirls of burning paint. That was the last thing Mickey remembered before he lost consciousness.

He woke up in a hospital room with his mother beside him holding his hand and Wendy on his other side. His head hurt something awful. "Is it gone?" Mickey asked weakly.

"You're going to be all right," Wendy said. "They got the tumor in time." Mickey had to think very slowly and clearly about what she was saying. Only now did he realize that his head was tightly bandaged.

"Tumor?"

"Yes," said a doctor looking down at him, smiling as doctors do. "One nasty brain tumor," he said. "The good news is that we got the whole thing, and we took it out without damaging any of the surrounding tissue. You're a very lucky young man."

Mickey's mom burst into tears.

"You're going to be all right, Mickey," she said. "You're going to be all right."

"In a way," said Wendy, "you tried to tell us. . . . Going out and painting those 'things,' then not remembering you did it. The doctor said it was your subconscious trying to warn us."

Mickey took a deep breath. He supposed he could wrestle with himself forever, trying to figure out whether the creature was real or just a hallucination brought on by a tumor. But thinking about that was a sure way to madness. The important thing was that the monster was out of his head, and out of his life for good. It was a memory he was happy to paint over, and lose forever.

Wendy gently held his hand. "I'm sorry about those nasty things I said to you."

Mickey smiled. "Hold that pose," he said, never wanting this moment with Wendy to end.

Meanwhile, deep down in the hospital basement, a med student tended to the pathology lab. With a sandwich in one hand and a medical instrument in the other, he studied a small, fleshy mass that had settled at the bottom of a jar of formaldehyde. It was a lump of brain tissue, with spidery, tentacle-like dendrites. The label on the jar read: M. BLAKE.

"So that's a brain tumor," the med student mumbled to himself. "That is one ugly sucker."

He put down his sandwich to clean up the table and then picked it up again on his way out. He didn't notice that the jar of formaldehyde was now empty. He didn't notice that there was something moving between the slices of his bread as he took a bite of his sandwich.

But a few minutes later, he did notice a sudden headache coming on.

RALPHY SHERMAN'S INSIDE STORY

• •

Of course you don't have to believe it, but this is a true story. As true as my dad being a spy, and my mom being abducted by aliens. And if you don't believe me, you can ask my sister.

I suppose I should start before the frogs and the ants. I suppose I should start even before my cousins arrived.

As usual, Dad was away on top-secret business when we got news that my cousins were coming, and Mom, well, we haven't seen her much since she was taken from our time-space continuum. So it was only me, my sister Roxanne, and our new nanny all alone in our immense house. (Actually, our nannies are always new, because none of them has ever lasted more than a couple of weeks, can't say why.) At any rate, we got E-mail from Aunt Millicent and Uncle Bernard that they were going on vacation, and since we had our big, empty house all to ourselves, could we watch our darling little cousins for them?

"Gag me," said Roxanne when she read the note. "I think I'm gonna hurl breakfast."

I knew how she felt, but Olga the nanny had no sense of the problem.

"Dey are your cousins," she said in a thick accent. She was from a country whose name I couldn't pronounce even if you paid me in rubles. "You should be happy to see your cousins."

To which I replied, "You don't know Candida and Bratt."

"Nonsense—I cannot wait to meet them," Olga chimed. "They cannot be worse than the two of you." Which in most cases, would probably be true—after all, most of our nannies leave with a scream, rather than a smile on their lips, can't say why. But rumor has it that Bratt and Candida had populated entire mental institutions with the mentally—and sometimes physically—shattered remnants of their former nannies.

Roxanne and I counted the days until they arrived, like convicts numbering the days till execution. Two weeks . . . one week . . . and finally the dreaded day was here. Similar to the beginning of most natural disasters, I could hear the neighborhood dogs bark as their car pulled up in front of our house. The doorbell rang, and we found them there, deposited on our doorstep, with three trunks. It looked as if they were prepared for a long siege.

Aunt Millicent was already running back to the car, which Uncle Bernard kept impatiently idling by the curb. "I'm sure you'll all have a wonderful time together," lied Aunt Millicent, trying to brush Bratt's sticky fingerprints off her mink as she ran. She leapt into the car, and Uncle Bernard burned rubber even before the door was closed, in no small hurry to escape.

So here they were, standing in our foyer. Seven-year-old Candida was in her typical pink frilly dress, looking like a grinning fugitive from "It's a Small World." She had a smile from ear to ear and looked like a human happyface. Beside her stood five-year-old Bratt. His hair was even messier and his face dirtier than I remembered, which was quite an accomplishment. His real name had once been Brett, but so many people called him Bratt that even his parents started calling him that. In fact, they might have had his name legally changed, although I'm not certain. In any case, there stood Bratt with his left index finger lodged so deeply into his nose that he was pulling boogers from the next county.

"Well, hello!" chimed Olga the nanny, throwing out her foreign arms to greet my cousins as if they were normal children. Bratt gave her a grimace, revealing his missing front teeth.

"I'm bored," he said. "This place is boring. And you're ugly."

Although Olga made no move to deny the charge, she was not thrilled by the observation.

Candida shook her head with a broad, knowing smile.

"Bratt," she said, "you're so *incorrigible*." Which is one of the tamer words people used to describe Bratt. Then Candida turned to my sister. She ratcheted her smile up a few notches. "Hey, Roxanne," she said brightly. "I brought my 'Golly Miss Molly Happy Time Plastic Tea Set.' Let's go have a tea party!"

Roxanne narrowed her eyes to slits. "I'd rather die," she said, but Candida just giggled happily.

"Oh, Roxanne, you're so funny!" she said. "Isn't she funny, Helga?"

"Olga," corrected our nanny.

"Whatever!" said Candida, and she dragged Roxanne into the den for Chinese tea torture. As for Bratt, he was already swinging from the chandelier.

* * *

The day quickly became a festival of shattered glass and splintered wood, compliments of Bratt. Five broken banister rails, four demolished vases, three shredded sofas, two dented appliances, and that weird-looking bird he nailed with a baseball in our pear tree. At first, poor Olga tried to clean up after him, but not even her days as an Olympic wrestler could prepare her for this challenge. As for Candida, she was accustomed to making her way through Bratt's mounting debris, and she flitted around the house with a carefree smile so bright, you needed sunscreen. This was all to be expected—you have to understand, this was normal for our cousins. It was at dinner that things started to get weird.

Olga, rather than put up with Bratt's nagging, agreed to serve us all his favorite thing for dinner. Lamb-aroni. It was while we were picking through our Lamb-aroni that a frog fell out of nowhere into Bratt's bowl. Tomato sauce splattered onto everyone.

"What is this?" said Olga. "Who has dropped a frog into the Lamb-aroni?"

"Oops!" said Bratt. Then he grabbed the frog, tomato sauce and all, and put it in his shirt pocket. This wouldn't have bugged me in the least, because after all, Bratt has been known to bring worse things than frogs to the table with him. But you see, Bratt didn't have a frog in his pocket when he sat down, and for the life of me I had no idea where that frog had come from.

Then that night, while we were watching sing-along videos (at Candida's request of course), another strange thing made an appearance in the room. I saw it out of the corner of my eye as it came hurtling across the room, bouncing with a *clink* off the glass of the TV. Olga picked it up and examined it. It was a tiny glass unicorn, perfectly molded, and just the size of your fingernail.

"How beautiful," she cooed. "Isn't that nice." But when she asked us whose it was, nobody claimed it.

It was as we were getting ready for bed that Roxanne pulled me aside and whispered to me.

"I don't know where that thing came from," she said, "but I do know one thing: Candida sneezed just before it hit the TV."

Around three in the morning, I was awakened by something cold and slimy hopping across my face. I brushed it away and sat up in bed. For a moment I thought it was a dream. But then I saw the covers undulating. I flung back the covers to find . . .

. . . frogs!

Not just one frog or two, but a dozen of them, hopping madly in every direction. It was almost biblical, if you know what I mean. A plague of frogs. I bailed out of bed.

"Oh, Olga!" I called. "Amphibian alert!"

Olga came running. When she saw the plague, she raced around trying to catch the frogs with a trash basket, but her efforts were wasted. There were simply too many of them . . .

. . . and that's when I noticed where they were coming from. I was sharing my room with Bratt tonight. I had the lower bunk, he had the upper, and the frogs were all hopping down from his bed. The little snot-bucket had taken an entire collection of frogs to bed with him and didn't tell anyone!

Roxanne stood in the doorway, not wanting to join in our frogathon. And through all this, little Bratt slept, his mouth open and drooling.

Candida arrived dragging her Raggedy Ann doll by its red-yarn head. "Oh, I'll take care of it," she said. We were all more than happy to let her deal with her brother's plague of frogs. "My poor brother," she said, "he really is a holy terror sometimes."

"There's nothing 'holy' about it," mumbled Roxanne.

Olga made Roxy and me some hot chocolate, and we left Candida alone to contend with the frogs. She got rid of them somehow, but I had no idea where she put them.

In the morning it was Roxanne's turn.

"Oh, yuck! No way!" Her yells woke me up at dawn, and I hurried into her room. There was a colony of ants running in black rivers up and down her walls and covers. But if Roxanne was tormented by ants, it was nothing compared to what they were doing to Candida, who had just awakened in the spare bed. You could barely see her beneath the moving army of insects.

"Oh! Oh! Dear me!" cried Candida, while Roxanne screeched out much more colorful words.

It took three cans of Raid and half the day to rid the house of the ants.

"Where did they come from?" Olga kept mumbling as she sponged ant guts off the wall, but I knew *that* wasn't the question we ought to be asking. The question was *why* had they come. This whole situation was a nuisance, and it was irritating to have nuisances that we didn't create. Roxanne took it upon herself to solve the mystery, while I spent the day chasing after Bratt.

I used to think that I had mastered being a pain in the rear, but I really have to hand it to Bratt: He is the true baron of butt pain.

"See, I can play golf," he said as he ran off swinging the club like a midget samurai. He proceeded to decapitate every plant in our garden.

"See, I can drive!" he said as he backed Dad's precious

sports car out of the garage . . . and right into the fountain.

"See, I can swim good," he said and dove head first into
a scummy, stagnant pond in the woods behind our property. I think it was the pond that finally slowed him down,
because just before dinner, he claimed to feel sick.

"Feel my throat," he ordered me. "Do I got swollen
glands?" He showed his neck to reveal so many dirt rings
that you could probably tell his age by counting them,
like a tree. I reached out to feel his glands.

They were swollen all right, but there was something
else about them that wasn't right, because as I held them
beneath my thumb and forefinger . . . *I could swear they
were moving*.

There was something strangely familiar about the feel
of Bratt's swollen glands. They reminded me of something that I couldn't quite place. . . .

Shortly before dinner, Roxanne came out of hiding to report her findings to me. You see, she had been avoiding
Candida all day because Candida wanted Roxanne to play
with her Dental Hygienist Barbie. Roxanne would rather
have swallowed hot coals.

Roxanne called me into the den and shoved a little
glass vial under my nose.

"Sniff this," she said, "and tell me what it smells like."

I took a deep whiff and cringed. It was an aroma all too
familiar. "Candida!" I said. "It smells like Candida. What
is it?"

Roxanne leaned closer to me and whispered, "Equal
amounts of cinnamon, ginger, and nutmeg. Plus a pinch
of ground clove."

I wrinkled my forehead, not getting it. "That's weird."

"But that's not all. Take a look at this!" She revealed a

small cup and inside were tiny, white, crystalline gran-
ules.

"What is it?" I asked.

"Taste it."

Reluctantly, I dipped my finger into the cup and lifted
it to my mouth. The taste was unmistakable.

"Sugar!"

"It was all over Candida's sheets," Roxanne told me.
"That's why the ants came."

"Candida went to bed with candy?" I suggested.

Roxanne shook her head. "Are you kidding me? Little
Miss Perfect doesn't even eat candy."

I thought it all through. There had to be a good explanation for this. "Sugar and spice . . ." I mumbled.

". . . and everything nice," added Roxanne. She opened
her palm to reveal a whole menagerie of tiny glass fig-
urines—the kind that seemed to fly across the room every
time Candida sneezed."That's what little girls are made
of."

My jaw dropped as it all began to come together, and I
realized what Roxanne was trying to tell me. It made
sense in its own strange and unusual way. I tried to recall
what the matching nursery rhyme for boys was, and although I couldn't recall the whole thing, I remembered
enough of it, and now it finally dawned on me exactly
what Bratt's moving, swollen glands felt like.

They felt like snails.

Suddenly a cry rang out from the backyard, and Candida ran inside in a panic. For the first time in her life the
smile had left her face. I hardly recognized her.

"You have to help! Hurry! Bratt's hurt himself really
bad. Inga!" she called "Inga!"

"Olga," I corrected, and calmed her down long enough
to find out what had happened. Apparently her little

brother was out back chasing squirrels with a pitchfork when he tripped and had the kind of accident that only happens in a mother's nightmares.

We all ran out back to help our poor little cousin. Bratt was lying in the grass, crying his eyes out. He had a big hole in his side where the pitchfork had speared him, but he wasn't bleeding. Not a drop. Instead, he was wallowing in a pool of frogs and snails and furry, squirming things that I could not identify.

"What are those?" I asked, pointing.

Bratt snuffled, then shouted at me, "They're puppy dog tails, butthead!"

Well, Olga took one good look at those tails and she was a nanny no more. She turned and ran off into the sunset and we haven't seen her since.

Meanwhile, Bratt's condition had gotten serious. Bratt's three primary ingredients were hopping, slithering, and squirming away faster than any one of us could catch them.

"We have to get him to the hospital!" screamed Candida. "He'll need a transfusion."

And although I shuddered to think where they would get enough puppy dog tails for a transfusion, I did as I was told. I called 911 and put it in the hands of the paramedics.

Modern medicine is an amazing thing. I don't know how the doctors did it, but they had Bratt stitched up and shipped back to us in less than a week.

His parents, having heard about the accident, reluctantly cut their 'round-the-world vacation short.

A week after the accident, we all sat at the breakfast table together. Candida sat primly, eating Shredded Wheat like a good little girl, and Bratt scarfed down Sugar-Frosted Cookie Dough cereal. Everything was back to normal.

"Well," said Uncle Bernard ruffling Bratt's tangled hair, "sounds like you had quite an adventure!"

"It stunk," grumbled Bratt. "The hospital was even more boring than here." Bratt hiccuped, and a small tree frog hopped from his mouth into the cereal.

"Don't open your mouth so wide dear," said his mother. She scooped up the frog and popped it back into her son's mouth. "It's rude."

Uncle Bernard sipped his coffee, then frowned. "A little sweeter," he said. Then he tipped Candida's head, and a stream of sugar ran from her left ear into his coffee. "I think you've learned your lesson, Bratt," he said. "No playing with pitchforks unless it's under adult supervision."

Bratt only grunted and continued to gum his soggy cereal.

It was as they were leaving that I asked the final question that would solve the last remaining riddle about my cousins' unique family.

"Candida?" I asked as they were heading out the door. "How is it that your parents can afford a 'round-the-world vacation?"

"That's simple," she said. "My parents are made of money."

Which explains why they jingle when they walk.

HE OPENS A WINDOW

....

You must never pull back the curtains," the kindly old woman always says. "You must never look out the window." Anna knows why it must be so; to risk anyone seeing her and her two young sisters will mean death or something worse. And so for many months Anna has obeyed, not daring to let anything but the faintest hint of daylight into the room. The old woman brings them food. Hearty stews when meat can be found, and undersized vegetables when that is all to be had, but always the best from the old woman's table.

"When will we see Momma and Poppa?" Gretchen, her youngest sister, asks. She is only four, and not old enough to understand that the answer might be "never."

"Soon," Anna tells her, and she tries to make herself believe it. Segrid, who is seven, looks up to Anna wide-eyed with hope. Hope of seeing their parents is all that keeps them going in this small, locked room that has become their lives.

* * *

The boy's father is a soldier, and his mother long buried.

The grocer keeps a bed for him at the back of the store, in exchange for delivering groceries twelve hours a day, throughout the wartime streets of Hamburg. When regiments of soldiers march past the boy, he always thinks he sees his father among them. He is hopeful, but even more, he is frightened by the dark soldiers he knows bring nothing but death. He can't stand to think of his father as one of them.

Or himself. He is fourteen now. If the war continues, he will be absorbed into the ranks of soldiers, to fight and die for the fatherland.

There used to be many children in Hamburg, but there are fewer now. Some families took refuge in the countryside when the war began, and others were driven from their homes and taken away in overcrowded buses and trains. Jews, mostly.

They were brought to the countryside, too, then thrown into the dark, mysterious camps, never to be seen again. He has lost many friends that way. Boys he had played with in the street, girls whose hands he longed to hold. He will not cry for them, because he knows if he starts crying, he may never stop.

There are some of them, though, that remain like ghosts, haunting the secret places of other peoples' homes.

Like the old woman's house on Baumeister Street.

He knows there are children hiding there, because he delivers enough vegetables and fruits for a family, although only one old woman is supposed to live there. And before he knocks, he often hears the faint whisper of children's voices from an upstairs window. So he is always sure to throw in some extra food without letting the grocer know.

Today as he approaches the old woman's door, he has some cabbages and onions slipped from under the grocer's nose while he wasn't looking . . . but today he hears no children's voices upstairs, and notices something strange about the house. He has been here enough to know that there are three upstairs windows—the center one always hidden behind heavy, dark curtains that never open. But today there are no curtains. In fact, today, there is no third window—only the bricks of the house where the window should be.

In Anna's eight-by-eight-foot world, strange things are happening. The thin hint of light that sneaks into the room has begun to change day to day. Her sisters don't notice, but Anna does. She has lived in Hamburg all her life and knows every color of the sky, from the pale clouds of winter, to the blue hues of summer, to the flickering night glow of lamplight. But lately the light peeking beneath the closed curtains is all wrong. One day the light seems red as fire, the next day green and shimmering, as if seen through the ocean. One day it's purple, and the next, there's no light at all. She doesn't dare tell the old woman, for Anna's certain it's just the madness of life in this room that's making her see these things.

But the sounds have been changing, too.

Some days, when the light is normal, she will hear cars in the street, and the terrible marching of soldiers. But on other days will come the caws of birds she can't identify, and the bellows of far-off beasts that cannot reside in Hamburg.

Until now, she has not dared to pull back the curtains and peek outside—but today is different from those days before, because the old woman has brought them neither breakfast nor lunch, and Anna begins to worry. The old woman had left for an early morning walk, but these days no streets are safe. Anna never heard her come back, and she fears the worst. Their secret room is locked from the outside, and if the woman doesn't return, they will have no way to get out. The only exit is through the window, in full sight of anyone and everyone who might turn them over to the Nazis. . . .

Yet she wonders if there are any Nazis at all outside her window today; because at this moment, a bright purple light peeks from beneath the curtains. It should be long past dusk but the window hints at an unearthly light of day. Even Gretchen notices it.

"It's like the sky has forgotten how to be blue," she says.

Finally Anna dares to do something she hasn't done for the five months she has been in the room. She reaches out her fingers, slips them between the thick fabric of the old curtains, and parts them wide enough to get a single eye's view of the outside world.

What she sees makes her dizzy. It makes her grip onto the curtain to keep herself from falling.

"What is out there?" asks Gretchen. "Are there troops? Are they going to find us?"

"No," says Anna in a whisper.

Just outside the window, there are dense purple clouds billowing heavenward and downward, stretching to the horizon. There is no earth out there. There is no Hamburg—only the purple clouds of a world Anna could never dare imagine. It's as if their tiny room is floating alone in some strange corner of heaven.

The boy gets no grocery orders from the old woman on Baumeister Street that day, or the next—no requests for the usual tomatoes, onions, and apples. Although part of him feels that she must have found a market she likes better, he knows this woman well enough to know that her habits define her.

And what troubles him even more is the missing window.

He can think of a few logical reasons for the window to be gone. Perhaps it had been closed in and the wall built to cover it—that could be done in a day. But as the window faces Baumeister Street, such remodeling would be certain to get the attention of the Gestapo. Or perhaps the window had never been there at all, in spite of his many memories of it. He would much rather believe his own mind has become faulty than believe the window has simply disappeared. True, disappearance has become a commonplace thing since the Nazis came to power, but this disappearance is different from any of the mysteries of the Third Reich.

And so he goes to the old woman's house, day after day, until the window finally reappears.

Three days with no food.

There is a sink and running water, but it hardly helps the hunger pangs. Her sisters complain continuously, and Anna does her best to quiet them, all the while thinking of the world beyond the window.

Gripping her stomach, Anna peers out through the curtains once more. It's different now. The mystical clouds have been replaced by an arid desert. Parched, cracked earth stretches toward a horizon, the sky the same vermilion red as the sand. It looks bleak and hot . . . still, it's more inviting than the room and the world behind the closed door.

She realizes she must have lost her mind to see such wondrous things, but if so, then she's not the only one, because her sisters have squeezed their way between the curtains and see the strange landscape as well.

"Who put that there?" says Gretchen, too young to know the impossible when she sees it. Segrid only looks to Anna, expecting some rational explanation, but Anna has none to give.

An hour later, the light beneath the curtains changes again, and Anna can't stop herself from looking. She has become addicted to the dazzling vistas that change like slides of places she will never visit. She pulls back the curtains, wider this time so that she might see with both eyes rather than just one whatever stunning view lies beyond the pane.

But to her dismay, there are only the gray cobblestones of the Hamburg street. Instantly she realizes her folly and how her own curiosity has led to her end . . .

. . . because down in the street, a boy looks up at her. His gaze holds her, and neither of them can look away. There is warmth in his eyes, and honesty. Even from a distance she feels she can trust him not to turn them in to the authorities, but in these strange days, she knows that no one is to be trusted.

She closes the curtain and prays that the boy's heart does not belong to the Nazis.

A tall man in a dark uniform waits in the grocery store for the boy.

The boy's heart seizes with unexpected joy, because he is certain it must be his father . . . but as the man turns, the boy sees nothing familiar in his face, except for the familiar stone-cold eyes of the Gestapo.

The man has been talking to the grocer—and now the grocer will not look the boy in the face. He only casts his eyes down as the Gestapo officer removes his leather gloves and saunters toward the boy. He smiles, but his smile is anything but warm.

"Herr Grottmann tells me you've been stealing food."

The boy thinks quickly. He can't afford a single error. "Herr Grottmann is mistaken," the boy says. "I only eat the food he gives me."

"I'm not talking about the food you eat," says the Gestapo officer, "I am talking about the food you give away." He grabs the boy by the arm firmly enough to leave bruises from his crushing fingertips. Then he pulls him into the back office.

"You could be a hero or you could be a traitor," the Gestapo officer announces. He has seated the boy in a chair in the small, windowless office—and although he speaks softly, there is poison in his voice.

"All you have to do is tell me who you've been stealing food for."

The boy wrinkles his nose. The man's breath smells like cigarettes and decay. It smells like death.

"I deliver what Herr Grottmann gives me. If food is missing, it's his doing, not mine."

But the hard man sees through his lie with his danger-ous eyes. "We know there are many enemies of the state in hiding. We also know you are bringing them food." He takes a long drag on his slim cigarette and blows the acrid smoke into the air. "Believe me, if you don't turn them in, we will find them without you . . . and when we do, you'll be sent to the concentration camps with them."

He has heard stories about what unthinkable things go on in the camps, though he doesn't want to believe them. And all he has to do to be free of this man is tell about the girl he saw today, peeking out through the blinds of the window that wasn't always there. But he can't imagine how this girl could possibly deserve the punishment that would be dealt to her.

"I'm sorry, sir," says the boy, "but I know no enemies of the state."

The interrogation ends as quickly as it began.

"Very well," says the man dismissively. "We will search every home on your delivery list until we find them."

And as soon as the officer leaves, the grocer, wanting no more trouble, fires the boy and sends him packing.

The boy doesn't worry about himself now. He hurries to the home on Baumeister Street, hoping that the window will be there when he arrives. It was there that morning, and a girl was behind it—thirteen or fourteen by the looks of her. Afraid, he runs all the way there. He doesn't know that he is being followed.

A view of Earth.

A sight so wondrous, Anna and her sisters lose their breath in the awe of the moment as they look through their strange and magical window. Wind whistles around the window frame into the vacuum of space. The glass of the window can barely contain the air in the room.

They must be millions of miles into space, and the globe before them looms peaceful and serene. Hard to imagine that this serene world could hold the pain and turmoil of this terrible war.

Then comes the sound from downstairs. At first, it seems like loud knocking—but in a moment she realizes that someone is kicking the door down. Anna lets the curtains fall, hiding the view from space.

Finally they hear the doorjamb splinter, and her sisters begin to wail. If there had been any way to save themselves, it is gone now. Heavy footsteps pound up the stairs, and in a moment the door explodes with the force of a heavy black boot.

Four guards scream at them in loud frightening voices. "Get up—let's go—hurry up!"

And then another voice. A young one.

"I'm sorry," the voice says. "I didn't mean to . . . they followed me!"

Anna spins around to see the boy in the iron grip of another nameless soldier. "I'm sorry," he says again. And in spite of her fear, Anna knows he is telling the truth. He had not meant to bring this fate upon them.

A guard grabs Gretchen, wrenching her off the radiator coil. The curtain ruffles a bit as he pulls her away. . . .

And suddenly, Anna realizes what she must do.

Still in the grip of the guard, she reaches out and pulls the curtain wide to reveal the star-filled space beyond the window.

In an instant, the guards and the boy turn to gape at the harsh Earth-light passing through the window.

"What is this?" says one of the guards, amazed by the wondrous sight.

Anna can waste no time now. She grabs the closest thing to her heavy enough to do the job: a picture of her parents—the only one she has left—surrounded by a heavy silver frame.

She wrenches free from the guard, grabs her sisters in with one arm, and with the other hurls the silver-framed picture at the window.

The whistling of air around the closed window explodes into an angry gale as the glass shatters and the air from the room sucks into the vacuum of space.

The four guards, unprepared, are barely able to utter a scream before they are sucked out of the room and into space. They spin end over end into the void, their screams silenced by the cosmos, where there is no air, no sound, and no life. Anna knows she may die as well, but this death is better than death in the camps.

Anna's hand is clenched tightly on the hot, hot radiator coil while her other hand desperately grips onto her sisters. The racing wind lifts her off the ground as it pours in through the broken door and out the shattered window. She can feel the pipe of the radiator begin to strain with her weight.

"Here! Grab my hand!"

The voice screams out against the violent wind. It is the boy! His hand tightly grips the doorknob, though his feet are dangling in midair, pulled by the wind, just as Anna's are.

"The radiator won't hold you!" he yells. "Grab my hand!"

Anna swings her arm away from the radiator and into the boy's hand, just as the radiator tears free from the floor and steam explodes from the wall. The radiator hits the window, smashing what's left of its frame, and disappears into orbit.

The boy grasps the doorknob. He knows his hands are strong, but not strong enough to survive in a force such as this. Finally the wind tears him from the knob and hurls him and the girls toward the window—and although he feels fear at the thought of his own death, greater still is the sorrow that these girls who have suffered so long in this room must also die.

He waits for the air to be sucked from his lungs . . . he waits for the cold of space . . . but instead he hits the floor with a heavy bump. And all is silence.

It is a long time before he can open his eyes, and when he does, the room is filled with a soft, green light.

The oldest girl stands, holding her crying sisters in her arms, and peers out the window. The boy stands beside her to see a rolling landscape of strange purple trees and green, glowing skies. They do not question each other, because they know no answer would ever be good enough.

Instead, the boy turns to the girl. "My name is Friedrich," he tells her.

"I'm Anna." She glances out the shattered window once more. "Will you come, or will you stay?" she asks him.

The decision is easier for him than he thought it would be. In a world of many dark unknowns, here is an unknown filled with hope.

They step out, and into the strange world of unfamiliar sights, smells, and sounds.

Gretchen and Segrid have stopped crying. Their eyes now follow the path of a blue butterfly the size of a kite across the sky.

She turns around to see the window disappear forever, sealing out the hopelessness of the small room. For five months the door to that room had been locked. Her parents once told her that when God closes a door, he opens a window. But they could never have dreamed of such a deliverance as this.

There will be peace here, Anna knows. Peace and freedom . . . and time. She is glad Friedrich has chosen to come . . . and yet there is a sadness without measure that fills her, and always will.

She cries as she thinks of the many small rooms and dark hiding places that know no such windows . . . and she cries for her parents whose memory spins through space in a silver frame, lost but not forgotten, in the powerful current of eternity.

CLOTHES MAKE THE MAN

· ·

An alarm blasts.

Then the carousel jerk-starts, slowly turning around and around. It's not the kind of carousel you find at the amusement park, but the kind you find in airports— that stainless-steel mechanical thingamabob that sends the luggage on a slow ride around and around the baggage claim area.

"What's taking so long?" barks my father impatiently as other people's suitcases come flying out of the dark chute. My father is an annoyed traveler. I don't know if he's like that when it comes to business travel, but whenever we come along, everything annoys him. There's a food cart in the aisle when he wants to go to the bathroom, for instance. Or the seat won't recline. Or our luggage is late in arriving.

"Logan, you and Leslie go to the other side of the carousel, and if our bag comes out that side, let me know."

My sister, Leslie, rolls her eyes at me as we trudge off to the other side. With my father, it's like a competition—an Olympic sport. We have to get our luggage and escape from the airport before all the other travelers, or we lose.

"Ah, he's just upset that our vacation's over," I tell Leslie. To be honest, so am I. Maui was like another world compared to Cleveland. And tomorrow we're supposed to go back to school with five-hour jet lag. What fun.

Dozens of people, wearing heavy winter coats over their flowery Hawaiian shirts, fight for space at the far end of the carousel. Since Leslie and I are smaller, we weave our way in between them and get to the front, where we have a clear view of the baggage slide. Mom and Dad's bag is the first of our luggage out—a big monster of a suitcase that barely fits through the hole. Leslie's is next—a little flowery thing Grandma got her last year.

I wait . . . and wait . . . and wait.

Across the carousel I can see Dad impatiently tapping his foot.

"Next time, we're packing everything in two big bags," he proclaims as he comes around to wait with me. "No more waiting around for little cases." He shakes his head disgustedly. I guess it's my fault the luggage handlers haven't gotten to my bag yet.

The crowd thins out as we wait. Outside, twilight quickly becomes night, and still my bag hasn't arrived.

"It figures," fumes Dad. He glances at his watch for the billionth time, and I grin. "Don't worry, Dad, it's only two in the afternoon . . . Hawaii time." Pretty funny. Until I notice that my dad isn't laughing.

He quickly adjusts his watch to Ohio time.

Finally, after every other bag has been pulled off the carousel and the rest of our flight has left the baggage claim area, my bag is spit out of the hole and slides down toward us.

"Hallelujah!" My dad throws up his hands and says, "Grab it, and let's go."

I pick up the bag. Although I crammed it full of souvenir seashells and a million other things, it feels light—but Dad is already storming his way out of the terminal with Mom and Leslie, so I don't have time to think about it. I just hurry along after him, pulling my suitcase behind me.

"You mean, you got the wrong suitcase?"

Leslie and I are still up that night around two in the morning. Mom and Dad are zonked out, and are snoring away, but Leslie and I aren't so lucky. Since I can't sleep, I figure I'd unpack—but when I zip open the case, nothing inside looks familiar.

Leslie reaches in, and pulls out a leather glove. "Aren't these your gloves?"

"No. Why would I take gloves to Maui?"

I pull out layer after layer of clothes. They're kids clothes all right, but not this kid's. I search for the address label attached to the handle, but there isn't one.

"You're gonna have to tell Dad," Leslie says.

The idea doesn't thrill me. Telling Dad will open up a nasty can of worms that I'd rather not deal with. I can just imagine Dad pacing around the kitchen at dawn, going on and on about how I should look before I leap. Then he'd drag us back to the airport and complain to the flunkies at Air Aloha, making a federal case out of it and embarrassing all of us in the process.

I try to remember what I had in the suitcase. Summer clothes that I'll outgrow by June. A bunch of shells that I wouldn't know what to do with anyway.

"Maybe I don't have to tell him," I suggest. "I mean . . . maybe these clothes will fit."

"What, are you nuts? You're gonna wear someone else's clothes? What if they're diseased?"

I pull out a T-shirt. I don't recognize the design on the front. It's not a sports team or rock group or anything— just a weird swirl of colors. I sniff it to see if it's clean, and Leslie practically gags. "Oh how gross!" she says. They're clean . . . but there's something about them that smells kind of strange. It's like the way everyone's house has its own unique smell. I suppose clothes must be that way, too . . . but the scent on these clothes seems totally unfamiliar. I kind of like it, though.

I slip on the T-shirt. It fits perfectly, and the fabric feels softer than any other T-shirt I've worn.

"Problem solved," I announce. "I'll try on the rest of the clothes in the morning, and we don't have to tell any-one."

I can tell that Leslie's not too happy about the idea of taking someone else's bag. "When you think about it," I explain, "it's a fair exchange. Mine for theirs." I figure if they want theirs back, they can find us, but until then, I have a new set of clothes.

I turn, heading toward my bed, but Leslie stops me.

"Logan," she says, "don't move!"

I freeze. The last time she said that, there was this big Hawaiian tarantula crawling on my beach blanket. Leslie moves toward me from behind, and I feel something on my back. I go stiff, until I realize it's only Leslie's fingers, tickling my back.

"Ha ha, very funny," I say. But then I realize that al-though I have a shirt on, there's no fabric between her fin-gers and my back. She's tickling me through a hole in the shirt. A pretty big one, by my guess.

"Great," I say. "I get a cool shirt from someone else's suitcase and it has holes in it."

"It's not a hole, Logan," says Leslie. "I think you should look in the mirror."

I step into the bathroom, my back to the mirror, and crane my head as far as it will go, to get a glimpse of my back.

"Hmm . . . that's weird," I say. It's another sleeve. I try twisting my neck further, to get a better look at it. Finally I take the shirt off. There's no denying that my new shirt has a third sleeve.

"Maybe it's an irregular," suggests Leslie. "Mom always buys irregular T-shirts. They're cheaper."

Maybe. But somehow I find it hard to imagine a T-shirt company making that sort of mistake and still selling it to people. Then again, I've heard of big corporations trying to sell people toxic waste, so you never know.

"Yeah, maybe," I say. Then I put the shirt back on. Extra sleeve or not, it feels comfortable enough to sleep in. More than comfortable—it feels . . . right. And somehow I feel more content. So content that I slip right off to sleep.

Mom, in her maternal wisdom, lets us miss a day of school, so we can sleep in and catch up with Ohio time. I don't wake up until noon, and the first thing I do is head for the suitcase.

I pull out the shirts on top and hang them up. Problem is, the shirts don't fit properly on the hangers. Could be because they all have three sleeves.

I search for tags, and any other kinds of labels or logos that might tell me what the deal is, but all the tags have been cut out—just like my own clothes. Whoever owns these clothes doesn't like the tags scratching their neck either.

Beneath the shirt are the pants. My heart speeds up a bit as I pull a pair out, worried that I might find three legs. But no—the pants look normal. I try a pair on. They look like jeans, but the weave seems much finer. They don't fit as well as the shirt. Kind of baggy.

I reach down to zip up the fly and realize that there's no zipper. No button either. Sure, the fly's there, but there's nothing to hold it closed. Great. Here's one pair of pants I won't be wearing in public.

"How come you're wearing those backward?" Leslie says from the doorway. I turn to see her standing there, still half asleep.

"They're not backward," I inform her. "They just don't fit, gel-brain."

"Oh," she answers and yawns.

Leslie shuffles off to the bathroom, still too tired to match my rank-out. I hitch up the pants on my hips, then remember what Leslie said. I take off the pants and put them on the other way.

They fit perfectly.

In fact, they fit more comfortably than any other pants I own. See, Mom says I'm always in between sizes, which means that my pants are always either too tight or falling off my hips. But these feel like they were made for me.

Only one problem: Why is there a zipperless fly in the seat of my pants?

Well, there's an obvious answer—and in fact, I've often wondered why they don't make butt-zippers for that other all-important bathroom trip. But that couldn't be what this hole is for—it's a little too high for that.

But, like the shirt I wore last night, the pants feel right. So rather than worry about it, I make sure my three-sleeved shirt is out over the pants instead of tucked in. That way it covers the little hole and no one has to know it's there. No one has to know about my shirts either, if I wear a jacket over them.

As Leslie passes by, on her way back from the bathroom, I call her into my room.

"So, what do you think of my outfit?" I ask her.

"Great, if you like wearing stolen clothes."

"They're not stolen," I remind her, "just accidentally borrowed." And then I turn my back to her. "Will you scratch my back?" I ask.

Leslie reaches in through the third sleeve and scratches me between the shoulder blades—where it's been itching all night.

"Hey," she suggests, "maybe that's what the hole in the shirt is for—back-scratch access."

Which is as good an explanation as any. I don't tell her about the hole in the pants.

"Looks like you're getting a rash," says Leslie. "Your back's getting all lumpy."

"Must be something I caught in Hawaii," I tell her.

There's a fresh layer of snow on the ground, so I put on my coat and head out, taking two of the three gloves in the suitcase. It isn't until I try to make snowballs that I notice there's a space for a sixth finger.

An hour later, I'm back in my room with the suitcase. I just can't seem to get it out of my mind—but I don't talk to anyone about it, not even Leslie. I'm usually bad at keeping secrets—when weird things happen, I'm the first one to announce it to the world. But somehow this little piece of baggage has become a very personal and private thing. I guess everyone has things they don't want to share with their family. Sometimes it's just dumb things, and other times it's earth-shattering stuff. I try not to think about which category the suitcase falls into.

There are other things in the case, too. Silver coins that float up off your palm, as if they're filled with helium. A pen that writes with light instead of ink. In a side pocket, I find an electronic device that kind of looks like a Walkman, but the earphones don't quite fit in my ears. I wouldn't call the sounds that it plays music—it's more like clicks and screeches—but the more I listen to it, the more soothing it feels. It does have an interesting rhythm, in a way.

And then there's the can.

It's small and looks just like any other can of food, although there's no label. In a way it's the most disturbing thing of all, simply because it's normal. What would normal canned goods be doing mixed in with this stuff?

I can't sleep that night, mainly because of the way my hands and back itch, as if I'd fallen in a potent patch of poison ivy. But deep down I know it's not poison ivy at all. Instead of sleeping, I turn on my flashlight and take a long look at a picture I found in the suitcase's side pocket. There are people in the picture, and although the snapshot is a bit blurry, I can make out their faces. I suppose it's a family. Two parents, two kids. I don't know them, and yet I feel something for them, as if I did. I want to know them, but I can't say why.

Mom slips into my room, and I quickly hide the picture.

"I brought you a snack," she says, offering me a plate. "You barely touched your dinner. I thought you might be hungry."

"No thanks," I tell her. Truth is, I haven't had much of an appetite since we've gotten home from Maui.

Mom sees me rubbing my itching back against the wall, and she offers to scratch it for me, but I don't let her, because I know she'll see how the rash is swelling.

She looks at me strangely for a moment and asks, "Where'd you get those pajamas?"

"Hawaii," I tell her, which isn't a total lie. They are more comfortable than any pajamas I've ever worn—especially now, because I don't quite fit into my regular clothes anymore. They've gotten tight in strange and unexpected places. I guess I'm having a growth spurt.

After Mom leaves, I finally fall asleep thinking of the people in the picture, and the little canister of food, which seems creepier the more I think about it.

The world changes forever the next day. Not the whole world, but the small part of it that I occupy. It starts with a fight—the kind of fight you have when you've packed day-old snow a little too tightly, so your snowball leaves a major raspberry on your friend's cheek when you throw it.

I hurl the ice-ball at Randy Small, because he threw one first. Problem is my throw is a lot stronger than Randy Small's. The ice-ball impacts on the side of his face, and he turns to me with eyes that scream schoolyard massacre. There's a dozen kids around us as Randy rushes me. He rams into me, and his momentum takes me down.

Randy's on the wrestling team, so it doesn't take long for him to pin me in the snow. As I look into his eyes, I can tell he's not about to use a wrestling move on me. Not unless loogie-hurl is an accepted wrestling maneuver. I struggle uselessly as he summons up a major midwinter-flu-season mass of phlegm, and then, before he can fire it at me, someone swings at him, punching him across the face with enough force to send him sprawling in the snow five feet away.

I look around to see who saved me but there's no one else close enough to have taken the shot.

Then I see my friends' eyes bug out. I see them back away. I see the hand that punched Randy Small. It's above my head, reaching down to flick some snow from my eyebrow. The hand—the arm, I realize, is mine.

Screaming, I tear off my coat. Although I can't see my back, I know what it looks like. There's an arm—looking just like my others—growing through the third sleeve in the middle of my back.

My friends all back away from me, then run.

"Wait!" I call after them. "Wait, I can explain." But I can't. Not really.

I feel something in the small of my back, too. Something growing out of that little backward fly. It's a tail, thin and curly, like the tail of a pig, and as I look at my gloves, I suddenly realize that the sixth finger-hole doesn't flop around limply anymore . . . because now there's something to fill it.

I race home screaming, trying to outrun my fear, but it follows behind me just as closely as my third arm.

It's dark. I've locked myself in my bathroom. Leslie keeps pounding, demanding to be let in, but I'm not opening the door for anyone. My parents don't know yet, but they will soon enough.

I tell myself that I didn't know what was happening, but that's a lie. Deep down, I knew. Maybe not at first, but somewhere along the way, I knew. And I guess I knew there was no way to stop it once it started. No matter how many two-sleeved shirts I put on, no matter how many five-fingered gloves, I would never be the way I was. Because the new clothes felt right.

On the counter in front of me is the can. Although it looks like any old can of tuna fish, I know there's no tuna inside. I know it without having to look. I hook on an old can opener and turn the crank. It turns in a slow circle, and I laugh, because it reminds me of the airport carousel that began this new chapter of my life.

I don't know why the suitcase chose me, but it did. Or maybe it was just dumb luck. Anyway, it doesn't matter now. As I turn the can opener with my other two arms, I bend my third elbow and press my new arm firmly against my back. I suppose we could move someplace, where no one knows about it. I could hide it in normal shirts, covered by bulky sweaters. Or maybe I could lock myself away in a basement somewhere, where no one can see. Maybe. But right now, I can't even think beyond tonight, and telling my parents. How do you tell your parents something like this—something that will change the way they see you forever?

The can opener makes a full circle, and I pull open the lid. I knew it. I knew it because I heard them. In the dead of the night I heard them moving inside the can.

Blue, wormlike things—hundreds of them sliding over one another, trying to hide from the light. I know I should be disgusted, but "knowing" and "being" are two different things. And the fact is, I haven't lost my appetite. I simply haven't been hungry for the food in the kitchen. I didn't know what I was hungry for until just now . . . although I did have a sneaking suspicion. That's why I brought a spoon.

They arrive the next day. Something told me that they would. So I pack a suitcase. I watch with Leslie and my parents as they land on our lawn in a ship that seems to me what a minivan might look like, if GM built them for interstellar travel instead of rush hour gridlock. Leslie cries silently, and my parents, well, they're still locked in the same shock they've been in since last night. Either they've accepted it or they're denying any of this is happening; I can't say which.

As I stride forward, suitcase in my third hand, the boy carrying my old suitcase steps forward as well, and we meet in the middle of the lawn. He's wearing my old Cleveland Indians shirt and my favorite jeans. He only has two hands with five fingers on each, but I know that's not the way he started. He started looking much like his family standing by the van.

"Hi," he says.

"Hi," I say back, and turn to take a look at my old family. "They're okay," I tell him. "You'll learn to love them."

But he just grins at me. I realize then that his English stops at the word hi. I suppose both of us will be learning new languages.

We look at each other for a moment more. He seems pleasant enough. We probably could have been friends, if circumstances were different. But now all we can do is pass each other as I move into the arms of his family, and he moves into the arms of mine.

My new father smiles at me, speaking strangely. He greets me by clasping my third hand above our heads, in a sort of bizarre high-five. My new mother smiles, and my new kid brother offers me a fresh can of food.

As I look at the worms squirming in the can, something suddenly strikes me as very funny. "Wow, what a nasty can of worms this is, huh?" I say, and laugh long and loud. My new family laughs as well, but they have no idea what they're laughing about. That's okay.

As I get into the van and strap myself in, my new brother hands me a book. On the first page is a picture of an odd-looking fruit.

⌐ is for ⌐⅂↷

Okay. I'll deal with this. Somehow I'll find a way to deal with this, I know I will.

My dad always said that life is like a game of poker. I suppose you learn to live with the hand you're dealt. Even when it's three of a kind.

THE BOB SQUAD

●●●●●●●●●●●●●●●●●●●●●●●●●●●●●●●●●●●●●●

This is highly irregular," said the visitor at the foot of Bobby Hartford's bed. Actually, it was one of seven visitors, standing there peering down at Bobby as if they had nothing better in the world to do but watch him sleep. None of them should have been there at two o'clock in the morning.

Just a moment ago, Bobby had been dreaming of scoring the winning goal for his ice hockey team. Eighth grade beauty Bonnie O'Lox was in the audience blowing him a kiss. It was the finest dream he had ever remembered having—so vivid and real that it hardly seemed a dream at all. Then all at once he found himself back in his bed with seven strangers scrutinizing him.

"What is this, some kind of dream?" he asked, only half-way out of sleep.

"I'm afraid it's no dream, Bobby." The man who spoke was tall and slim, with a shock of cotton-white hair. "I wish it were a dream, but it's not."

Bobby briefly wondered if he were in a hospital ward—after all, these men and women were all in white suits. But this was his room, not a hospital; and besides, these visitors weren't wearing doctor's outfits—these were tailored white business suits. Their shirts and blouses were all midnight blue, and in them, Bobby could swear he saw stars.

"Who are you?" Bobby pulled his knees up under his covers. "Mom!" he called, "Dad!"

A hand clapped gently over his mouth. Startled, he turned to see that the hand belonged to a wise-looking woman, tall and matronly. "You shouldn't speak now," she suggested. "Not until you understand."

"Yes," said the white-haired man. "Don't make this any worse than it already is." Another woman, plump with a grandmotherly smile, pushed the door to his room closed.

Bobby pushed the hand from his mouth. "What are you all doing in my room?"

No one spoke. The visitors just looked to one another, as if no one wanted to be the first to explain. Bobby had to admit this group didn't look very threatening, but anyone who mysteriously appeared in someone's room was highly suspect.

The white-haired man shook his head. "This won't do. This won't do at all."

A short, bespectacled man with a clipboard leaned in close to Bobby, studying him like a specimen in a petri dish. "Perhaps," he said, "he should go back to sleep."

"Quite right!" said the white-haired man. "Go back to sleep, Bobby. Maybe we'll be gone by morning."

"But . . ."

"No buts!"

"He never listens to anyone!" complained yet another one—this one with dark, spooky eyes.

"Close your eyes immediately!" insisted the white-haired man.

Bobby did as he was told, but opened his eyes only a moment later to find all seven of them still staring at him intently. All but the short one, who was jotting things down on his clipboard.

"Mom!" Bobby screamed. "Dad!!"

The white-haired man motioned to the plump woman. "Could you see that the parents' slumber is undisturbed?" The plump woman smiled and walked through the door. Not out of the door, not around the door, but *through* it, as if the door was not even there.

Although Bobby Hartford had never been accused of being the brightest kid in the world, he could put two and two together fairly easily. He knew that, odds were, when someone walked through a solid door, something out of the ordinary was going on. Bobby gasped, then groaned, feeling his dinner rising from the unspeakable depths of his gut.

The white-haired man raised an eyebrow, and the bespectacled man shook his head and made more notes on his clipboard.

Then a lithe, dark-skinned woman stepped forward. "I'll ease his way," she said, then produced from behind her a harp—a huge thing much taller than she was, and much too large to ever fit through the door of Bobby's room. He opened his mouth to ask how it had gotten there, but the moment she began to play, Bobby felt his jaw relaxing, along with every other muscle in his body. She played a soothing tune that lulled his concerns, and drew down the lids of his eyes. His mind began to drift, and soon he found himself sailing across the ice again, dreaming of hockey stardom.

*   *   *

"Rise and shine!"

Bobby's mother snapped open the curtains with a brightness in her voice that made Bobby want to crawl deeper under his covers. *There ought to be a law against "morning people,"* he thought. Especially when that morning person was your mother.

"Upski and outski!" she shrilled. "It's a beautiful day, and you don't want to be late for school."

Bobby opened his eyes. His mother stood by the window. His seven visitors stood around her.

"Aaaah!" screamed Bobby. He suddenly remembered that odd dream—but it hadn't been a dream, had it?

"What's wrong?" asked his mother.

He pointed to the unwelcome guests. "Those people—don't you see them?!"

His mother looked at him, then glanced around the room, then out of the window. "See who?"

The short, bespectacled man shook his head. "This is bad," he said.

"Yes, exceptionally bad," said the white-haired man.

The one in the back with spooky eyes and crazy hair pushed his way to the front. "What a waste of life you are, Bobby," he said, but almost instantly the plump woman came forward.

"Don't listen to him! You're special, Bobby. If you can see us, that proves you're very special."

"There!" said Bobby, turning to his mother. "Don't you hear them?"

He bounded out of bed, grabbed his mother by the shoulders and turned her to look at the seven, who just sighed and folded their arms. "Do you see them now?"

His mother shook her head. "Pleading insanity will not get you excused from school." Then she left to get breakfast ready.

When she was gone, the plump woman closed the door. "It will all be all right, Bobby. You'll see."

"It's the end of the world," announced the spooky-eyed guy.

"It's nothing of the sort," said the white-haired man, taking charge. "Now see here, Bobby—"

"No! *You* see here!" Bobby yelled. "This is my house, my room, so take all of your ghosts and go haunt somebody else!"

The white-haired man burst out laughing. "Ghosts? You think we're ghosts?" The rest began to chuckle as well.

Bobby frowned, not sure what to think anymore. "Aren't you?"

The white-haired man took a step closer. "Why don't you take a better look?"

And so Bobby did. As far as he could tell, they were still wearing the same white suits from the day before, but then he noticed that their shirts and blouses were no longer midnight blue. Now they were a brisk morning blue, speckled with puffs of gray and white, mimicking the clouds just outside his window. Then as Bobby took in each of their faces, it occurred to him that there was something familiar about each of them. The white-haired man's decisive eyes; the plump woman's soft smile; the shifty stance of the spooky one; the gentle movements of the harp player's hands; the scrutinizing gaze of the bespectacled man; the whispers of the tall woman. Even the pretty, silent girl who sat in the background as if waiting for a time that had not yet come seemed familiar.

"I know you," Bobby said, confused. "All of you . . ."

"Yes," answered the white-haired man, "and no."

Bobby noticed something odd about the fabric of their suits. It wasn't like anything he'd ever seen before. He reached out and ran his fingers along the white-haired man's sleeve. It was smoother than velvet, and finer than silk. "What is it?" Bobby asked.

"Watch," he said.

All at once their suit coats lifted open, as if from a billowing breeze, and they stretched outward until Bobby could see that they weren't tailored suits at all. They were wings.

Bobby gasped in astonishment.

"Allow me to introduce myself," said the white-haired man. "I am Bartholomew, and we . . . are your guardian angels."

Bobby heard it, but he was still too dazzled by the spectacle of their open wings to say anything.

"You see," explained Bartholomew, "every human is attended to by a host of seven angels."

"We monitor you," said the bespectacled one.

"We advise you," said the tall woman.

"We caress your moods and emotions," said the harp player.

"We tend your inner fire," said the patient, pretty one.

"We comfort you," said the plump woman.

"We put obstacles in your way to challenge you," said the creepy one, with an even creepier little laugh.

Then Bartholomew gestured to the others and the fluttering of wings ceased. Bobby watched, entranced as the wings folded over them, becoming simple white suits once more. "There are thirty-five billion of us," Bartholomew said, "seven for every human, and we travel unseen within the lives of humankind."

"But . . . I can see you."

"Yes, you can." Bartholomew thoughtfully rubbed his chin. "Now you understand our problem."

Bobby sat back down on his bed, trying to come to grips with what he had been told. He had always thought—hoped—that there were such things as guardian angels, protecting him, guiding him. But *hoping* for such things—even *believing* in them—was very different from seeing them standing in his room taking notes. He suddenly found his bladder several sizes too small.

"I gotta use the bathroom." Bobby slipped out the door, and across the hall to the bathroom, glad to be away from them. But to his horror, he found all seven of them waiting in there for him. The bathroom was small even for one person, but now it held Bobby and seven angels. Three stood in the bathtub, two stood on the toilet tank, one hovered above the sink and another hung from the shower curtain rod.

"Do you mind?" asked Bobby. "Can't I even take a whiz by myself?"

"Not a chance," said the bespectacled man, busy scribbling. "We're with you everywhere. We see every pick of your nose, every scratch of your butt, every cookie you steal from the cookie jar. We always have, and always will."

"And man, you are one gross dude," said the spooky one.

"But we don't mind," said the plump woman. "It's our job."

"Now go ahead and do your business," said Bartholomew, "or we'll be late for school."

Bobby failed his math test that day, even though math was his best subject. It wasn't that he didn't know the work, he just couldn't concentrate. How could anyone concentrate with an entourage of seven angels hovering around you, taking notes, looking over your shoulder and constantly telling you what to do?

"Do the easy math problems first," one suggested.

"No, do the hard ones first; get them out of the way," suggested another.

"Don't do any of them, run out the back door."

"Copy the answers from the kid next to you."

They were like a living multiple-choice test. So many voices, so much advice, and not all of it good.

Hockey practice was a crash-and-burn. Although their voices were mostly drowned out by the action around him, they were still there, gliding across the ice around him, making it impossible for him to see the puck through the gaggle of angels. And then the creepy one kept tripping him on purpose!

"Just doing my job," he would say. "What's life without a little challenge?"

His coach wondered why Bobby was so clumsy, his friends couldn't figure out why he kept looking off and mumbling to himself.

But if all that was bad, nothing could compare to what happened on Bobby's first date with Bonnie O'Lox.

It was eight o'clock at the multiplex, and the lights had barely gone down when the angels got to work.

"You really should put your arm around her," whispered the pretty angel in his ear—the first time she had offered any advice on anything at all. So surprised was Bobby that he flinched, flinging popcorn all over Bonnie.

"Is something wrong?" Bonnie asked.

"No. No, nothing. I just slipped, that's all."

"So are you going to put your arm around her or not?" asked the pretty angel.

"He's too much of a wimp," said the creepy one.

"He's a good boy," said the plump one. "He won't do anything too forward."

"Enough!" Bobby grumbled

Bonnie turned to him. "Enough of what?"

"Uh . . . enough coming attractions," he said. "When's the movie going to start?"

The bespectacled angel put a check on his clipboard, and gave Bobby a thumbs-up. "Good recovery."

"Put your arm around her!" insisted the pretty angel. Finally Bobby complied, slipping his arm around her shoulder. Bonnie didn't seem to mind. The angels applauded.

"Can't you leave me alone!"

It had burst out of his mouth before the matronly angel could cup her hand over his lips. Bonnie turned to him, understandably annoyed. "What did you say?"

But now the angel of silence's hand was over his mouth, and he found himself tongue-tied. It took all his will to push her hand away. "I didn't mean you!" he finally said.

"Then who did you mean?"

And that's when the angels began a full scale offensive on his brain.

"Just shut up and pretend it didn't happen," said one.

"Run to the bathroom quick!" said another.

"You're such a loser," said the creepy one.

"Let's all go get some ice cream," suggested the plump one.

So many voices and choices—all so confusing.

"Kiss her!" screeched the pretty angel, and Bobby found himself taking her advice. He leaned forward and planted a popcorn and soda-pop kiss on Bonnie O'Lox's unsuspecting lips.

For a moment at least seven different emotions played on Bonnie's face before she slapped him so hard across the face his retainer flew into the next row.

Bonnie got up and stormed out.

"Smooth move, moron," said the creepy one.

"At least your mother still loves you," said the plump one.

And then Bartholomew pushed his way to the front. Until now he had been content to just orchestrate the others, but now he stepped forward for some decisive action. "Sorry about this Bobby," he said, then he punched Bobby in the stomach. Bobby folded over, the wind knocked out of him. The feeling spread through his body feeling more like a wave of embarrassment and humiliation than a punch to the gut. "Nothing personal," Bartholomew said. "It's just part of the job."

It was the same for weeks. Seven voices, seven courses of action. Words of comfort and praise, accusations and condemnations. Warm hugs and the occasional punch to the gut. Living with it didn't make it any easier—if anything, Bobby became more frazzled as time went on. In those first few weeks, he was regularly caught talking to himself, but it was just assumed to be a standard variation of eighth-grade weirdness.

"I'm worried about you, Bobby," his mother said one afternoon. That was nothing new—she worried about him even before he was blessed by a plague of angels that no one could see but him. But this time he knew she had reason to worry. These angels were driving him crazy—in fact, the only thing that kept him sane was the knowledge that there was one place they could not go. They could be in his face twenty-four hours a day, but they couldn't be in his head. They couldn't read his mind, and could never truly know what he was thinking.

When he went to the library and pulled down every volume he could find on angels, he told them, "I'm just studying all bout you. If I have to live with you I might as well understand what angels are all about." Since the angels didn't believe it possible for Bobby to keep anything from them, they never suspected the true nature of his studies. Even when he began to research the authors of the darker, stranger books. Even when he found one of those authors living in his town.

"The boy has a healthy interest," Bartholomew told his colleagues.

"I think it's sick," said the creepy one, who found most everything Bobby did to be sick.

The most interesting, weirdest book on angels Bobby found was by a man named Terrence Daktill—who, according to the bio, lived right there in town. From the things Mr. Daktill wrote, it was very clear to Bobby that he was different from the other authors. He knew too much—which meant, perhaps, that he saw his own angels, too.

Terrence Daktill lived in a mansion in the most exclusive part of town, with a gate so far from the main residence that the house couldn't even be seen from the street. Although the man had only one book to his credit, he appeared rich beyond reckoning.

"Does Mr. Daktill come from a rich family?" Bobby asked the butler who led him toward the morning room.

"No—Mr. Daktill came into his wealth rather recently," said the butler. "Good investments."

As they sat in the morning room, the angels flitted about in their standard orbits around Bobby, some flying, some pacing, some trying to distract him, console him, or challenge him, as they always did

"I don't like this place," Bartholomew commented.

Then Terrence Daktill made his grand entrance. He was a man dressed in a thousand-dollar suit, with a gold watch and a glittering diamond earring. "You've come to speak to me about my book?"

"Yes," said Bobby, introducing himself. Mr. Daktill

gestured for him to sit down, with a smooth wave of his
hand that seemed more like a magician revealing a secret
card. Bobby sat in a plush leather armchair, and got right
to the point, ignoring the whispers and comments of his
angelic entourage. "You see your angels too, don't you,
Mr. Daktill?"

The man didn't seem surprised at all by the question.
"Yes, I did see my angels for a time. If we dream too
vividly, they become visible to us—but you already know
that from my book."

"You don't see them anymore?" Bobby asked.

"No, I don't."

Bartholomew perked up. "Splendid!" he cried. "Get
him to tell us how we might become hidden from you
again!"

Bobby shushed him, and Daktill smiled knowingly.

Then the butler entered with a pot of tea, pouring two
cups, then left.

"Please have some," Daktill offered. "I think you'll
find the brew exceptional."

It was exceptional, all right; exceptionally disgusting.
It tasted more like mud than tea, but Bobby just smiled,
not wanting to be rude. Meanwhile, the angels chattered
away, trying to tell him what to do.

"Run away."

"Tell him he's a nutcase."

"No—listen to what he has to say."

"Ask him if he has a daughter your age."

"See if there's anything good for dinner."

Bobby put his hands over his ears. "Shut up!!"

Daktill grinned. "Are they giving you too much advice?"

"All day long," Bobby confessed, "and they're always
there, watching me eat and sleep. They won't leave me
alone!"

"It's their job, you know," said Daktill. "Now drink your tea—it will ease your mind."

The plump angel took offense to that. "Don't you believe him, Bobby. It's *my* job to ease your mind!"

Daktill slowly wove the fingers of his right hand into the fingers of his left. "I once saw my angels," he told Bobby. "And then I educated myself. You see, they do have one weakness. They can advise you, they can watch you, but they can't make you *do* anything—which means they can't *stop* you from doing anything either.

The angels began to grumble uncomfortably. Bartholomew leaned forward. "Let's leave," he said. "Let's leave right away."

"No," Bobby said, "I want to stay."

"Good for you!" said Daktill. "Exert your free will!"

Bobby smiled. Perhaps he had more power than he realized.

Daktill reached his slender fingers down to a small snuff box that sat on an antique table beside him. "This box dates back six hundred years," he explained. "It's priceless, like most of the things in this house. But it's what's inside that makes it most valuable to you and me." Daktill opened the snuff box to reveal that it was full of straight pins, each about two inches long.

"Select a pin," Daktill instructed.

"What for?"

"You'll see."

Bobby pulled out a pin. It was ordinary in every way.

"Now prick your right thumb with it."

All at once the angels erupted into a noisy argument, no longer advising him but fighting with each other as to what they should do. Bobby jabbed the pin into his thumb, and instantly the angels fell eerily silent, watching. Bobby withdrew the pin, and a tiny bead of blood bubbled up on his thumb. Suddenly Daktill grabbed

Bobby's hand and thrust his thumb into his cup of tea.

"Hey! That's hot!" But even as he said it Bobby realized that the tea was chilling, as if his thumb were an ice cube cooling the water. In a moment the tea was freezing cold, and the liquid had changed from muddy brown to clear.

"Once you see your angels, they'll never be far from your sight," said Daktill. "Unless you remove them completely."

"Remove them?"

The angels suddenly cried out, demanding that Bobby leave, trying to turn his will—but he remained steadfast, and they could do nothing against his resolve.

"The removal of one's angels," continued Daktill, "requires a potion consisting of hummingbird wings and manatee tears, boiled in a purée of unicorn horn and the adrenal gland of a Himalayan Yeti. That's what you've been drinking."

Bobby began to feel sick to his stomach, but forced the feeling away.

"The final and most important ingredient was a drop of your blood," said Daktill. "Now only one part of the ritual remains. Do you truly wish to rid yourself of your angels, Bobby Hartford?"

"Yes," said Bobby, "yes, I do."

"Then repeat after me. . . ."

"Don't do it!" shouted the angels.

"We love you!"

"We hate you!"

"Who will comfort you?"

"Who will frighten you?"

"Who will make you feel?"

"Who will make you sleep?"

"Who will hold your tongue?"

"Who will push you to action?"

"Don't do it, Bobby!"

Daktill held Bobby's hand deep in the tea that was quickly turning into ice. "With this brew," said Daktill.

And Bobby repeated, "With this brew,"

"I thee absolve."

"I thee absolve!"

There came a flutter of wings and kicking up of dust, seven sudden gasps of air . . . and all the shouts were enveloped by sweet, sweet silence. The angels were gone.

"Where'd they go?" Bobby asked.

"Look at the pin." Daktill handed him back the pin, and a huge magnifying glass. Bobby looked through the lense to see seven tiny angels stuck to the head of the pin.

"This is highly irregular," Bartholomew cried in a faint, high-pitched voice. "Highly irregular indeed!"

"And that's that," said Daktill. Then he took the pin from Bobby and stuck it into a little red pincushion that was already bristling with pins. "I've been collecting them," explained Daktill, "from other unfortunate souls like yourself." He slid the pincushion into a drawer in a roll-top desk.

Bobby didn't know how he could ever thank the man. "I should pay you something," Bobby said. "I don't have much, but—"

Daktill just laughed. "Having your angels is payment enough," he said. "They're good luck, you know." Since I've started collecting them, I've won the lottery and every sweepstakes I enter." Then he handed Bobby five hundred-dollar bills. "This is for you—payment for your angels."

Bobby took the money, wondering if perhaps angels might be worth something more—but in the end, it didn't matter, because they both got what they wanted. Bobby left a very happy boy.

That night, Bobby slept quietly and contentedly. In his dream he was alone at last on the ice—no one but him and the open goal ahead. There in the stands was Bonnie O'Lox, waving at him, forgiving him for being so strange on their one and only date. It was a dream for the record books, more vivid, more real than any dream he could remember. But then he was awakened by a nasty twist of his big toe.

"Ouch!"

He opened his eyes to a sea of faces around him. Not just seven, but many, many more.

"You nasty, nasty boy!" said the leader of this tribe of angels, all with silver wings and bodies glowing as bright as the sun.

"No!" shouted Bobby. "I just got rid of my angels. What's going on here? Who are you?"

The lead angel leaned forward menacingly. "Do you think that you humans are the only ones who have guardian angels? Ha! We are the seven squads of archangels who attend to the lives of *your* angels . . . but now that you've banished them to the head of a pin, there's not much for us to do, is there? So we've come to you."

Bobby swallowed hard. "You mean—"

"That's right, Bobby. We're *your* angels now . . . and we're not happy about it."

Bobby buried himself under his covers, but his blanket was quickly ripped away. "Things are going to change around here," the lead archangel said. "There will be no more whining, no more nose-picking, no more nail-biting or fiddling with your toe jam. You will live by *our* standards now . . . because we'll always be watching you, Bobby. *All forty-nine of us.*"

Bobby looked at the crowd of disgruntled faces scowling at him, and suddenly thought he might just wet his bed.

"I . . . I gotta use the bathroom," he told them.

The lead angel rolled his eyes. "Very well, if you must. Just give us a moment."

Bobby sighed with sad resignation. It was going to be one very crowded bathroom.

THE LIVING
PLACE

....

The old woman fills her porch rocker like it was built just for her, and she slowly shifts forward and back, forward and back. I think I might get seasick just looking at her. Her hair is as silver as a spider web on a dewy morning, and her skin is as dark as a moonless night. Her name is Delilah. She's the first person we met when we moved into the neighborhood last week.

"Prime property you got there, Katie," she tells me as my brother Tyler and I sit on her porch, sipping her sun tea sweetened with fresh comb honey. "Finest property in the county."

I turn around to look at our house across the street. It's not much to look at—gray roof shingles that have gone green from too much rain and a porch sagging in the middle from the weight of five generations. I mean, the place is old, filled with mysterious relics from vanished days—like the old coal furnace that no longer works, or the light fixtures which have been painted over so many times they now look like barnacles growing from the ceiling. The place is full of radiator coils like steel anacondas that groan and complain, then summon out legions of overgrown bugs from their depths every time they begin to heat.

"I hate that house," grumbles Tyler, who's seven and hates most everything. "I don't even know why we had to move here."

But he knows. We both do. It was living in the city that made Mom sick—all that stress. But she's better now. Total remission, the doctors said—sometimes it happens like that. She's putting some weight back on her bones, and her hair's growing back, too. Life in the country is what she needs, so we bought this little house, and about a gazillion acres of land behind it.

The old woman hurls a handful of seed out at the birds on her lawn, whose numbers grow with each handful thrown at them. "You can hate the house, but not the land it sits on," she tells us. "The land is something special."

Tyler flicks some bird seed off the porch. "I wish we could move back to the city."

Delilah shakes her head. "Cities!" she says, pursing her lips as if the word was a sour lemon. "Cities are places that suck life away—just suck it away like a cat sleeping on your chest."

I feel a chill release itself on my spine, echoing through to my fingers and toes. Tyler looks at me, and looks down. I can hear his breath beginning to get raspy, and he reflexively taps the asthma inhaler to make sure it's in his pocket. It wasn't just Mom who lost bits and pieces of her life to the city.

Delilah looks up at the trees around us. "But this place is nothing like the city. This place is *abundant*."

"Abundant," I repeat, letting the musical sound of the word somersault off my tongue.

Delilah takes a long sip of her honey-sweet tea. "Have you been out back of your place yet?" she asks.

I shake my head. "Our parents won't let us. There could be rattlers, or gators."

"And ticks," adds Tyler. "Don't forget the ticks!"

"Nonsense," says Delilah. "Haven't been rattlers around here since I was your age, and we don't get gators—this place ain't exactly the bayou."

Back and forth goes her rocker. Birdseed crackles beneath its curved, blunt blades. Then she moves her chair as far forward as it will go without toppling over. Leaning toward us she whispers, "You know . . . there are powerful places around these parts."

Now she's caught my attention. "What do you mean . . . powerful?"

"I'll show you."

We help her out of her chair and hand her a birch cane with an ivory handle. As we cross the lawn, the birds take wing, sweeping a frantic path toward the setting sun.

The field behind our house is huge. It's full of tall wheat grass, windswept and wild like a mop of morning bed-hair, stretching for fifty yards. The property would have been big enough if it ended there, but it doesn't. Behind the field is a grove of oaks. "No good for wood, though," Dad had said, as if everything had to be milled, distilled, or processed for it to be useful.

According to the real estate agent, the property goes back more than half a mile; twenty-six acres in all. Mom and Dad had intended to survey the property with a notebook and a canteen, trekking through the woods like Lewis and Clark, cataloguing everything our little Louisiana purchase had in store for us . . . but like so many things, real life came first. Unpacking before exploring. So far, our property was mostly unexplored by us.

Delilah leads us through the wheat grass, toward the woods. "I knew the folks who owned the property before you. Nice folks, for a time."

"For a time?" I ask.

Delilah takes her time answering, as if weighing what she should say and what she shouldn't. "People get funny now and again. You see those signs?" She points at some trees around us.

"Yes," I tell her. To be honest, the signs are hard to miss: NO TRESPASSING in big red letters, on iron signs rusting around the edges. There's one on our front fence, and one on the tree in our side yard. Out back, those signs seem to be everywhere.

"And they meant it," Delilah says. "Nobody came onto their property, not for any reason under the sun." Then she sighs. "Of course, they weren't always like that. There were times I remember when I was a young woman, they used to have parties and picnics like the rest of us. Then one day they just shut the gate, and put up those signs. I suppose they would have put up electric fences if they could afford 'em."

"But why would they do that?" Tyler asks.

"Got greedy, I suppose. Wanted all that beautiful land for themselves."

I think back to when we met the old man who sold us the property. His face was deeply cragged with wrinkles, and his limbs as gnarled as the branches of a juniper. When he signed the papers and handed over the keys to my dad, he had said, "It's not my responsibility anymore," as if leaving the place took the weight of the world from his shoulders.

The grass flattens before us, leaving a green trench that betrays our path. We wear long pants to protect us from the swarms of mosquitoes, but I can still feel the coarse grass brushing across my legs. A rich chlorophyll aroma is pressed out of the grass as we make our way towards the woods.

"I don't know about this," says Tyler, slowing down as we reach the woods. "Mom and Dad won't like this at all."

But I remind him that Mom and Dad don't have to know; they're off buying wallpaper to cover the mildewed bedroom walls.

Delilah laughs when she hears that. "Nothing wrong with a little mildew," she says. "It's just one form of life changing into another. It reminds us that we're part of the circle. There, you see?" Delilah says cheerfully, pointing to several saplings sprouting from the moss-covered remains of a felled oak. "It's all recycled in the end."

Tyler continues walking, but not before double-checking that his inhaler is still in his pocket. Strange he should worry about that, because right now his breathing sounds clearer than it has in weeks.

We move deeper into the woods. The trees are thick and tall, and the light is dim. I wonder if it's getting dark, or if it's just the canopy above us. Birds call to one another. We hear something scurry past in the brush and dart out of sight.

Finally Delilah stops. "Look here," she says, pointing to a moss-covered rock.

"Just a bunch of moss," says Tyler.

"No . . . look closer."

"Let me see." I bring my hand across the stone, and flake away the thick layer of moss, to reveal something carved into the stone. "Wow." The markings are badly weathered, and appear to be very old, but I can clearly make out the shape of a circle, with swirls coming out of it.

"Who made them?" Tyler asks. "Indians?"

"No one can say," answers Delilah. "These marks are as old as time itself."

"Do you think this was some sort of ancient burial ground?" I ask.

"Cool!" says Tyler, thrilled and terrified by the thought.

"No," says Delilah. "Not a burial place . . . a *living* place."

Tyler and I look at each other, not sure what she means. As I turn back to Delilah, I notice the boulder beside her is more than a mere boulder. It's a piece of stone carved into a wedge, like an arrow . . . and it points deeper into the woods, where a rusted barbed wire fence cuts between the trees.

"What does it point to?" I ask.

Delilah seems a bit less sure of herself now. With her cane for balance, she shifts her weight from one hip to the other. "Can't be sure," she tells us. "When I was young and foolish I came out here and found the stone. But something about it gave me the willies."

"You got scared?"

"Scared enough to turn and run. It wasn't long after that the fences and 'no trespassing' signs went up."

I take a deep breath. "Well, this is our property now, and no one can stop us from going on in." Now I lead the way instead of Delilah. Finding a gap in the barbed wire, we climb through.

The deeper we move into the forest, the more I understand what Delilah means by "a living place." The emerald green of the trees; the sound of birds and insects filling the air; the rich smell of peat, like a spring garden—every inch of the place seems to be alive. I begin to feel lightheaded and wonder if, like the rainforests, this air is rich in oxygen. This truly is a living place, where all life thrives and even my brother breathes clearly, without a hint of an asthmatic wheeze.

At last we come to a clearing within a circle of tall, straight oaks, and between each oak is another triangular stone pointing toward the center. The sky above is a patch of early twilight blue surrounded by shimmering green leaves, and the clearing is filled with wispy gossamer grass and wildflowers bursting with such powerful color you could swear you feel those blues, yellows, and pinks caressing your brain.

"Lord Almighty, will you look at this place!" says Delilah, her breath taken away. "What a wonder!"

Tyler lopes out into the clearing with an enthusiastic stride, instead of shuffling his feet like he usually does.

"Maybe it's like an ancient temple," he suggests, "like I seen on TV! People come secretly at night and make human sacrifices!"

"It's no such thing!" I tell him, and I instinctively know that I'm right. This is a place of life, not death. Maybe it once was a place of worship, but not of dark deeds. Not here.

Yet, as I look at Delilah, I can see that her wonder is quickly dissolving into concern, and then fear. Her fear becomes contagious, and I can't help but to feel that we shouldn't be here—and that something terrible is going to happen.

"That's enough," Delilah calls out to Tyler. "I'd best be getting you two back home."

But Tyler is in his element, prancing around the grassy clearing, kicking up the rich scent of wildflowers and weaving fantasies.

"Maybe it's a pirate place," he says.

"We're a hundred miles from the ocean!" I remind him.

"So? Pirates can walk. Even if they got peg legs. Maybe pirates hauled their gold here, and buried it right in the middle of this clearing!"

Then he takes off toward the center of the clearing.

"Tyler, you get back here!" I yell, but he's not listening. "Tyler!"

And then suddenly he's gone. He just disappears into thin air—or so it seems to me—but old Miss Delilah, thick glasses and all, sees the whole thing better than I do. She drops her cane, and goes running right to the center of the field, throwing herself on the ground.

"Katie, help me!" she cries.

I hurry to her and see Tyler's face looking up at me from a dark hole in the ground, less than two feet across. His hands cling to the grass at the edge of the hole, and I can only thank heaven that the grass is healthy and that its roots are strong enough to hold firm.

"Help," shouts Tyler. "Don't let me fall!"

"I got you, Tyler," says Delilah. Not bothering with his hand, she grabs him by his mop of hair. He was supposed to get a crew cut for the summer, but it's a good thing he didn't.

"Ow!" he yells, but with her hand snagged in his hair like that, there's no way he's going to fall. I grab his arm and pull, then pull again. Finally, between the two of us, we haul Tyler out of the hole. Lying there on the grass, he sobs for a few moments, but gets over it quickly, determined not to let us see his tears.

"I told you pirates were here!" he says. "It's a pirate cave!"

"It's no cave," I tell him flatly. "It's just an old well."

Tyler peers down into the well, disappointed. "So . . . it *could* have been a pirate cave."

Now that Tyler is safe, Delilah trembles with the fright of it all. "Lordy, we almost lost you down there."

I think about the stories I've heard about kids who've been trapped in wells. Someone digs the wells then forgets them, or they board them up but the boards rot. Kids and animals fall in. Sometimes they die—especially when the well is hidden in tall grass, like this one. Tyler got lucky today.

He leans over the well, tempting fate. "Tyler!" I scold, gripping onto the waistband of his pants, just in case he loses his footing. He is consumed with curiosity. I guess I can't blame him.

"How deep do you suppose it goes?" I ask.

"To the center of the earth, I'll bet," says Tyler.

I look to Delilah, but her face is clouded with thoughts as deep as the well. She knows something—but it's not something she wants to share with us.

A breeze blows past us, and I can hear it whisper across the lip of the well, conjuring forth a raspy moan. "Sounds like something's down there," I say.

"Just the breath of the wind," says Delilah. Once more her fear lays itself upon me like a yawn. "You two come on now." She fishes her cane from the grass. "Got to get home while there's still some light left."

We leave together, but as we reach the circle of trees, I have to look back. From here the hole is hidden by the grass around it.

Delilah takes my arm. "Come along. Maybe its best you keep to the other side of the barbed wire."

We wind through trails and over logs and boulders until we're on our back porch once more. Only then do I hear that Tyler's wheezing has returned.

There are some places that draw you to them. They grab you so deep in your soul that you find yourself drifting toward them, even in your dreams. That's how it is with the Living Place. It isn't just that we're drawn there; things had felt different there, too. That first time out there with Delilah, we had felt full of ourselves, full of life, and even as we left, I knew we would be going back.

We don't tell Mom and Dad about the well, or the stones, or the old barbed wire fence. Our parents' boundaries have not yet reached beyond the tall grass in our yard—and even then, Dad has only managed to mow half of it. At this rate it will be months before they venture deep enough to find our secret little spot. We keep it to ourselves. We don't even talk to Delilah about it anymore.

The next time we go back, Tyler takes his soccer ball. It's a shiny one, still as smooth as the day Dad got it for him, because Tyler never uses it much. Not that he doesn't want to, his asthma just won't let him. One time he had an attack just running for the school bus, and ever since he's been too worried to play much of any sport. And yet it doesn't surprise me that he grabs the ball when we go back to the Living Place.

"You be careful out there," Mom calls to us from the back porch.

"Don't worry," I tell her, "we won't go far."

The second we cross from the tall grass into the woods, Tyler drops his ball and begins dribbling it around rocks and gnarled tree roots. The closer he gets to the Living Place the faster he moves, and I have to jog to keep up with him. As I run, I can feel the pores on my face open as if I'm in a steam bath, and I know that being out here will even help my acne.

Tyler stops as we near the clearing that hides the well. He won't go into that clearing again. Neither will I. Instead we stay just outside of it, kicking the ball back and forth between the trees.

"You be goalie," insists Tyler, bouncing the ball from one knee to another, high-stepping like the leader of a parade, no sign of asthma or worry.

"Okay," I tell him, "but if you aim at my head, you're dead meat!"

"I won't aim at your head," he tells me, then takes a shot directly at my face.

I throw up my hands a moment too late—the ball painfully ricochets off of my ear, and between two trees.

"Goal!" shouts Tyler, jumping up and down.

"Why you little—"

"Katie—the ball!"

I turn to see the ball bouncing into the clearing, over the brightly colored wildflowers. I know exactly where it's headed.

"Stop it!" yells Tyler, as if I have arms that could stretch out that far and bring the ball back. I race out, but it is too far away, and I can only watch as the ball disappears into the well.

"Oh, great!" says Tyler. "You owe me a new ball!"

"*You* kicked it!"

"It hit *your* head!"

I step up to the well and look down, seeing nothing but darkness. Then I hear something: a distant sucking sound. Then silence. Until that moment I hadn't realized there had been any noise in the air at all—I guess my ears had just become accustomed to the faint rasp of wind across the well, but now that airy hiss is gone.

Instantly things begin to change.

At first I think it's just my imagination. "Tyler! Look at the grass and flowers. Do they look funny to you?"

He looks around, and shrugs. "No."

"See how they're lying? They're not as tall as they were before. It's as if the whole field has flattened out a bit."

"That's because we just ran across it," he says.

"But we didn't walk everywhere," I say pointing to the other side, where the flowers have definitely begun to wilt.

He furrows his eyebrows, the way Dad does when something confuses him. "That's weird."

Tyler looks into the hole again. Dark and silent. "What about my ball?"

"We'll get you a new one."

"You're paying for it."

"Fine," I say, just to get him moving. "Let's just get out of here."

By the time we reach the circle of trees just beyond the clearing, I notice some leaves have begun to turn yellow.

A summer blight, the neighbors call it. A new breed of weevil, or something like that. Trees, grasses, and shrubs brown and yellow around us within the next three weeks. At first it's just our property, but the blight spreads in twisting spokes like brown tentacles of death, following the banks of streams and the veins of canyons. Birds fall dead from their perches on trees. Worms crawl up through the earth only to bake and dry in the sun. From my window I can see the brown wasteland of our backyard. The dead grass blows away like chaff in the wind, leaving behind mud.

The town begins a slow simmer, boiling toward panic as the arms of the blight stretch toward farmland.

Tyler doesn't play soccer anymore. He barely gets out of bed. At night his wheezing keeps me awake—not because it's so loud, but because I'm terrified that it might suddenly stop.

And then there's my parents.

One morning, after a breakfast as somber as a funeral, I dare to ask my father a question that I've been afraid to hear the answer to.

"Dad," I ask, "When did your hair start going gray?"

He looks at me as if it's a forbidden subject. It's Mom who answers. "It's just stress, dear," she says. "That happens sometimes."

But it's not just Dad's hair and Tyler's asthma—there are other things. Like the way the food I eat doesn't seem to nourish me anymore. I'm losing weight. My summer tan has begun to pale long before the summer is over, and you can see the veins through my translucent skin. Now all I ever want to do is sleep.

"What's happening around here?" I ask them.

They sense the urgency in my voice, and look to each other as if communicating in some sort of parental telepathy.

"Honey," Dad says, "You don't have to worry about Mom. It's probably nothing; the Doctor said so."

I'm caught completely off guard. "*What's* probably nothing?"

They turn to each other again, realizing they've opened a can of worms. Now that I look at Mom, I can see the dark rings under her eyes and the failing expression on her face, like a hillside about to give way.

"I just have to go back in for a few tests, that's all."

"The doctors say it's probably nothing," repeats Dad.

I bolt from the room, not ready to hear any more, not wanting to face the possibility that the cancer is back, growing through Mom's body like the blight spreading through town.

But it's more than just a "blight." I know that. I've known it from the beginning, but I hadn't dared to think what it's really all about. Now I have no choice.

As I burst out into the street the despair is everywhere—I hear hacking coughs from windows down the road. I pass a bone-thin dog, its coat mange-torn and its eyes large and hopeless. The stench and sounds of slow death rise in the air around me—it fills the air *within* me. I can feel my own body winding down.

I burst into Delilah's unlocked door. She always keeps it unlocked. She says she trusts in the safety of the world. I wonder if she trusts in it now.

I find her lying on her bed. At first I think she's asleep, but her head slowly turns to me. "Katie," she says. "I suppose you've been wondering about me. I've been tired, is all." She smiles and gazes at me through rheumy eyes.

"I need to know something, Delilah," I tell her gently. "I need to understand. You know what's happening around here, don't you? Please, tell me."

She nods sadly. "It's dying."

"What's dying?"

"Everything. The birds, the trees, the land, and the sea. All dying. All dying."

"What should I do?"

"Nothing to do," she says weakly. "The Living Place is dead. No telling why."

"What *is* the living place?" I ask her. Afraid to hear her answer, but more afraid not to.

She sighs and shifts in her bed, not even trying to sit up. "Every living thing has a breath of life, child," she tells me, "and everything that breathes needs a place to do it from." I sit back in my chair beginning to understand what she is telling me. "I knew it the moment I saw it. I've heard tell of such a place, but never dreamed it was real."

I just shake my head, not wanting to believe it.

"I thought you understood, child," her voice gets weaker with every passing word. "The world . . . has stopped . . . breathing. . . ."

And in a moment, so does Delilah. She just closes here eyes, takes one deep breath, then a shallow one, then a shallower one still, and she is gone.

I let go of her hand and it falls limply to the bed. I want to cry, but I know I have other things to do now. Delilah would not want me to cry. *It's part of the circle,* she would say. Flesh to dirt, to daisies, to flesh once more. I realize now that the best thing I can do for Delilah is to make sure the cycle doesn't end with her. That the renewal continues.

I leave Delilah's house, stepping into my own house

just long enough to fish out my dad's Swiss army knife from a junk drawer. Then I head straight out into the backyard, tramping through the mud toward the barren trees beyond. The abundance of life Delilah was so fond of talking about is gone. All the moss is brown and the rich smell of peat has turned bitter. The bodies of rats and rabbits litter the ground as I get closer to the Living Place. They are uneaten, yet they are undecayed. *Even the bacteria has died here,* I think, and I wonder which is worse: the indignance of flesh breaking down into dust or the crime of it not being returned to the earth at all. I push forward past the wedge of stone pointing toward the center of life.

The hole stands bare now; the grass and flowers have been blown away, like flesh torn from a skeleton, and the bare, hard earth is cracked and mottled in sickly shades of gray. I imagine the blight stretching out from this place; a slow shock wave of death enveloping the whole Earth, leaving it a voiceless, soulless rock drifting in silent space until time itself ceases.

I stand at the lip of the hole. How long has it been since Tyler's ball went down there? Four weeks? Five? "There's nothing to be done," Delilah had said—but she didn't know the ailment. I do, and if there can be a cure, it's up to me.

This is for Delilah, I say to myself, *and for my brother, and my mom and dad. . . .*

And although I am terrified, I know that my fear means little, for if I succeed, even if I die, the life I save will be well worth my own. Before I can change my mind, I dive into the hole headfirst, with my eyes closed.

Rocks scrape me, tearing my shirt and jeans as I fall, until I am tightly wedged in the hole. With my hands before me, I must wriggle deeper and deeper, slithering in the darkness, feeling the blood rush to my head, pounding in my ears, and finally when I can fall no deeper, my hands come across something cold and round, blocking the tight hole ahead.

The ball is wedged in the hole too tightly to pull out, so I don't even try. Instead I find the knife in my pocket. I pull out a stubby little blade and stab at the ball with all my strength. At first the knife just bounces off the hard leather surface, but I try again and again until the blade sinks deep, and I hear the telltale hiss of air escaping from the popped soccer ball.

I grab the flattened ball, pulling it free from the hole, and as I do I can hear the sucking of wind growing stronger and stronger. I push out my elbows and knees to keep from being sucked any deeper, and just when I feel that I can't hold on anymore, the air being drawn into the earth stops . . . and then it begins to reverse with such force that the ground around me shakes.

I feel myself moving up and up, with a blast of moist air! Suddenly I'm being coughed up out of the bowels of the earth at an impossible speed. The darkness gives way to light, I see sky, and earth, and trees. I am airborne, but only for an instant before I fall in a heap on the hard, gray ground. A flash of light—I seem to see stars, like they do in cartoons, and then darkness, as I lose consciousness.

I wake to the sound of birds. Just one or two. It takes a moment for me to orient myself, remembering where I am and what I have done. I sit up, my head still spinning from the concussion. Around me is the clearing, still gray and bare . . . but something is different. I hear the faint rasp of air slipping into the hole at the center, and the smell of the air is fresh again. A few feet away is the flattened soccer ball. It's covered in dark, dark mud. In fact, so am I—it covers every inch of me, as thick as tar . . . yet I don't feel dirty, for I know that this dirt is clean. I sit

there for a few minutes more, then take the soccer ball
and head out of the woods.

We spread Delilah's ashes out over the Living Place. I
know it's what she would have wanted. And now in the
clearing the wildflowers grow taller and brighter for it. In
turn, they attract more bees, who take the nectar and turn
it into honey for someone else to use in their sun tea.

The blight ended as quickly as it came, and now the
Living Place is back to its full green glory. I go back to
the clearing every once in a while, to lie out there in the
flowers. I never bring a soccer ball, and always keep a re-
spectful distance from the "well." Usually I just go there
to think, and to breathe in the sweet air. I took Mom here
once. Of course, I didn't tell her anything about the place,
but she was impressed by the flowers nonetheless. A few
days later, her doctors informed her that her treatment
was successful, and that she was back in remission again,
just as quickly as Tyler's asthma had subsided. Diseases
come and go, I guess. Sometimes they take the best of us,
sometimes they take all of us. And other times they visit
just long enough to remind us we're alive.

As for me, I'm just content with the way things are,
and happy for the chance to lie out in the Living Place
now and again, looking up at the fingerprint swirls of
clouds above and the face of the man in the moon. I remember when I was little, I once asked Mom if people on
the moon talk about "the man in the earth," and if so, was
the man in the earth smiling?

I guess I don't have to wonder anymore. All I have to
do is lie out among the wildflowers to know that he is.

RALPHY SHERMAN'S PATTY MELT ON RYE

•••

O f course, you don't have to believe a word of it, but I swear it's all true—even the parts I made up.

It all began in Hawaii. . . .

We were on vacation, Dad, my sister Roxanne, and me, on the Big Island, right in the shadow of Mauna Loa, the most massive mountain in the world and an active volcano that's always blowing its stack.

You have to understand that my dad's gotten to be a pretty lonely guy. Sure, he's a world-class spy, but all that James Bond, ladies'-man stuff isn't true in the real spy world. The fact is, when your business is international espionage, you're pretty much on your own. Roxy and I don't even see him all that much, and when we do, he's usually in disguise.

Anyway, Dad's never had much luck with women— our mom got abducted by aliens ten years ago, and then e-mailed us that she had met a Polarian smuggler who had three heads, each one of which was a better kisser than Dad. Then there was Vermelda, whom Roxy and I didn't really care for, so we weren't too crushed when she got eaten by the Loch Ness Monster. Honey-Lou was nice to us, and it seemed that she and Dad might have a future—until we discovered that she was just a beehive cleverly disguised as a human being. So here we were in Hawaii, Dad on the rebound after being stung by Honey-Lou. That's when we met Patty.

I saw her first. I woke up early one morning and went out onto the terrace of our hotel room. Our hotel, Volcano House, sits right on the rim of the Kilauea volcano crater, so I supposed we would be the first ones to go in case of an eruption. Anyway, I was standing on the terrace when I happened to see a woman down there, walking over the steaming, crusted surface of the crater. I had seen geologists down there the day before, but they all wore silvery heat-protection gear. This woman wore nothing but a bikini top and a grass skirt. I wasn't quite sure, but I think she was also barefoot.

She looked up at me and caught my gaze. Then I heard Dad back in the hotel room, mumbling something in his sleep. Launch codes, or something like that. I turned—it was just for a second, but when I turned back, she was gone. She just vanished in a puff of toxic volcanic gas. Now, I'm no stranger to ghosts—in fact, I have several of them trapped in pickling jars on a shelf back home—so at first I just figured this was just your run-of-the-mill ecto-plasmic manifestation. Turns out I couldn't be further from the truth.

That afternoon, while driving our rental car around Crater Rim Drive, we came upon a woman hitchhiking. Dad always cautioned us on the dangers of picking up hitchhikers, but I guess he was willing to throw caution to the wind when it came to beautiful Hawaiian women in black silk dresses with flowers in their hair. He hit those brakes so hard the anti-lock system engaged.

"Thank you," said the woman as she stepped into the car. She had a voice that was both sultry and gravelly. "It was kind of you to pick me up." I had a feeling right away that she was trouble—but, then, Dad was kind of a magnet for beautiful women who were trouble.

"My pleasure." Dad put the car in gear. "Where are you headed, Miss?"

"My name is Patty, and I'm headed home to Halemaumau, just five miles along the rim of Kilauea." Patty had the kind of stunning face I couldn't look away from, and her long hair was so dark and shiny you could almost see your face reflected in it. She also looked familiar.

"Halemaumau," said Dad. "Too bad."

"Why is that?" asked Patty

"Well, it's such a beautiful day, it's too bad you can't share it with us."

Roxy pinched the space between her eyes, like she was getting a sinus headache. "Oh, brother," she said. "Here we go again."

Dad was turning on the charm—and Dad's charm was an ill wind that never blew anyone any good. I checked my seat belt, figuring Dad's mind was no longer on the road.

Patty smiled. "I would like that," she said. "Maybe I could show you the sights of Kilauea."

Dad beamed. That's when I noticed something. I looked at Roxanne, and from the look on her face, I could tell that she had noticed it, too. There was an aroma about Patty like the faint smell of rotten eggs, as if she had been near one of the *fumaroles*—the toxic sulfuric gas vents that speckled the many craters of the Kilauea Caldera. I guess she tried to mask the stink beneath the pungent perfume of all those flowers she wore in her hair, but it was there all the same. Then I remembered where I had seen her before. She was the woman I had seen walking on the crater beneath our hotel window!

"Uh . . . Dad," I said, my brain already on red alert, "maybe Patty has better things to do than spend the day with us. Like maybe walk on some hot coals."

Dad threw me a fusion gaze in the rearview mirror. "You'll have to pardon my son," snapped Dad. "He's turned rudeness into an art form."

"Hey," grumbled Roxanne, insulted. "I have, too—how come he gets all the credit?"

Patty laughed, and leaned in closer to my father. "I'll fire-walk some other time," she said. "But right now there's nothing in the world I would rather do than show you my island."

She spent the whole day with us, clinging to my father's arm like a fast-growing vine, and when night fell, Roxy and I were predictably on our own.

"Patty and I are going to take in the Hawaiian nightlife," he told us as he left us at the hotel. "Here's a credit card. Don't wait up for me."

I sighed as they drove away. "It sounds like we just heard the mating call of the North American Loon."

That night Roxy and I went to a luau by ourselves. Dancers dressed in little more than long grass and seashells did fire dances to the powerful beat of drums. A huge pig roasted in banana leaves.

"It looks like Marvin McShultz," Roxy said.

Indeed, the pig did bear a striking resemblance to Marvin, a kid we knew back home. And, so, when they began to serve him up with a side of pineapple wedges, Roxy and I just couldn't bring ourselves to eat it. Instead, we settled for a bowl of poi, which was apparently the sound you made after you put some in your mouth. It tasted like

Elmer's glue mixed with potting soil. In any case, it adhered nicely to our intestinal walls, and we slept well.

When we woke up in the morning, Dad had still not returned.

"Do you think he got called off on a secret espionage assignment?" Roxy asked.

"Nah," I told her. "Whenever he vanishes in the middle of the night, there's usually a coded note and a new nanny on the doorstep."

By noon, we had maxed out Dad's credit card at the gift shops up and down the street, and still he was nowhere to be found. We really began to worry.

"Maybe we should try to find him," I suggested, as we stood on a corner waiting for a light to change. "Where was that place Patty said she lived? Holy moo-moo, or something like that?"

"Halemaumau," said a voice behind us. We turned to see a withered old Hawaiian man. He stood in a booth on the street, selling beautiful statuettes carved from volcanic rock. "It's the Halemaumau crater you speak of. You must be looking for Pele!"

"No. Patty," I corrected. "Her name is Patty."

The old man nodded. The sun painted deep creases in his worn face. At first I thought he was squinting from the sun, but then I realized he had only one eye—the other was just an empty dark socket, as if it had been seared away by a glob of hot lava.

"She has as many names as she has faces," the street vendor told us, "but Pele is her one true name. Madame Pele, the fire-goddess. The breath of the volcano."

Roxy and I turned to each other. "Either he's totally *loco*," Roxy said, "or we're in deep magma."

I turned back to the one-eyed street vendor and listened.

"Flooded at every turn by her sea-goddess sister," continued the vendor, "tormented by Kama Pu'a, the pig god, Pele is easy to anger and slow to forgive. I once looked at her the wrong way, and she spit in my eye."

"Great," said Roxy. "Why does Dad always fall for women with so much personal baggage?"

Well, I had to admit, Dad sure knew how to pick 'em— and, as usual, it was up to us to pluck him from harm's way.

"Could you direct us to Halemaumau?" I asked.

He pointed west. "An hour's journey, toward the setting sun," he said. "Follow the trail, and the screams of birds." Then he reached behind his little booth. "The path is overgrown. You'll need this." He produced a shining machete with a bone handle. I don't know what a street vendor would be doing with a machete, but hey, what the man does on his free time is his own business. We graciously took the machete, and headed out toward the Halemaumau crater.

The hour walk turned into two, and then three, following the chilling screams of native birds and the growing smell of sulfur. We slashed our way through vines and ferns, and finally we came out of the lush forest and over a ridge to see the devastation of Halemaumau crater.

The change was sudden and shocking. There was no plant life, no birds. Halemaumau crater was a place of death. The rock was twisted and braided like black rope, and the center of the crater was a barren badlands filled with steaming sulfur *fumaroles* that smelled so bad, you had to hold your nose.

"Yuck," said Roxy. "Who let one loose?"

In the very center of the rugged rock that plugged the crater sat our father, locked in a little bamboo cage.

"Dad!" we called.

"Ralphy! Roxy!" he called back. "Get out of here, it's too dangerous. Run—save yourselves!"

Of course he always said that when trapped in life-threatening situations—but the one time we did run and save ourselves, he grounded us for two months once he got out of traction. So now we know that "run—save yourselves" really means "get your butts over here or suffer the consequences."

As we approached the bamboo cage, we felt the ground beneath us begin to shift, and cracks appeared in the hardened lava rock. Then, ten yards away, a fissure opened up, and through it we could see a lake of lava bubbling just a few feet beneath the surface of the rock, reminding us that this was still a very active volcano.

Then a tongue of lava licked up from the fissure and took the shape of a beautiful woman. The lava cooled, resolving itself into flesh. It was Patty—but the heat of the fire was still in her eyes.

"You come to Halemaumau uninvited," said the volcano goddess. "Leave now, and I will forget your infraction."

"Not without our Dad," I told her.

She laughed. "Your father now belongs to me. Today I, Pele, take a husband. Soon we will descend together into the flaming heart of the earth."

Roxy looked at Dad and shook her head. "You and your hot dates."

He gave us an apologetic shrug.

"Leave," she ordered us, "before I singe off your eyebrows."

That's when I pulled out the machete that I was hiding behind my back. Pele gasped and stepped back when she saw it. "No!" she said, terrified. "Not the Bone Blade of Pu'u Loa! No! Keep it away from me!"

Realizing that I suddenly had the upper hand, and that this machete was like a Hawaiian Excalibur, I took a step closer and spun the machete like a ninja, nearly cutting off my arm in the process.

"Release my father," I demanded, "or face the Bone Blade of Pu'u Loa."

"You are too weak to wield the Bone Blade!" she yelled, but I could tell she wasn't so sure, because she took a step back and hesitated.

That moment of hesitation was all I needed. I turned, hacked apart the cage with the machete, and dear old Dad fell out, onto the hot ground.

Pele tried to advance on us, but I held the machete in both hands. "Come any closer," I warned her, "and I'll run the Bone Blade of Pu'u Loa through your flaming heart."

"You don't have the guts." said Pele.

I have to admit, she was right about that, because Roxy, Dad, and I turned and bailed as fast as we could . . . but we didn't get far before the ground beneath us began to break up, leaving islands of rock rapidly melting in a seething lake of magma.

We jumped from one rock to another, knowing that a single misplaced foot would leave us more well-done than Marvin the luau pig.

At last we reached the edge of the crater, as the lake behind us began to bubble higher and higher with the fury of Pele's anger.

"You will suffer for your impudence!" she shrieked.

"I guess we really dissed her," I said.

"Just keep moving," said Dad.

We reached the rim and leapt from the desolation into the fern forest. Then, an instant later the ground shook, the air seemed to explode, and fountains of lava exploded from Halemaumau crater. It was a full-fledged eruption! The forest fell beneath a fast-moving river of molten rock, its leading edge burning on our heels.

"Vacation over," Dad said.

I dropped the machete, because it was slowing me down, and together we tried to outrace the lava. The heat was unbearable, singeing my eyebrows, and seriously defeating Dad's antiperspirant. We charged through a lava tube, a solid rock tunnel made by an earlier eruption, and were backlit by the caustic orange glow of magma that shot through the tunnel behind us like pop through a straw. We came out at the far end, into the fern forest again, and beside us was a solid wall of dark, volcanic rock full of holes and crags for hands and feet to grab.

"Okay, guys," said Dad, "here's where all your rock climbing experience pays off." Climbing on the indoor rock climbing wall in our rec room wasn't exactly scaling the face of Kilauea. But potential death was an excellent motivator. We scaled that sheer mountain wall just as the magma incinerated the ferns behind us, melting the rubber trim of my sneakers.

"Don't put your hands too deeply into the holes in the rock," Dad warned as we climbed. "There could be snakes and tarantulas."

"Gee, thanks, Dad," Roxy said, disgusted. "As if I need to hear that right now."

Once we reached the ridge and were out of the lava's path, we made our way back to the road and hitched a ride directly to the airport without even picking up our things at the hotel. We took the next flight out, with nothing more than the singed clothes on our back.

As our plane picked up altitude, shaking from the violent turbulence of the eruption, we watched from our window as a dozen glowing lava rivers spilled into the sea, sending up a cloud of angry steam that would blanket the entire island for days.

Back home, Roxy and I were content to just lie around, happy to be safe from the volcanic ordeal. We even in-

vited Marvin McSchultz over and pretended to roast him
on a spit.

Each day we watched the news. Reports from Hawaii
told of lava flows that leveled whole villages before siz-
zling into the sea. Kilauea was popping like a geologic zit
that wouldn't quit, expanding the size of the island by a
million cubic yards a day. But by far the most dramatic
display of Earth's power was the blast in the Halemaumau crater: a single discharge that shook the ground and
blew out windows as far away as Honolulu. They de-
scribed it as a pyroclastic belch of gas that dislodged a
chunk of molten lava, sending it skyward on a ballistic arc
across the Pacific. In layman's terms, mighty Mauna Loa
had coughed up a wad of magma and was spitting it in
our direction. It didn't take a vulcanologist to figure out
what happened, or where that burning bolide was headed.
Halemaumau was Pele's home . . . and it looked like she
had decided to relocate.

We watched from our backyard that afternoon as the
bright orange ball zeroed in on us and dropped from the
sky. The lava-loogie left a trail of smoke in the air like a
crashing DC-10 and came straight down on our tool shed
at the far end of the yard. The shed detonated with the im-
pact, sending wood and tools splintering in all directions.

When the smoke cleared, there she stood—Patty, a.k.a.
the goddess Pele, spurned and burning with red-hot
anger. Apparently it wasn't a good idea to dump a goddess of fire after the first date. Although she was in human
form now, her eyes still glowed with the heat of the
magma that flamed within her.

"How dare you mock the Volcano Goddess?" she bellowed. "You and your father shall feel the breath of my
wrath!"

I turned to Roxy. "Them's fightin' words," I said.

"How are we supposed to fight that?"

"I'm still working on it."

As for Dad, he had been whisked away by a dark sedan at dawn to be briefed on one international crisis or another, so Roxy and I were pretty much on our own for this one.

The goddess strode toward us across the wispy winter rye grass, setting the rye aflame and burning it to ash by the mere trample of her footfalls.

"You're wasting your time," I told her. "Our father's not here."

"Then I'll have to settle for both of you." She picked up her pace.

"We're toast," said Roxy. "Literally."

"Not yet," I told her. "I've got an idea."

By now the whole field of rye was aflame. Behind us was nothing but our pool, our house, and the lawnmower. It was one of those big sit-down mowers, more like a tractor than a grass cutter. I leaped on it, started it, and began to mow my way across the flame toward the Hawaiian goddess of fire.

"What insolence to pursue me with your infernal contraption!" she bellowed.

"Ah, stuff a sock in it," I told her—which I know is kind of a rude thing to say to someone, especially to a divinity—but you see, I was trying to get her so mad she wouldn't think straight.

It worked. She leapt right onto the grille of that mower, reaching for me with her killing hands. "I will boil the marrow in your bones, Ralphy Sherman."

"Sounds like fun," I said, then spun the mower around and headed for the pool. She didn't see where we were going—she was too intent on boiling my marrow.

The mower crashed through the chain-link fence that

surrounded our pool. With flames licking up all around
me and the soles of my sneakers melting, I jumped from
the mower, landing on the concrete deck.

Goddess and mower plunged into the pool, and
Madame Pele sunk as if she was made of stone—which
she was. In less than five seconds, the entire pool began to
boil furiously.

"We don't have much time," I called to Roxanne. "The
water will boil away in a few minutes, and she'll be able
to get out. We have to stop her once and for all."

"What do you have in mind?"

"I think a phone call to Kryo-Rama® might do the
trick."

Roxy smiled, quickly figuring out what I was thinking.

Kryo-Rama® was just down the street. It was a place
where they cut off people's heads and froze them in liquid
nitrogen for all eternity, or at least until some future genius
could figure out what you could do with a frozen head. It
was a favorite town establishment, because everyone
knew that Kryo-Rama® was the best place to go during a
heat wave—and, in the name of community relations, they
had a nice big lobby where they let the neighborhood keep
cool on those really hot days. Anyway, business had gotten
tough lately. Their two-for-one Christmas sale hadn't gone
over very well, which meant they had a surplus of liquid
nitrogen lying around just waiting for someone to make an
offer on it. Which we did.

With our pool boiled halfway down, we quickly
drained our fish tank. We're talkin' one big aquarium. It's
a huge cylindrical tank—the centerpiece of our living
room, eight feet high and three feet in diameter. Filled
with a thousand gallons, it stood in our living room, floor-
to-ceiling, like a massive glass of water. We used to keep
it full of piranhas until they devoured one of our nannies.

Now it held less carnivorous sea life. With the fish re-
moved, we now filled the tank with liquid nitrogen, and
set our trap.

We heard the sizzle as the last of the water boiled from
the bottom of our pool. In a few moments there was a
pounding on our door, and the door burst into flames.
Through the flaming doorway stepped Pele, fit to be tied,
her eyes almost white-hot with rage. Every step she took
singed the carpet, like a hot iron scorching a shirt.

"You're going to burn for this, Ralphy Sherman," she
promised. It wasn't the first time I'd heard that threat, but
this time I knew it was more than an idle boast.

"Gotta catch me first," I said, and raced up the stairs.
She continued the chase, setting the steps aflame.

Upstairs, I turned right and darted into the guest room.
Roxanne had put a tiny little masking-tape X on the floor.
I crossed over it and stood about two feet away from the
spot.

That's when she entered the room. Now her figure was
dripping with hot lava. Licks of flame curled her hair, and
her eyes were like a solar eclipse: pitch black in the center, surrounded by a corona of flame.

"Pity we don't have any marshmallows," said Roxanne.

Pele slowly strode forward. "Your pain will be exqui-
site in my blistering embrace."

"Yeah, yeah, whatever."

She took one more step—right onto the 'X' marking
the floor.

"Wait!" I shouted, stalling. "You're forgetting about
the Bone Blade of Pu'u Loa."

She stood on the X, the wooden floor beneath her turning black. "The Bone Blade was consumed in flames."

"Well, we have another," blurted Roxanne, eying the
burning floor beneath Pele.

"Yeah," I said. "We bought it off the Internet at BoneBlades.com."

"Didn't even have to pay sales tax," added Roxanne.

Pele was not amused. "The more you mock, the greater your suffering will be."

I smiled. "I don't think so." Just then, the wooden floor burned through, just as Roxy and I had planned. "Bye-bye, Pele," I told her. "Time to chill."

"No!" She screamed, and plummeted through the floor, leaving a rim of fire around the scorched hole in the wood. Next came a splash and the sputtering hiss of nitrogen steam. We raced downstairs.

The spot where Pele had stood had been directly over the tank filled with liquid nitrogen. Now, through the glass of the cylindrical tank, I saw a furious Pele, still red-hot and molten, thrashing about, trying to free herself of the super-frigid liquid, but it was no use.

"Now, Roxy, now!" I shouted. Roxy stood on a ladder on the other side of the tank, and with all her strength she pulled on a rope, which was attached to a pulley, that was tied to a manhole cover we had taken from the street. The manhole came down on top of the tank with a heavy clang, sealing it shut.

Roxy came down from the ladder and the two of us stood, admiring our handiwork. Inside the tank, Pele wriggled and squirmed, but the frosty liquid dampened her strength—she couldn't even keep herself in human form anymore, and just became an angry, amorphous globule of magma. There was no way she'd be able to lift up that manhole cover before we had it permanently welded shut!

"Dad'll be proud of us," Roxy said, "although we're going to have to find a new place for our fish."

The room glowed red with the heat of Pele's spirit, and it has stayed that way to this very day. Even trapped in a tank of ice-cold liquid nitrogen, her anger still keeps her molten hot; but the most she can do is bubble and stew, just a shapeless blob, unable to take human form—which is perfectly all right with Roxy and me. We always wanted a lava lamp.

OPEN HOUSE

•••

Barbara sits at her kitchen table staring at her cup of lukewarm tea. The windows tell of a gray day, and the gloom pours in, blanketing the room like a ground fog. The oven is always cold, for nothing ever cooks there, and although the TV sits against a living room wall, it never brings in a picture.

Barbara slowly sips her tea, its color gray-brown, its taste bland and bitter. She does not wish to know the nature of the brew—some things are better left unknown. She looks at the unmoving hands of her wristwatch. He's been gone almost a day now, and she's beginning to worry when he'll be back. But that decision is not hers to make; nor is it Kenneth's.

She hears footsteps and then, all at once, the north wall of the kitchen—indeed, the north wall of the entire house—slowly swings open . . .

. . . to an unthinkable expanse of a bedroom, with a ceiling that touches the sky and a far wall that seems a mile distant. There, staring her in the face, is the monster-child.

"Good morning," she says, "did you have sweet dreams?" She speaks with a pronounced lisp, and the word comes out "Thweet." The monster-child is all of five years old, with brown hair in pigtails and bundles of energy in her massive muscles.

"What have you done with Kenneth?" Barbara asks, backing away from her rickety kitchen table.

The huge child then bounces on her bed, which is the size of a stadium. The heavy quilt that covers it is fringed in a hundred tassels the size of horse's tails. "I have him right here," she says. She pulls him out of a pocket in her pink overalls. Barbara can see the grimace of pain on his face and knows there's something different about him even before she realizes what it is.

"Kenneth, oh no!"

"The dog got him," says the girl. She jumps off her bed, carries Kenneth through the air, and sits him down on the chair opposite Barbara as if she still has to do it for him—as if he couldn't sit in the chair by himself.

"He has a boo-boo, but I made it all better with a Band-Aid." The beige fabric bandage is glued across Kenneth's chest like a wide sash.

"Does it hurt?" Barbara asks.

Kenneth offers her a slight smile that doesn't compare to the bright-toothed smile he's always had. "I try not to think about it," he says. Barbara clasps his hand across the table to comfort him. "You look nice," says Kenneth, but then she always does.

The giant girl goes over to her desk and opens a tray that holds little cakes of watercolor paint. They watch as she busily dips a wet paintbrush into the paint, then into the water, then into the paint, over and over again until the water takes on a cloudy, muddy tone. Then she brings the little plastic cup of water over and spills a drop of it into the small teacup sitting in front of Kenneth.

"I made you some more magic tea," she says. "Drink up, it's good for you."

Kenneth forces a "thank you" and sips the paint-water. Barbara can barely stomach it, but she tries not to let the girl know.

"How's yours?" she asks Barbara.

"It's fine," she says, "just the way I like it." She fears saying anything else to the monster-child, who could snap their necks with a twist of her thumb.

"Let's go out to the swimming pool!" The girl's voice booms with high-pitched enthusiasm. "Let's play water games!"

Barbara and Kenneth shudder in unison at the very thought.

"No thanks," says Kenneth, trying to sound as pleasant as possible. "I think we'll stay home today."

The monster-child frowns—and they both know that can't be a good thing.

"I liked you both better," she says, "before my magic tea brought you to life." Then she slams the wall of their home so hard that the plastic bed bounces down the stairs.

"We've got to get out of here," Kenneth whispers.

It's night now. A pocked, mournful moon shines in from the little girl's window. The monster-child sleeps, her breath rising and falling in a rhythmic gale. Kenneth paces while Barbara brushes her hair with long, drawn-out strokes in front of a vanity with fake light bulbs.

"It was better before," she says, thinking back to the days before the magic brew, when their thoughts had no more substance than the air between their plastic ears and their polyurethane limbs would not move unless the monster-child chose to move them. "Yes," repeats Barbara, "it was much better before we became aware."

Kenneth comes up behind her gently touching her long blonde hair. "Never say that," he says. "Don't even think it. We'll get through this."

But Kenneth's words have no comfort for her, and for the first time in her life, Barbara cries, shedding little cellophane tears that drift to the floor. "How much longer do we have to go on having tea parties and dressing up in day-glo clothes?"

Kenneth takes a deep breath. "It ends here," he says finally, decisively.

Barbara stands up, looking deep into his opaque blue eyes, "You're not going out there," she says. "You can't go—it's not safe out there!"

Kenneth leans against the wall and the face of the house pushes open, leaving a space wide enough for him to slip out.

"Be careful," whispers Barbara, and he disappears.

He is gone for three days. Three days alone with the wrath of the monster-child. Barbara hides beneath the little plastic bed, she hides beneath the kitchen table, she even hides in the small trunk in the attic space, but still the child finds her.

"You've been bad," the monster-child tells her, "both of you. If you don't tell me where Ken has gone, I'll have to punish you."

"I don't know where he's gone," Barbara tells her truthfully. The child scowls at her, narrowing her massive blue eyes. Barbara can see into those dark pupils, and sees nothing there. She wonders who is more empty inside: herself, or the girl. Barbara knows there is little more than air within the shell of her own plastic body, but what of the girl? Do flesh and blood necessarily mean the monster-child has a soul?

The girl's mother comes in now and again, a woman who stands so tall Barbara can't even get a good look at her face. The pleats of her skirt are like the ridges of a mountain, and her voice echoes from an unimaginable altitude, ordering the girl to clean her room or calling her down to dinner. Now, every time the mother comes in, the girl launches into a crying fit. "Ken ran away!" she cries. "You have to buy me a new one! You have to buy it now! Now! Now!" She kicks and screams—her pounding feet making all the furniture in Barbara's bright little house shake.

"He'll turn up," the mother says. "He always does."

And when the mother leaves, the girl is always angrier than before. This time she pulls open the wall of the little playhouse and drags Barbara out. "We'll have to force a confession out of you," she says with malevolent cheer, "just like I've seen on TV."

She then ties Barbara to the bedpost with some kite string, leaving her there for five agonizing minutes, before returning with leftovers from yesterday's dinner. The girl reaches onto her plate, grabs a hamburger patty, and rubs the greasy hamburger meat on Barbara. Then she opens the door.

"Mr. Cuddles!" she calls. "Where are you, Mr. Cuddles?"

"No!" cries Barbara. "Please! Please not that!" But it is too late. Barbara hears the jangling of dog tags, and then the beast enters the room—a black-nosed, curly-haired monstrosity. A malicious poodle named Mr. Cuddles.

Barbara screams as a tongue, foul-smelling and rough, rolls toward her like a tidal wave and envelops her. Fangs the size of stalactites gnaw at her, but she endures it, thinking only of the day when her slavery will end.

* * *

"There are places you would not believe," Kenneth tells her.

It is midnight. The girl sleeps, and the world is at blessed peace—but it will only last until morning. "There are great oval lakes with white walls, and bright plastic boats. There are building-block cities and fast wooden trains. There are cars that speed on a slim orange track. I have seen all these things!"

"I want to see them, too!" says Barbara. "I can't stay here a moment longer!"

"Tomorrow," he tells her. "We'll wait until tomorrow. I have a plan."

"I don't know if I can wait," she tells him, then she shows him the jagged gnaw marks, a living memory of the fanged poodle-beast, etched into her arm.

Kenneth grimaces. "We could sand that down," he tells her.

She smiles. "You say the nicest things."

They endure the monster-child for one more day, all the while working on their plan.

"We're so sorry we were bad," they tell the girl, as they drink their bitter watercolor tea. "We love you. We want to be with you always."

The girl grabs them and gives them sticky bubble-gum kisses. "You be good," she tells them, "and I'll never have to punish you again."

Then as evening approaches, they set their plan in action.

"We want to watch TV," Barbara tells the girl. So she lifts them up, and sits them in front of their little plastic television.

"No," says Kenneth, "*Real* TV. Downstairs."

"Yes, we want to watch with you!" Barbara adds.

"Oh, you sillies!" says the girl. "If I bring you downstairs to watch TV, Mr. Cuddles will be after you."

"We don't mind," says Barbara, trying not to sound horrified at the thought. "We like Mr. Cuddles."

The girl smiles, believing their every word, and after dinner, she takes the two of them downstairs, and sits them on her lap.

As the evening goes on, the girl's eyes begin to droop. Barbara feels the child's death grip on her begin to loosen.

"Now!" whispers Kenneth, and together they dive off her lap, scuttling across the plush fabric of the sofa, until finding the place where the cushion ends. Then they force themselves between the cushions into soft dusty, darkness. There, among popcorn fragments, coins, and gum wrappers, they listen to the muffled voices above.

"But I brought them down!" the monster-child complains to her father. "They were right here with me!"

"It's bedtime, honey," the father says. "We'll look for them tomorrow."

"I won't go upstairs without my dolls!" But her voice is weak and weighty with sleep. She doesn't have the strength to fight, and in the end, she gives up. Barbara peeks out to see the father carrying her up the stairs.

"Now?" asks Barbara.

"Not yet."

They wait until the mother puts Mr. Cuddles on a leash, and takes the beast out the back door.

"Now!"

The moment the dog is gone, they burst out from beneath the sofa cushions, racing along the hardwood floor. "This way!" says Kenneth. "Follow me! I've been there! I'm sure I can find my way back."

The wood gives way to the bright, flowery linoleum of the kitchen, and before them is a door, open just a crack.

It takes all of their strength to push that door wide enough for them to squeeze through. Ahead of them now is a flight of steep gray wooden stairs, disappearing into darkness.

"Down there?"

"Yes! Trust me!"

Together they leap from one stair to another until finally they reach the dusty cement floor of the basement. Up above they hear the telltale jangling of Mr. Cuddles's dog tags, and although he barks and scratches at the door, the mother pushes the door closed so the dog can't get down. They are safe at last.

But the space around them is anything but inviting. The basement is filled with sorrowful clutter. Disintegrating boxes, rusting paint cans, and the upturned bodies of a thousand dead insects stretch across an expanse of web-hung darkness.

"Oh, Kenneth," Barbara bites nervously on her knuckle. "Is this freedom? Is this bleak, awful place all there is? I thought you said there were wonders!"

He smiles at her. "Let me show you something." Then he leads her across the musty floor to a big black cavern: a heavy iron thing with a heavy iron grate. The bars of the grate are just wide enough for them to squeeze through.

What Barbara sees inside the gated cavern almost brings color to her peach-tinted face. Kenneth was right. "Oh! How wonderful!"

There in the center of the black, rugged earth of the cavern is a cabin! A beautiful log cabin, built of interlocking logs, with a green slat roof. Their dream house.

"I built it for you!" Kenneth tells her. "I knew you'd like it."

And although the walls of the cabin are bare, and void of furniture, they know they will be happy here, far away, hidden from the monster-child dwelling above.

For, surely, the child would not think to look for them in the basement, and even if she did, she would never find their little home in the huge iron cavern.

. It is as they sit there, inside their dream house, that a question occurs to Barbara.

"Kenneth," she asks, thinking of the small sign that was on the entrance to the iron cavern. "What does 'furnace' mean?"

Kenneth just shakes his head. "I don't know," he answers. "But there wasn't one in the plastic playhouse, so it must not be important."

He puts his arm around her, and she snuggles close to him. Barbara is confident that they will be safe here . . . and that even when the winds of winter blow in the world outside, their little dream house will stay very, very warm.

MAIL MERGE

....

<*****W**elcome. You are in "Hyperwarp" chat room***>

Barbarella:	So, like, what if there were an infinite number of parallel universes?
Wyrmhole:	**Yeah, but how could you get from one to another?**
Morlock:	*If you could get to another universe they wouldn't be parallel anymore.*
<u>StarWart:</u>	<u>How do you parallel park in a parallel universe?</u>
Barbarella:	If you could move faster than the speed of light, you could punch a hole in this universe.
Morlock:	*Very carefully.*
<u>StarWart:</u>	<u>:)</u>
Spacecadet:	My dad once got hit by a guy trying to parallel park.

Wyrmhole:	**Was he from a parallel universe?**
Spacecadet:	No, I think he was from the moron dimension.
Morlock:	*But you can't move faster than the speed of light.*
MCsquared:	Yeah—time dilation. Einstein predicted that.
StarWart:	I think half of my school is from the moron dimension.
Spacecadet:	What's time dilation?
StarWart:	It's what happens when your teacher is boring. A single period drags on for days.
Spacecadet:	I had my eyes dilated once. Things were blurry for an hour.
Barbarella:	It means that time slows down the closer you get to the speed of light.
MCsquared:	At the speed of light time stops.
Wyrmhole:	**And you become heavier.**

<***BBGIRL has entered the room***>

Spacecadet:	So if you go real slow, you lose weight?
BBGIRL:	HELLO. WHO'S IN HERE?
Barbarella:	Mass, not weight.
Spacecadet:	I went to Midnight Mass last Christmas.
Wyrmhole:	**Hi, BBGIRL.**
StarWart:	So how do you reach a parallel universe?
Spacecadet:	My friends said the Pope would show up, but he didn't.
Barbarella:	You don't.
Morlock:	*Hi, BB.*
BBGIRL:	WHO ARE YOU PEOPLE?
Wyrmhole:	**Maybe time travel can send you to alternate dimensions.**

Morlock:	*Maybe there's a different dimension for every moment in time.*
MCsquared:	Huh?
BBGIRL:	WHAT IS EVERYONE TALKING ABOUT?
StarWart:	Stop shouting, BBGIRL.
Morlock:	*Think about it. You go back in time, but you're really not going back in time, you're jumping to a parallel dimension where everything's exactly the same as this universe, just ten years back.*
BBGIRL:	IS THIS THE BEENY BABY CHAT ROOM?
MCsquared:	Why ten years?
Spacecadet:	I was only three ten years ago.
BBGIRL:	I GOT SOME NEET BEENY BABIES TO TRADE.
Morlock:	*It doesn't have to be ten years.*
BBGIRL:	I GOT PINKY PYTHON—SHE'S REALLY RARE.
Barbarella:	If you go back before you were born, you could become your own father.
Morlock:	*I'd rather die.*
Spacecadet:	I still don't understand.
BBGIRL:	I GOT OSWALD THE OCTOPUS—AN IR-REGULAR WITH 9 LEGS INSTEAD OF EIGHT.
Barbarella:	Take a hike, BBGIRL, you're in the wrong room.
Wyrmhole:	**I understand your parallel temporal dimension theory, Morlock. In fact, I have a similar theory myself.**
Morlock:	*I'm glad someone understands.*
Wyrmhole:	**There's a different universe for every single quantum of time, right?**
Morlock:	*Yeah, that's what I'm saying.*

Wyrmhole:	**What about infinite universes that are identical, except for one small difference?**
Morlock:	*I was just about to say that!*
Barbarella:	They say time and space are interchangeable.
StarWart:	<u>My mom says I'm good at taking up time and space.</u>
BBGIRL:	WHAT BEENY BABIES DO YOU HAVE?
Barbarella:	Will somebody punt her off line?
MCsquared:	Einstein predicted parallel universes.
StarWart:	<u>No he didn't.</u>
MCsquared:	Yes he did. It was in my report.

<***BBGIRL has left the room***>

Barbarella:	Good riddance.
StarWart:	<u>Isn't Quantum an airline?</u>
Morlock:	*I think that's Quantas.*
Spacecadet:	I flew Quantas once. I had the chicken lasagna.
MCsquared:	Einstein died in a plane crash.
StarWart:	<u>No he didn't!</u>
Barbarella:	And then there are black holes . . .
MCsquared:	Well, he could have, in a parallel universe.
StarWart:	<u>My parents say my bedroom is a black hole.</u>
Spacecadet:	I took a bus tour through a black hole once. It wasn't that bad.
Wyrmhole:	**You can't go in a black hole, bozo—you would be crushed to subatomic particles.**
Morlock:	*You can't go into a black hole, dweeb—you would be crushed to subatomic particles.*

Wyrmhole: **Hey, we both said the same thing! How did you know I was going to say that?**

Morlock: *I'm spychic.*

StarWart: Black holes are in space, spacecadet.

Spacecadet: Can you see them with a telescope?

Morlock: *I mean psychic.*

StarWart: If you could, they wouldn't be black.

MCsquared: Stephen Hawking predicted black holes.

Barbarella: I like spy chic better.

StarWart: :)

Morlock: *Stephen Hawking is cool.*

Wyrmhole: **Stephen Hawking is cool.**

Morlock: *There we go again. Spy chic!*

Wyrmhole: **Spy chic!**

StarWart: My Mom was a Spy Chick.

Morlock: *Hawking's amazing—the greatest mind in the world, in a ruined body.*

Spacecadet: What about green holes and blue holes?

Barbarella: I think maybe Morlock and Wyrmhole are the same person.

Wyrmhole: **As opposed to me, the greatest body in the world, with a ruined mind.**

MCsquared: No, they only come in one color—black.

Barbarella: Hey—maybe you two are the same person in parallel universes!

Morlock: *Not very likely.*

Wyrmhole: **Not very likely.**

Morlock: *There it goes again.*

Wyrmhole: **There it goes again.**

Spacecadet"   Didn't Stephen Hawking write "The Shining"?

StarWart: No, gel brain, that was Stephen King.

Barbarella: What do you think happens when two parallel universes collide?

StarWart:	<u>Traffic jam on the interstellar highway.</u>
MCsquared:	Big explosion.
Morlock:	*The end of life as we know it.*
Barbarella:	Maybe not. Maybe one just absorbs the other.
Wyrmhole:	**You mean kind of like two raindrops that get too close?**
Morlock:	*Kind of like raindrops that get too close.*
Barbarella:	Wow—you guys really are kindred spirits.
StarWart:	<u>My Mom says I'm in my own universe.</u>
Spacecadet:	I went to Universal Studios once. I got wet on Jurassic Park.
Wyrmhole:	**Hey, Morlock—are you really psychic, or are you just repeating me?**
Morlock:	*Neither—I'm typing the same things you are, at the same time.*
MCsquared:	Stephen Hawking is my uncle.
StarWart:	<u>No he's not.</u>
MCsquared:	How do you know?
StarWart:	<u>Because he's from England, and you're not.</u>
Barbarella:	What if you guys really are parallel beings?
Morlock:	*We couldn't be, we'd have to have more in common.*
Wyrmhole:	**Naah, we'd have to have more things in common.**
MCsquared:	Maybe I am from England.
StarWart:	<u>Then why did you write "color" instead of "colour," like the British do?</u>
Morlock:	*Hey, Wyrmhole—what's your mother's name?*
Wyrmhole:	**Angela.**
MCsquared:	Well, he's my friend's uncle.
Morlock:	*That's my mother's name, too!*

Wyrmhole:	**You're lying!**
Morlock:	*Am not!*
MCsquared:	Am not!
Wyrmhole:	**Oh, now MCsquared is repeating us, too.**
MCsquared:	Am not!
<u>StarWart:</u>	<u>Guys, this is a sinking ship, and I'm bailing.</u>
Barbarella:	Bye, StarWart.

<***StarWart has left the room***>

Wyrmhole:	**You have a sister, Morlock?**
Morlock:	*Yeah—her name's Wynona.*
Spacecadet:	I saw Wynona in concert once.
Wyrmhole:	**No way—that's my sister's name, too!**
Barbarella:	You guys are making this up, aren't you?
MCsquared:	You're all a bunch of liars! And Stephen Hawking is my friend's uncle. So was Einstein.
Wyrmhole:	**No, we're telling the truth.**
Morlock:	*No, it's all true!*

<***MCsquared has left the room***>

Barbarella:	Two colliding universes . . . do you think they would just merge?
Morlock:	*I hope so, better than blowing up.*
Wyrmhole:	**I hope so, it's better than blowing up.**
Barbarella:	You guys are really starting to freak me out.
Wyrmhole:	**Maybe great minds just think alike.**
Morlock:	*Hey, great minds think alike.*
Spacecadet:	This is all too confusing, and I've got homework to do. Bye.

Morlock:	*See ya.*
Wyrmhole:	**See ya.**

<***Spacecadet has left the room***>

Barbarella:	So what's going on here?
Wyrmhole:	**Beats me.**
Morlock:	*Beats me.*
Barbarella:	Are you guys friends, just sitting next to each other, laughing at the rest of us?
Wyrmhole:	**No, I'm in Idaho—I don't know where he's from.**
Morlock:	*No, I'm from Odahi—I don't know where he's from.*
Wyrmhole:	**Odahi?**
Morlock:	*Idaho?*
Barbarella:	Parallel universes, with just a few small differences. Cool.
Wyrmhole:	**There's no such place as Odahi**
Morlock:	*There's no such place as Idaho.*
Barbarella:	I'm gonna call some friends and tell them about this. Talk to you later!
Wyrmhole:	**No don't go!**
Morlock:	*Don't leave us like this.*
Wyrmhole:	**It's too scary.**
Morlock:	*It's too scary.*

<***Barbarella has left the room***>

Wyrmhole:	**Now what are we going to do?**
Morlock:	*Now what are we going to do?*
Wyrmhole:	**Stop that!**
Morlock:	*Stop that!*
Wyrmhole:	**No you stop it!**
Morlock:	*No you stop it!*

Wyrmhole: **I feel kind of weird . . . do you feel weird?**

Morlock: *I feel kind of weird . . . do you feel weird.*

Wyrmhole: **Like the air is changing**

Morlock: *Like the air is changing*

Wyrmhole: **And I'm seeing double.**

Morlock: *And I'm seeing double.*

Wyrmlock: **Wait. Wait. I feel better now.**

Wyrmlock: **Hello?**

Wyrmlock: **Hey, is anyone else in the room?**

Wyrmlock: **Anybody?**

Wyrmlock: **Darn. I hate it when everybody leaves a chat room.**

<***Wyrmlock has left the room***>

THE PETER PAN SOLUTION

. . . .

From behind the blinds, John could see them playing in the yard, their identical blond heads in constant motion as the football spiraled back and forth between them. From this distance it was difficult for John to tell them apart.

The football hit the ground and Daniel (John decided it was Daniel) tripped, hitting the hard earth. His brother, Steven, laughed loud enough for John to hear behind the closed window. The laugh was malicious. Almost evil. John tried to shake it out of his mind, but it left an imprint. He could remember the days of his own youth, when people actually laughed at the folly and pain of others. Slapstick, it was called.

But things had changed, and laughing at slapstick, well, it wasn't a sign of abnormality in and of itself . . . but the tone of the boy's laugh was unsettling. It reminded John that the twins were reaching that age of independence, the age where John had no idea what was going through those adolescent minds as they laughed.

Momentarily, Daniel stood, rubbing his bruised shoulder and cursing at Steven at the top of his lungs. John winced, for he knew how their voices carried out of the privacy of the yard to other homes in the neighborhood. It wouldn't take long for word to trickle down the thorn-laden grapevine, and soon the whole neighborhood would accuse John and Anne of being unable to control their sons. Where in God's name did the twins learn those foul words anyway? They weren't spoken in conversation, or even in films anymore. Of course, the parents would be blamed.

Well, what was he supposed to do? "Overcorrection" and all those other nice little behavioral intervention strategies failed miserably with the twins. Now that they were thirteen, not even Acute Anticognition Therapy would disrupt the pattern—and it *was* a pattern, there was no doubt about that.

If it had only been foul language and nothing more, John would have been able to deal with it. The pecking from neighbors and government agencies could be quelled. John Woods was simply too important to be bothered by it, and once he convinced the Genotechnic Commission of that, they would be left alone. After all, profanity didn't always imply organic misevolution.

Unfortunately, the twins did not stop at words.

By now Daniel's shoulder felt better, and he turned to his brother, who was still obviously quite entertained by Daniel's clumsiness. Still spewing curses, Daniel hurled himself at his brother, hitting him at mid-waist. They rolled, began to fight, and John lost track of who was who. He closed the blinds and the room became dark.

His sons were fighting.

Not playing, not arguing, but throwing punches, trying desperately to hurt one another. Just like their brother Joe. Joe would have been thirty-one this year.

This was the final symptom, the one that would make him helpless when he had to face the Juvenile Board—and oh, what a field day the tabloids would have:

NOBEL LAUREATE'S SONS SUFFER FROM MISEVOLUTION.
MASTER GENETICIST'S FOUL BREED

And of course they'd blame it on his own engineering. Was it his fault that the procedures weren't perfect? Here he was, slowly beating violence to death in the human species, and they're ready to hurl his own sons back in his face.

Two years earlier, Daniel and Steven had been the perfect children—more so than any other children John, or anyone else for that matter, had spliced. It was the procedure. The smallest change in the gene-splicing pattern. While most children had been patterned docile, and fairly joyless, John had taken the next step: to weed out aggression, but leave the rest of the emotional system intact.

Joe had been the first.

Joe had been perfect, just like the twins; but then something happened to him at the onset of puberty, some unforeseen snafu in the splice caused his personality to deteriorate as his body changed, reintroducing a violence into the system that nothing could reconcile. The twins were the same. They were halfway through that vicious metamorphosis, and there was nothing that could be done about it.

Now, at thirteen, they fought. Not only with each other, but with other children, children who no longer knew how to fight. It wouldn't be long before the authorities would haul them off to Correctional Camp, where they'd stay for the rest of their lives. Just like their brother Joe.

It was all inevitable. They were destined to change from the beginning, and John often wondered if those first twelve years would make up for the years ahead.

There was a warm pressure on John's shoulders as Anne began to massage his neck, releasing some of the tension there.

"We still have some time with them," his wife reminded him.

"Maybe so." He relaxed as he felt her thumbs rolling in small soothing circles on his neck.

Then the front door opened and slammed. Two loud voices were heard, but the cursing had at last stopped. John put his hand to his shoulder and clasped Anne's, then went out of the bedroom to confront the twins. He hated to confront them. He had no defense; all he had were words and reason, and they were immune to that.

As John entered the living room, the twins were lying down, sprawled on the sofa and love seat. They abruptly became quiet as their father entered.

"All right, what's going on here?" John asked, knowing full well what was going on and what the answer would be.

"Nothing," said Daniel—or was it Steven? They always wore each other's clothes, and without close scrutiny it was hard to tell, even for John.

Steven turned to look at John, already bored with a lecture his father hadn't even begun, and John caught sight of a puffy eye, mottled purple.

At this point Anne entered the living room, glanced at Steven, opened her mouth as if to speak, but gave up. She turned to John with a mild glare, as if to say "they're all yours," then marched off into the kitchen, closing the swinging door behind her.

"The fighting has to stop now!" said John.

"It's a free world," said Steven. "We'll do what we want."

"Not as long as I'm your father and you're living in this house." John stared Steven down. He was still good at that, but its effects were minimal. John took a deep breath and changed the tone of his voice. It became soft and caring. "C'mon, Steven, I'll help you take care of that black eye."

"It's Daniel." The twin with the black eye stood and stormed off into his bedroom, with smug indignation. The other twin looked at his father as if to say something to alleviate the tension, but thought better of it and followed his brother into the bedroom. The door was closed and John heard the click as the door was locked from the inside. He entered the kitchen.

"Anything new and wonderful besides the black eye?" said Anne, slicing potatoes with all the determination of an executioner. "How long are you going to let this go on?"

"Well, what do you want me to do about it?" The last person John wanted flack from was Anne. There was enough of it permeating the air without hers. "Go ahead, I'm open for suggestions."

Anne gave up on the potatoes and turned to him. She might have had a tear or two in her eyes if John hadn't been there, but she would not show them in his presence. "I don't know. Maybe some therapy."

"What now? None of the others have helped. Should we toss them in for anticognition? Selectively shock it out of their little brains? Well, I've got news for you, it's not going to work for them because it didn't work for Joe." John tried to bite back those last few words, but they slipped away. Joe was a subject not to be mentioned. If there was a chink in Anne's armor, that was it. No more potatoes were sliced. No words were said for a while. Anne simply stood there, her back to the counter, head down, composing herself.

"Stop yelling," she said quietly, after a long time. "I don't want to give them any more satisfaction or ammunition."

"I'm sorry."

"No, you're right. Therapy won't work." She looked up at him and forced a smile, but when the smile was gone John could see the lines in her forehead wrinkle up, filled with shadow. He went to touch her forehead with his fingers, and she relaxed it, closing her eyes.

"They *are* . . . so much like Joseph." she said.

"Well, you knew it had to be that way."

Anne turned back to the counter as if ready to continue dinner again, but when she gazed at what lay in front of her, she didn't seem all that interested anymore. "I thought by raising them differently, in a different place . . ."

"It was a pipe dream. Environment this, environment that—it just doesn't work." The words of a hard-core geneticist, he thought. He knew his science. No psychologist could change genes. A dog could not be conditioned into being an ape.

Anne reluctantly continued with dinner. "I suppose they'll take the twins away in a year or so," she said.

John felt an urge to pace come over him, and rather than succumb, he pulled out a chair and sat down. "I suppose."

"I still love them, you know." Anne glanced at him on her way to the refrigerator, but broke the gaze quickly. "I mean, despite that they're changing, I'm still their mother." She reached for a dishtowel, trying to hide the fact that she was blotting her eyes with it. John might have cried too, if he still could.

* * *

When John returned home from the lab on the following Tuesday, it was quite obvious that something was wrong from the instant he stepped in the door.

Anne was standing stiffly, as if holding up the living room wall, and the twins were strewn on the furniture again, both surprisingly quiet. John felt a boulder slip off of a ledge somewhere, and it was about to hit the pit of his stomach.

"They robbed a store today," said Anne.

"We didn't rob it."

"Well, then what would you call it?" Anne was surprisingly calm. Numb, thought John.

The twins looked at each other and one of them spoke up—Steven it was. "We were caught shoplifting, all right? That's not exactly stealing."

"Are you listening to this?" said Anne. "Go ahead, tell him the whole story."

"Why don't *you?*" Steven rolled over on the couch with the annoyed indifference of a cat.

"I had to pick them up at the police station," said Anne. "They had shoved everything from batteries to candy in their jackets, then just walked out of the store. Security caught it all on disc."

"Guess we should've checked for cameras, huh?" said Steven.

John fumed. "I want to know why you did this—and look at me when I talk to you, Steven!"

"It's Daniel!" Daniel rolled over and looked at his father.

"Did you do it to get back at your mother and I for something? Is that it?"

"We did it because we wanted to, all right?" screamed Steven, standing up. "The stuff was there, we wanted it, and we didn't feel like paying. There's your damn answer."

Anne winced. Steven glanced at his mother, then at his father. "I'm sorry," he said as he looked into his father's eyes, but it was clear that he wasn't sorry for anything. Nothing at all. John might have been satisfied if there were the slightest bit of conscience left, a twinge of guilt; but if there was, it certainly didn't show in either of their eyes.

"You'll end up like your brother, you know that, don't you?"

"Here we go again," mumbled Daniel.

"You're acting just like he did."

"How would we know?" said Steven. "He died a year before we were born, remember. For all we know, you made it all up just to scare us."

"Maybe he didn't die in 'Camp' at all," added Daniel. "Maybe you lectured him to death."

John stood speechless, void of ammunition. Would his sons suffer their lives away in the camps, or would they be lucky, and somehow live to terrorize? They might even evolve into full-fledged sociopaths, learning how to appear respectable while all the time manipulating, plotting, discarding people who were no longer useful to them. A perversion of decency.

"I suppose it's punishment time," grumbled Daniel. "What is it today? No TV? No dinner? Grounded for three years?"

"Why don't you hit us?" suggested Steven.

Now that was the perfect blow, thought John. They knew he would not touch them. He could never bring himself to do that, it just wasn't done anymore. Still, John continued the game, not willing to back down. He undid his belt and pulled it out in his father's best fashion, remembering the stinging spankings he had been given as a child. He looped the belt and gazed threateningly at the twins.

"If that's what you want," he said.

And the twins laughed at him.

Immediately John felt like a fool—the emperor with no clothes.

"You won't do it," taunted Steven.

"Besides, we're too old," said the other.

"We'll sue you if you do."

"And anyway, you'll only be able to catch one of us . . . and you won't even know which one!" They both laughed. Duplicates of that hideous laugh John had heard so many times before, both blending into one. The twins stood and brushed right past him.

"Don't be too angry, Dad," said Steven, rapping him lightly on the arm as he passed, and then he laughed again as the two went off into their room, locking it.

Anne rubbed her eyes, and continued to hold up the wall. "There's more," she said softly.

Anne glanced at the twins door, then said, so that they couldn't hear, "They've been reclassified as juvenile delinquents." She closed her eyes and swallowed, and held out a handful of colorful brochures. "We have three weeks to choose a Correctional Camp."

"We could do it again," said John as he slipped into bed. Anne didn't answer right away; probably surprised to hear a voice in the bedroom that lately had begun to resemble a tomb.

"No." Anne rolled over, away from him. "I'm too old."

"Nonsense." John climbed into bed. "Nowadays sixty-year-old women are giving birth left and right—and you're only fifty-three."

"And you can't *have* children anymore, John." He could only laugh at her bluntness. "I don't want to rely on some strange computer splice, no matter how well you've got the thing programmed." Anne yawned and shifted the blanket towards her side.

"No, I mean we can do *exactly* what we did before." John waited, giving Anne a few moments to think about it.

"You mean like with Joe . . . but with the twins instead?" She sat up. "I don't know. What will they think?"

"They'll never know," said John with a grin. Anne seemed unsettled by his grin. He tried to wipe it from his face but couldn't.

"Because they'll be at Correctional Camp?" she asked.

"We'll see." John gave her a grinning kiss, and then settled into bed. He waited until he saw a pensive grin appear on Anne's face as well, before he turned out the light, then quickly fell asleep with visions of faultlessly gorgeous blonde boys playing in the sun. Boys too young to be juvenile delinquents.

Anne consented to his plan.

It took all of two weeks of clandestine discussions that never lasted for more than a minute, since Anne was so quick to change the subject, but she finally agreed as long as John didn't involve her until he had to. She wanted the situation glazed over, as it would be for the neighbors, or anyone else who knew them. He knew she would come around—there was simply too much to gain.

John waited until the Juvenile Board called him at work, a few days later. Then he made final preparations.

That afternoon the twins were their usual rambunctious selves when John arrived home, arguing over some unpleasant incident at school. They didn't know they were to be sent away—both Anne and John had agreed to keep that, and a good many other things, secret. John wondered if the twins would have run away if they knew.

As John entered the kitchen, Anne was preparing dinner, with the radio turned up loud enough to drown out the twins' "discussion" in the bedroom. It was amazing how she had been able to divorce herself entirely from the twins over those three weeks. To her, it was as if they were already gone.

"The Juvenile Board called me at work," he told her.

"And?"

"And we have three days to chose a Correctional Camp, or they'll make the choice for us."

Anne diligently washed the salad, stopped for a moment then turned to look at him. "Well, nice to know they're efficient."

She returned to her work, with an angry passion.

"What's for dinner?" he asked.

"Spaghetti, salad. Nothing special."

John crossed to the refrigerator, which had already been raided by the boys and was fairly empty.

"And to drink?" asked John.

"Not much. I thought I'd mix up some punch."

"Fine. Do that." said John. Anne was busy at the chopping block, slicing a green pepper. John came up behind her, and placing his hands on her shoulders, he leaned forward and whispered in her ear.

"Don't drink the punch," he told her, softly.

The steady slicing sound stopped, but only for a moment. Anne closed her eyes and tensed her shoulders a bit. Then she nodded and continued slicing the pepper.

"I'm pregnant," said Anne, sitting in the breakfast nook. They didn't use the dining room much anymore. "Triplets," she said slyly. "Who would have thought!"

John smiled. "I didn't get that award for nothing."

Anne sipped her coffee. "If you're so wonderful, then why do you need me at all? I'm sure they make petri dishes in all sizes."

"Don't laugh," he said.

"Do you think anyone will give us trouble?" Anne asked, for the umpteenth time.

"Why should they? The twins were to be sent to 'Camp,' and they ran away. The police have been unable to find them. It happens every day, and nobody asks too many questions about delinquent kids that vanish. Not anymore."

John drained his cup, and Anne refilled it. No, nobody would disturb them. Even if they were given a hard time, John could just talk to the Genotechnic Commission. He was still too important to be bothered by the government.

"You know, they would have died anyway," she said, still rationalizing a month after the fact. "I mean, they were destined to be *exactly* like Joe, weren't they?"

"Of course, perfect duplicates," said John.

"Well, then it's better this way. They didn't suffer in camp, like Joe did. There's some cake in the fridge, would you like some?"

"Fine."

She went to the refrigerator and returned with half of a cake. It was slightly stale with no one around to eat it.

"I've got a surprise for you," John smiled and ate some cake, leaving Anne in suspense.

"Go on, tell me, don't just stuff your face!"

"Well, you know my work has been steadily progres[-]sing. . . . Genetic engineering isn't perfect yet, but it is getting better. . . ."

"Spare me the dissertation and tell me what you did."

"I changed the pattern."

"You *what?*" Anne's worry lines darkened.

"Don't be upset, I just changed it a little." John took a sip of his coffee, and carefully assessed Anne's response.

"I see. And I'm the guinea pig, right? So you're telling me they'll be different?"

"No, I didn't change the cloning procedure at all, I just fixed something, so to speak. Their personalities won't change."

Anne didn't respond to that right away. She regarded him in her cool analytical way. "So they won't grow up to be delinquent?"

"Well, either that or they'll just stop aging at eleven, I'm not sure yet. Like I said, genetic engineering isn't as exact as we'd like it to be."

Anne smiled, and her worry lines faded. "I like your surprise." She put her hand down and touched her abdomen—as if she actually expected to feel a kick already. "We can't take a chance people will recognize them," she said. "We'll have to move again."

"The company has offices all over the world," answered John.

They slept that night lying comfortably back to back. There were no noises in the next room to disturb them; there, only memories remained—memories of the good times, for there was no room for the bad. They thought of the two boys running along the beach laughing—an innocent laugh. They thought of the same scene with Joe, years before, and now they could do it again, giving Joey, Danny, and Stevey a new lease on life. No other children could share their childhood with their parents longer than John and Anne's children had, and would continue to in the years ahead.

Anne had fallen asleep and John lingered on the edge.

Just before dreams set in, it occurred to him that they were probably the first to ever do something of this sort. John fell asleep pleased.

How wonderful to be unique.

THE BODY ELECTRIC

· ·

You are not in your right mind.

You knew it from the moment the lightning struck you, and as you stumble through the whipping, windswept branches of December-bare trees, you are certain your mind has gone terribly wrong. You know because the trees were green and alive in a steamy summer storm only a moment before. Now they are as dormant as death, and the rain is now mixed with frigid, stinging sleet. You know because it was daylight when the lightning descended upon you, crashing from the heavens like the fist of God. It was only seconds earlier . . . but now it is night, not day, and the only thing lighting your path are the blinding flashes that the angry clouds discharge.

Stumbling over sharp rocks, you count the seconds between lightning and thunder. One . . . two . . . three. Three seconds. A mile away. The storm is moving away, beginning to ease, and although you feel relief, one question fills your thoughts. Why weren't you hurt when the lightning struck you? It had blinded you for an instant—you felt it coursing around you and through you, penetrating your mind, your spirit—and then it was gone, leaving summer turned to winter and day turned to night.

No, you are not in your right mind . . . and you're afraid to find out how wrong your mind truly is.

The rushing of water fills your ears, and you burst through the trees, almost falling into a river swollen by the icy rain. To your right is a small brick house, its windows lit by a gentle flickering light. You don't know this place, but it is far more inviting than the forest or the river. A woman stands on the porch; you can see her as you approach. She's wrapped in a heavy winter shawl.

"Al?" she cries. "Al, is that you? Get in here right away! You must be crazy to be gallivanting out in a storm like this!"

As you get closer, you figure the woman will see that she's mistaken. You are not Al, whoever Al might be. Stepping onto the covered porch, you shake the rain from yourself like a wet dog.

"Hi," you say. "Would it be all right if I came inside? I have to call home."

She looks at you with an odd expression on her face. "Call home what?"

You're not sure what she means—but you're more troubled by your own voice than by anything she says. The timbre of your voice is completely wrong. You must be getting a cold. "Maybe I should just page my father."

The woman shakes her head. "Your father has enough pages with all those newspapers he reads. Come inside, dinner's ready."

Does she know my father? you wonder. Probably not—because your dad never reads the newspaper; he gets all his news from the Internet.

Inside, the house is warmed by a fireplace and lit by

flickering bulbs. No, not bulbs—gas lamps, like the kind they used a hundred years ago.

"That's weird," you say, clearing your throat to get rid of its strange sound.

In the kitchen, a man sits behind a newspaper. The table before him is set with a serving platter of chicken and dumplings, making you suddenly realize how hungry you are.

The woman hands you a towel, and a beige button-down shirt. Its stitching feels funny; so does its collar. Just a little bit too small. "Better change into this before you catch your death of cold," she says.

"Hurry up, Al, so we can all eat," says the man.

"My name's not Al."

The man puts down his newspaper not sure he has heard correctly, and looks you over. "One week working for the railroad, and the boy's already putting on airs!"

"Perhaps you'd prefer we call you 'Tom,' " says the woman, "or 'Tommy.' "

But that's not your name either. You are about to inform them of this, but then you catch a glimpse of yourself in the big hallway mirror, and the truth hits you like a second bolt of lightning.

You *are* in·your right mind after all. Unfortunately, you're in the wrong body.

In the mirror you see a thirteen-year-old boy. It's not the kid you saw in the mirror yesterday! You look at your hands and your arms. You peel off your wet shirt and examine your birthmarks, freckles, and moles, which are as unknown to you as stars over an alien sky. You slip on the shirt and button it so you don't have to see that unfamiliar body.

"Well, what's it gonna be, boy?" says the man. "Do we call you by your first or middle name, now?"

Too dumbfounded to speak, you sit down in the hard

wooden chair, then after several deep breaths you say, "Whatever you want to call me."

Satisfied, they continue to call you Al, and with nothing else to do, you begin to eat. Thankfully, at least, chicken and dumplings is still the same as you remember it.

Later, the woman douses the light in a bedroom she claims is yours. "Goodnight, Al," she says. "Don't forget to say your prayers."

The woman's name, you've learned, is Nancy, but you've also learned that there's another term by which you should address her.

"Goodnight . . . Mother." You feel so strange calling her that, the words stick in your throat.

After she is gone, you study the room. There are several books on shelves, a tablet with handwriting that's far neater than your own.

Everything you see makes you realize just how desperate your situation is—but nothing could have been worse than the glimpse you got of the man's newspaper. The date was December third . . . 1860.

Now you know why the lightning did not harm you—its powerful electrical surge was absorbed elsewhere, short-circuiting time and space, thrusting you into the body of an unremarkable boy named Al, in the unremarkable town of Port Huron, Michigan.

A void deepens within you as you try to fathom all the things lost. Your own parents are three generations from being conceived. Your great-great-grandmother has not even been born, and your friends are lost in a future too distant for people here to imagine. There are no cars, no phones, no World Wide Web, no Saturday horror movies at the local multiplex. There won't be video games for at least a hundred and ten years, and you'll never hear rock music again because not even the plastic of your precious CDs has been invented.

Say your prayers, the woman told you, and so you kneel at the foot of your bed and pray, your eyes filling with tears, because if there ever was a time to pray, this is it.

You dream of fast cars and fighter jets, but you wake only to find that the world you now occupy considers such things to be wild flights of fancy. Absurd science fiction.

"Hurry, Al," you hear the woman you must call "Mother" shout to you from the kitchen. "Better get up or you'll be late for work."

Work, you think. Yes—that's right—last night your "father" said you worked at the railroads . . . but doing what? How could you show up there, not even knowing your job? So you head into the kitchen, and strike up a conversation with your mother, who cooks up some dark pancakes she calls flapjacks.

"I'm tired of working for the railroad," you tell her. She takes it in stride, without even looking up at you.

"It's only been a week. Give it time."

"Yes," you say, "but it's the same old thing every day."

"No it's not," she says as she serves you up some piping hot flapjacks. "The newspaper is different every day. If you get there early enough, maybe you can read the paper before you start selling them to passengers."

You gloat happily. *So, I sell newspapers on the train,* you think. "I guess you're right," you say. "But it's such a long walk to the train station."

She scoffs. "What a complainer you are! I would hardly call a half mile downriver a long walk!"

Scarfing down your flapjacks, you slip out the door, with all the information you need. "Later, Mom!"

"What's later?" she asks, not quite getting your futuristic lingo. You're out the door too quickly to explain yourself.

"Morning, Al," says the round, runny-nosed man who hands you a stack of papers. "Better run, the 8:40's about to pull out. Miss the train, miss a day's pay." The bundle of papers feels lead-heavy. Are you expected to carry these things?

You hear a train whistle, and the man glares at you. "Waiting for an invitation, son?"

Heaving the bundle of papers on a shoulder, you plod off toward the train. About halfway there, the steam engine begins to move—you can hear a series of clanks running down the spine of the train as each coupler tugs at the car behind it. The wheels grind into motion, and the whole train begins to move.

"Oh no!" You pick up the pace, but the train's already pulling out of the station. There's a baggage compartment, its door wide open. You cut a diagonal path, hoping to intercept the door before the train picks up too much speed.

Your legs pumping at full strength, you reach the open doorway and hurl the newspapers into the car. So far so good. You leap, figuring you just made it—but your legs are too tired to give you any momentum. You fall short and your fingernails scrape on the wooden floor of the baggage car. Halfway in and halfway out, your legs dangle beneath the spinning wheels of the accelerating train. You're slipping! If you fall, you'll be sliced in two! No surgeon in this time—or even your own—would be able to save you.

Your nails slip, and your body begins to fall beneath the train. You scream . . .

. . . and a pair of hands reaches out, grabbing you by the ears.

"I've got you, Al," the deep voice of the conductor says. He tugs you up by your ears so hard, you feel something snap inside your head. Your ears burn, they're ringing—but he doesn't release his grip. He lifts you by your agonized ears into the baggage car. The stinging pain in your ears brings a flood of tears to your eyes.

"Close call," says the conductor, not even noticing. You feel like screaming at him, but instead you try not to show the pain. After all, you should be grateful; the man saved your life.

Thanking him, you take your stack of newspapers and begin making your way through the stuffy, overly heated train, selling your papers for two pennies apiece.

The passengers are all what you expect. Well-dressed businessmen, dainty women. The women are strongly perfumed, but it doesn't hide the stench of sweat already in the air. "Someone ought to invent deodorant," you mumble to yourself.

A man next to you chuckles, and says "Why don't you, Al? You've got enough chemicals in that cellar of yours to do the job!" The man must be a friend of your family. You return his smile as if you know him.

"Hey," he suggests, "maybe you can invent something that will stop perspiration dead in its tracks!"

"An antiperspirant," you tell him, thinking back to a familiar TV commercial " *'Made with aluminum chlorohydrate. Roll-on or spray. Strong enough for a man, but made for a woman.'* "

The man laughs, thinking it all very funny. However, there's someone else on the train who takes you seriously. He's a kid—same age as you—with reddish hair and a piercing gaze. He's staring at you from the far end of the car. It makes you uncomfortable.

"Paper?" you ask him, as you reach his end of the car.

The boy shrugs, and speaks in a heavy Scottish accent. "No point in it. It's all old news."

"Suit yourself."

You're about to go on into the next car, when the kids says something that stops you in your tracks.

"What I wouldn't give for a high-speed modem and a nice chat room," he says.

You snap your head around so quickly, it makes your aching ears ring louder.

"What did you say?"

"I'm thinkin' that you heard me." The kid's smile is about as wide as the train. You look to the woman sitting next to him, who isn't fazed in the least. "That's me mum," he tells you. "She's deaf, you know—but even if she could hear, she'd be thinkin' it's gibberish we're talking."

You sit down in a seat facing his, dropping your pile of newspapers. "You're from the future!"

"Not anymore," he tells you. "I'm from the present, now. And a fine place it is, too!"

"Fine?" you say, incredulous. "No cars, no electricity, no phones. What's fine about it?"

"The possibilities, Al! The possibilities."

"How come you know my name?"

He leans back, silent for a moment, grinning all the while, like he knows something you don't. Then he holds out his hand. "My name's Aleck," he says. "Got switched here in a thunderstorm, same as you, I'll fathom. I even had to learn me accent."

"No way!"

"Way! I convinced my mother to make this trip to America. I told her I wanted to see the world. But the truth is, I came to find you!"

"Me?"

Then he leans in and whispers. "We're going to be great adversaries, you and I. I thought we should begin it with a friendship. Like two boxers shaking hands before the fight."

"I don't understand."

"Aye, but you will," he says, so sure of himself it makes you angry.

Then a man clears his throat behind you, and you turn to see the conductor standing in the aisle, hands on his hips, not too pleased with you.

You stand up, and pick up your bundle of newspapers.

"Sorry, sir," you say, not even knowing his name. "I'll get back to selling papers."

"You'd better do just that," he says in a voice suitably menacing, then he turns to Aleck.

"I'm sorry about that, young Master Bell."

"That's all right. I rather enjoyed chatting."

It takes a moment, but you make the connection, like a circuit finally closing. "Aleck Bell? As in Alexander *Graham* Bell?"

He nods. "Remember the name," he says, "you'll be hearing no end of it soon."

The train vibrates and rolls beneath your feet, but its more than just the train. You feel dizzy and dazzled by the presence of such greatness before you. Alexander Graham Bell! You even did a report on him, back in sixth grade. It's hard to believe that this grinning kid sitting here is only a few short years away from inventing the telephone!

The conductor roughly nudges you away. "Move on! The next car needs papers, too."

"Goodbye, Al," says young Master Bell. "Or should I call you 'Tom'?"

And in a daze you say, "Call me Al. Everybody calls me Al."

* * *

With your feet still feeling as if they're on the train, you walk home. It was a long day, but that's okay. It's given you time to think; time to accept the end of your old life, and the beginning of a new one. You wonder how the real Al will do, a hundred and forty years from now, when he finds himself trapped in your old body, wearing Nikes, playing video games, and trying to comprehend the mysteries of America OnLine. You wish you could be there, but you know that you won't. You'll die somewhere around 1930, a very old man. That much you remember.

"Good evening, Mother," you say, as you enter, giving her a peck on the cheek.

She laughs, looking up from the dinner she's preparing. "What's gotten into you?"

"Nothing," you tell her. "It's just a great time to be alive."

Then you open the door to the cellar. In the dim light spilling through the cellar window, you see a table down there, covered with jars full of chemicals and all kinds of little gadgets. You take a deep breath of joyful anticipation. The future rests down in that cellar—and someday there will be records, there will be movies, and there will be electric light.

"Thomas Alva Edison!" calls your Mother, "are you going to spend the whole evening tinkering around in that cellar again?"

You toss her a grin before you descend the stairs. "Remember the name," you tell her. "You'll be hearing no end of it soon."

BAD FORTUNE
AT WONG LEE'S

●●●●●●●●●●●●●●●●●●●●●●●●●●●●●●●●●●

The Greenblatts settled down for another Chinese dinner at Wong Lee's Cantonese Emporium, which advertised a little piece of China in Brooklyn. They came to Wong Lee's every Friday night, every Sunday night, and for the occasional mid-week take-out order. In short, the Greenblatts loved their Chinese food with a passion.

Except, that is, for Lauren.

Her parents and brothers could have lived solely on the stuff—they could have had it pumped into their bloodstream intravenously, and they would have been as happy as Sweet and Pungent Clams (Number 26 on the dinner menu). But Lauren prayed that one day their tastes would change, and maybe she wouldn't be forced to suffer through yet another endless multi-course meal. It wasn't the food she objected to; actually, she enjoyed that part of it.

The problem was the cookies.

It started back when Lauren was seven.

* * *

Aunt Edna was visiting from Buffalo. She rarely came
down to Brooklyn, but when she did, the traditional meal
at Wong Lee's Cantonese Emporium was always the first
order of business. And so the whole Greenblatt family
had piled into the minivan and headed to Wong Lee's:
Mom, Dad, Michael, Seth, and Lauren—who, at the age
of seven, already knew how to use chopsticks like a pro.

The meal was delicious. Six courses spun around the
lazy Susan in the center of the big round table until everyone was so stuffed they could hardly breathe. Next came
the tiny scoop of pistachio ice cream in a little silver cup.

And then the cookies.

Oh, how Lauren used to love the cookies. Sweet
vanilla and almond flavors carefully folded into that familiar crescent shape, with a surprise inside its hollow
shell. Since she had begun reading at six, fortune cookies
were a special, delightful challenge, because they always
contained big words that only Confucius would use.
Everyone selected their cookie and snapped it in half.

"What does yours say, Lauren?" Mom asked.

Lauren read slowly. " *'You are generous of spirit, and
will move mountains.'* "

And then it went around the table counterclockwise, as
was the family tradition.

" *'Love many, trust few, paddle your own canoe,'* "
read Dad.

Seth and Michael began snickering.

" *'You have many secret admirers,'* " read Mom,
glancing slyly at Dad.

" *'You are a glorious fountain of golden water,'* " read
Michael, and snickered some more. It was a perfect toilet-
humor opportunity, but her brothers mercifully let it pass.

" *'Your wild spirit soars into a thrilling future,'* " read
Seth. "What does *that* mean?"

"It means," said Dad, "that you'll still be a wild maniac when you grow up."

Seth smiled, proud to know his place in the world.

"How about you, Aunt Edna?" asked Lauren.

Aunt Edna broke the cookie in half with a loud snap and peeled out the tiny piece of paper, holding it at arm's length so that her far-sighted eyes could read. " *'Confucius says: You will die on Tuesday in freak accident.'* "

Mom gasped and Dad's spoon clattered to his silver ice-cream plate, which was instantly taken away by the waiter who hovered in wait of empty plates like a vulture over a lion's kill.

Seth and Michael, who had been ready to burst out laughing a moment ago, suddenly dropped their jaws, and sunk into their seats. If they could have disappeared into a hole in the floor, they would have.

"Let me see that," said Dad, growing red in the face. He snatched the little piece of paper from Aunt Edna, and motioned to the hovering waiter.

"Do you find this funny?" he demanded.

It was Mom who realized who the real culprits were. Seth and Michael had guilt painted on their face in a neon glow. Mom glared at them with accusing eyes.

"What did you do?"

"It was Seth's idea," Michael blurted out.

"Yeah, but Michael bought the gag fortune cookies," shot Seth.

"And, anyway, they were supposed to be funny, not sick, y'know—they were supposed to say things like *'help, I'm being held prisoner in a fortune cookie factory.'* Y'know, stuff like that." They started elbowing and pushing each other. It was Aunt Edna who saved the day. She began to laugh, not just any laugh, but an Aunt Edna laugh. Other relatives often whispered that there was insanity on that side of the family, and perhaps that's why

Aunt Edna had inherited such a crazy laugh. Her laughter was always long and loud and contagious. In a few moments the whole family was laughing, and soon even the table next to us was in stitches as well, without even knowing why they were laughing.

They had Chinese food every night during her stay. Luckily, the fortunes were all pretty normal, and everyone forgot about the bad fortune. Then on Tuesday they all said their goodbyes as Aunt Edna boarded her bus back to Buffalo. And somewhere in the Catskill Mountains, the bus plunged off the road, down into the freezing cold of Kiamesha Lake. Everyone survived except for Aunt Edna.

It was then that Lauren stopped reading her fortunes.

It was a secret she kept for six long years. After every meal at Wong Lee's Lauren held the offensive little pastry in her hand, while the others read their little phrases of wisdom and fate. Finally, it would be Lauren's turn. She would hold that cookie in her lap, where no one could see, hating the awful cookie with every ounce of her being.

"Go on, Lauren," her father would prompt. "Aren't you going to open it?"

No, she wanted to say. *I refuse to read it!* For deep in her heart she felt certain that no one should know the future, no one should try to guess, and no one should serve up tiny shreds of destiny and pretend it was just in fun. There was nothing fun about it. Lauren had already *seen* the results of a bad fortune.

She couldn't tell her parents; they wouldn't understand. So week after week, she would take the little cookie, keep it hidden in her lap, unbroken, and, like a magician, she would pull out a blank strip of paper that she had cut from a notebook. Then she would hold up that blank paper and pretend to read, saying something like, *"Love will rain on you like stars rain from the heavens,"* or, *"For every smile you give, it will be returned one hundredfold,"* or something else that sounded both wise and vacant at the same time. Having heard the fortunes of her family a thousand times over, she knew how to fake it, and no one ever suspected that her fortune cookies went unopened. She would slip them into her pocket, dispose of them in her own special way when no one was looking, and they would never be seen again.

Or so she thought.

The first day of the year of the Dragon. Chinese New Year. That's when Lauren's little cookie world began to unravel.

The Greenblatts were eating at Wong Lee's on that particular night. Business as usual for Lauren. She cracked an almond cookie in her hands beneath the table pretending it was her fortune cookie, then picked up a blank scrap of paper she had brought from home, and pretended to read her fortune. All went according to plan. Then, just before she left, she went to the restroom, got rid of the cookie, and rejoined her family.

At home that night, however, she was disturbed to find something strange and mushy in the medicine chest, right beside the dental floss.

"Gross!" She flicked it out, and it landed on the bathroom counter, inert and lifeless. It was a wet fortune cookie. This was strange, because no one brought home unopened fortune cookies in their house—it was almost a sacrilegious thing to do. She was certain that she had flushed hers at Wong Lee's. But, then where had this one come from?

"Michael! Seth!" she called, but there was no answer. She scraped up the soggy cookie, and stormed downstairs to where her brothers were veging in front of the TV.

Michael, now sixteen, never pulled tricks on Lauren anymore, unless they were really good tricks, and Seth . . . well, at fifteen, a fortune cookie in the medicine chest was too childish even for him.

"Who put this in the medicine cabinet?" She said, trying to sound as innocent and unbothered by it as possible.

"What is it?" asked Michael, not looking up from the TV.

"It looks like a fortune cookie," said Lauren. "Or something."

Michael shrugged, and Seth said, "Not me."

"Well, someone had to put it there."

"Maybe we have mice," suggested Michael.

"Or squirrels," offered Seth. "They hoard nuts, you know. Maybe they could go for fortune cookies, too."

Lauren decided not to push the issue. She took it out to the back porch, and crushed the thing beneath her heel. It made a sickening, squishy sound, like a snail crunched on pavement.

There, thought Lauren. *That's the end of it.* She went to bed and slept soundly, putting thoughts of the rogue cookie out of her mind.

And in the morning she awoke to find another one on her pillow.

"Mom!"

Her mother came running. "Lauren, honey, what is it? What's wrong."

She was about to tell her about the mysterious reappearance of the cookie, but thought better of it. Instead, she held the cookie behind her back and tried to make something up, but her mind drew a blank.

"Um. . . . ummm."

Then her attention was drawn to something skittering across the carpet. She gasped. "A mouse!"

Her mother jumped. "Where?"

Lauren pointed, but her mom turned too late, just missing the small blur that ducked under Lauren's bureau.

"Uh . . . that's why I called you in," said Lauren. "There's a mouse in my room." Once more Lauren saw the light-colored blur dart off beneath her bed.

"Did you hear that?" Lauren looked up.

Her mother looked up too, as if she could see through the ceiling. "I don't hear anything."

It sounded like a rodent crawling around in the attic. Then Lauren heard skittering inside the wall. "There—do you hear it this time?"

Mrs. Greenblatt listened, then shook her head, but took her daughter's word for it. "Great. Mice—just what we need."

But while Mrs. Greenblatt was disgusted, Lauren left for school feeling oddly relieved. Mice must have been dragging all sorts of munchies around the house. The mystery was solved. The universe was back in order. Although there was one question she kept in the back of her mind all day. Where did the mice find fortune cookies?

A cloud of dust billowed downward as the exterminator climbed down his ladder from the attic. Mom and Dad waited in the hallway. Mom nervously scratched the dry skin of her elbows, and Dad looked gloomy, probably wondering what all this was going to cost. Lauren sat in her room doing her homework, but kept glancing at them through the open door of her room.

"Well," began the exterminator, "the good news is I can't find signs of any mice or rats anywhere in your house. But you *should* have mice, with all of *these* things lying around."

Lauren bolted upright in her chair. What was he talking

about? She leaned back until she could see him through the open door. He was holding a handful of jagged little pastries in his hand. Fortune cookies.

Lauren lost her balance and fell over backwards in her chair.

"How strange," said Mr. Greenblatt, examining the dusty relics the exterminator had given him. "These cookies must have been left there by the previous owner."

The exterminator shrugged, and wrote out a bill that made Dad grimace.

The whole family spent the following Saturday cleaning up the attic, where they were amazed to find at least a hundred unopened fortune cookies scattered about the floor boards.

"Weird," Seth said. "I can't believe the family that used to live here would hoard fortune cookies in the attic."

"Total slobs," Michael responded. He made a move to crack open one of the stale cookies, but Lauren quickly slapped it out of his hand.

"Hey, what was that for?"

"We just got this place cleaned up," Lauren replied. "Do you want to get crumbs everywhere?" Maybe the others didn't know, but Lauren had been in the attic before, and knew the cookies hadn't been there when they moved in.

"How about dinner out tonight?" Dad said that evening. Lauren suggested Italian and crossed her fingers. But majority ruled, and the majority wanted Wong Lee's.

For the entire meal Lauren poked at her rice and toyed with her Mongolian beef, wishing she could be anywhere else in the world.

The rest of the family shoveled down the food without speaking, and when the meal was over, the waiter approached with a plate of fortune cookies.

The Greenblatts looked at one another, and everyone but Lauren burst out laughing. After the day's ordeal, the last thing anyone wanted was a fortune cookie. For a moment Lauren felt relief wash over her, figuring that, for once, the ritual fortune reading would be canceled tonight—and maybe every night thereafter. But her father was a creature of habit, and couldn't let it go.

"Aw, what the heck," he said. "Let's see what they say."

"I'll go first," said Michael. He snapped the cookie open and pulled the paper out, studying it with a furrowed brow before reading it aloud. "Here's a weird one," he said. " *'Take care, for the fortune you shun today may consume you tomorrow.'* "

Dad went next. "Ooh," he said. " 'Someone you love is about to leave you.' "

Mom chuckled. "Probably me," she said, then cracked her own cookie, and peeled out the fortune. To Lauren the paper seemed to squirm in her mother's hand like a white worm. She couldn't stop staring at it, as her mother read: " 'Set your dinner table for four. Begin tomorrow.' "

Lauren could feel the panic silently well up inside her. Didn't her family know? Couldn't they see what was happening? It was those vile cookies. They were plotting against her!

Crack! Seth ripped his cookie open, and drew out the slithering piece of paper. " 'The Sister of False Fortune receives judgment at dawn.' " Seth flipped the paper over to see if there was more. "What does *that* mean?"

Blank stares from Mom and Dad, a shrug from Michael, and nothing from Lauren, who couldn't even look up from table.

"Your turn, Lauren," prompted Dad. Lauren had to fight to keep herself from hyperventilating.

"C'mon, Lauren," Seth said impatiently, "we don't have all night."

She had her slip of blank paper in her pocket, but her fingers trembled so much that she couldn't get it—and even if she did, she wouldn't be able to think of any false fortune to say. Still, they all stared at her, waiting for her to tell them what the Fates said.

"Lauren?" Mom asked.

"Excuse me." Lauren stood up, and her chair scraped itself back on the floor, a loud, jarring noise. In a moment she found herself in the bathroom, staring at her own wild eyes in the mirror.

Stop it, Lauren, she told herself. *This is crazy—they're only cookies.*

But they were more than mere cookies—Lauren had always suspected that. She thought back to poor Aunt Edna—how she had laughed away her own bad fortune, only to be devoured by it. Deep down she had always felt that the cookie hadn't merely predicted Aunt Edna's fate. Somehow it had caused it!

Frantically, Lauren reached into her purse, finding a felt-tipped pen. In the other hand she still held the offensive cookie, its secret message still trapped in the dark crevices of its twisted folds. If these hideous little pastries were the makers of fate, she would defy them to the end. With the pen she wrote on the surface of the cookie "NO FATE!" like a bright red tattoo, and she hurled the cookie into the toilet. She watched as the swirling waters spun it around and around the bowl, fighting to take it down into eternal sewer darkness.

When she finally stepped from the bathroom, hands cold and wet, her dad was signing the check, and her family was preparing to go. It was as if nothing had happened. But how could they not know? Didn't they understand what those fortunes had said? How could they not see the look on her face as she raced off into the bathroom.

Or maybe they did see, thought Lauren, *and they're a part of it. . . .*

As soon as the thought dawned on her, it mushroomed and multiplied until it filled every ounce of her mind. If this was a conspiracy, how deep did it go? Was it her brothers? Her parents, too? The exterminator—was he involved? How about the waiter, who so innocently handed out those malevolent cookies today. Suddenly, something in Lauren snapped like the crust of a fortune cookie, and she felt herself slip out of the arms of those she loved, and into a place where everyone was suspect. Yes. This was a conspiracy—it had to be, and everyone was out to get her.

"Get your coat on Lauren, it's cold tonight," said Mom.

"What's that supposed to mean?" snapped Lauren, suddenly realizing that there may be hidden secret messages in everything the people around her said. Was it a warning that her life would be cold and empty? Did it mean her parents had decided to start giving her the cold shoulder? Then Mom threw Dad a glance. What did that glance mean? What were they planning to torment Lauren with now?

"Lauren," asked her father, "what's gotten into you?"

"As if you didn't know," was all she said.

She held her silence on the way home, and through the evening. While the others settled in for a pleasant evening of pay-per-view, Lauren locked herself up in her room, sitting knees to chest in the corner of her bed. When sleep came it was cold and fraught with disjointed nightmares.

It was near dawn when the strange sound dragged her up from the depths of her troubled sleep.

Boink-boink-gurgle-boink.

It was a familiar enough night sound. Just like the creaking of their settling house, or the skittering of leaves across the roof, it was a sound she had grown used to, or at least learned to tolerate.

Blurble-boink-glubb-glubb.

It was, of course, the toilet—its porcelain intestines echoing a complaint as water slipped through an imperfect seal. Fixing the noise was simple—just a matter of jiggling the handle. But no one was getting up to do it. No one but Lauren. Slowly she opened her door.

Gurgle-hiss-glubb-glubb.

It was louder than usual tonight. She turned on the bathroom light to see the clean waters of the bowl shimmering slightly. Mom was positively psychotic about clean bathrooms, and so the bowl was immaculate, full of Caribbean blue waters.

But tonight something was causing a little tempest in that particular teapot. Lauren narrowed her eyes as she noticed something in the very bottom of the bowl.

"Gross."

It seemed to be moving; crawling its way up the drain. She slammed down the handle, but the water did not flush. Instead, the water swirled and slowly began to rise, brimming, and delivering the crawling little mass to the surface; soggy and beige. She didn't need any closer inspection to know what it was, because on its waterlogged surface the words "NO FATE" were scrawled in her own handwriting, the deep red letters bleeding into one another.

Lauren had to bite her lip to keep herself from screaming. With the water flooding the floor like the great flood itself, Lauren slammed the door and hurried back toward her room . . . but something stopped her. A sound. Another sound. This one outside.

She went to the open hallway window and looked out across the lawn.

Crunch-crunch, skitch-skitch. Something was moving beneath the piles of dead winter leaves. Something was burrowing beneath the ground. Many things. She could see the crisscrossing, slithering patterns they made in the ground, like a thousand moles burrowing closer and closer to—

She slammed the window to lock out the noise, but that wasn't enough. She had to seal them out any way she could. Tearing through the house as fast as her ice-cold feet could carry her, Lauren went to every window and every door, bolting them and double-bolting them. She stuffed a pillow in the little cat door, she plugged up the garbage disposal, she closed the air conditioning vent.

Her parents and brothers still hadn't woken up—and she wouldn't wake them either, for fear that somehow, in some insane way, they were allies of those evil little fortunes. Finally, when she was certain the house was secure, she took a moment to sit down on the couch and catch her breath.

They would not catch her tonight. And tomorrow she would run. She would go far away where the Fates could not find her and fortunes were not yet written. Surely there had to be a place like that—she just had to find it.

At first, the skittering she heard didn't register in her mind. It was just another one of those night noises she had grown accustomed to: ashes slipping down the chimney.

The chimney?

Instantly, Lauren realized her fatal mistake. The flue was wide open, and she dared not go near it now, for they were already tumbling down.

She broke for her bedroom, letting lose a scream that might have woken the dead, and most certainly woke up everyone living in the house. Her parents and bothers came barreling out of their rooms as Lauren crashed past, her arms flailing madly. She ducked into her room slammed the door, locked it, put a chair in front of it, and sat in it, her head in her hands, sobbing.

"Lauren, what's wrong?" wailed her parents, pounding on the door. "What is it? What's happened."

She wouldn't answer them. How did she know she could trust them? What if, when she opened the door, they weren't really her parents at all, but were beige shells of flesh, hollow except for a single message scrawled on a squirming white sheet? She couldn't open the door now. She didn't dare.

"Lauren, please . . ."

She opened her eyes for an instant . . . and in that instant, she saw it. There, alone on the little round rug in front of her closet, right in the center of the rug's concentric rings . . . a single fortune cookie.

It didn't move. It didn't squirm. It merely waited. For her. As it had waited for her since that first day at Wong Lee's after Aunt Edna's bus plunge.

As she stared at it, the truth came to her in bright clarity. A truth she had been hiding from herself as well as the others.

"What have I done?" She whispered.

She had never thrown all those fortunes away, had she? All these years, she had told herself that she had flushed them, or crumbled them, or shoved them into the trash. She had made herself believe her own lies. But the truth was, she kept them—because as much as she despised them, deep down, she was far too superstitious to throw away an unread fortune. Now a corner of her mind that she had always kept locked sprung open, and the truth spilled out. *She* was the one who had hurled the cookies into the attic. *She* was the one who slipped a cookie into the medicine chest the other night. *She* was the one who buried them in the yard the way a dog buries bones, knowing they were always there, waiting. And she was the one who plunged the grungy toilet at Wong Lee's, desperate to get back her "NO FATE" fortune before it could be irretrievably lost in the sewers of Brooklyn.

Slowly, she made her way to the little cookie in the middle of the rug, and picked it up. It was the perfect fortune cookie. Some cookies had their fortunes sticking slightly out of the end, like the flag on a Hershey's kiss. But not this one. Its message of fate was well concealed within its snug but fragile folds.

With the thumbs of both hands, she pulled on the two ends until the cookie wrenched in two, spilling forth its white paper soul. And for the first time in six years, Lauren cast her eyes upon her fortune.

Had she remembered the closet, she could have saved herself. Had she looked at it—seen the way the closet door bulged like a boiler ready to blow . . . but she was too focused on that fortune—so she didn't stand a chance when the closet door exploded open, sending a suffocating slide of thousands upon thousands of fortune cookies on top of her, so much denser than they appeared, carrying so much more weight than anyone could have guessed.

The world went dark as the cookies began to cover her, spilling forth from the closet in an endless flood. All the fortunes she had hoarded over the years—all the fortunes in the world, it seemed—had at last spilled out upon Lauren in a cascade of sweet-smelling destiny, impossible to ever deny. And as Lauren felt the last remnants of her mind slip away forever, she began a chilling fit of insane laughter, still clutching in her hand the tiny slip of paper that read: " *'You will be buried in good fortune.'* "

OBSIDIAN SKY

....

Watch," says the girl. "They'll be coming soon."
The sun rides low on the horizon, slowly dousing the south Texas plane into red dusk. I stand there, wondering what it is about this strange ten-year-old girl that makes me want to stay here. She bothers me. Not enough to make me want to leave, but enough to tease my curiosity into wispy strands of wonder and fear.

"*Who* will be coming soon?"

"Not *who*," she says calmly, "but *what*."

The girl is ugly, there's no question about it. "Ugly as mud on a door," as my mom would say; but my mom's not here to say it. No, she and my dad are off on their second honeymoon, so I have to spend two weeks at my Uncle Weldon's farm.

Now, to be clear about things, I don't usually go around playing with girls that are almost three years younger than me. But there are no boys my age in Uncle Weldon and Aunt Marion's family; their kids are grown and gone.

Even though it's just my first day here, I can already sense that there are very few kids around at all. The fields reek of "maturity." There's not a ball or bike or video game between here and San Antonio. I think the ugly girl is the only other kid within ten square miles of this place. She's even got a name as strange as her: Zephyr.

Well, I figure it might not be so bad, on account of Zephyr knows things. She knows how to find snakes and hold them so they won't bite. She can catch bugs in midair and never misses.

But now she's getting weird, standing here looking at the setting sun like it's gonna jump up and do a dance for us.

"Listen," I tell her, "it's been fun, but I've gotta get back for dinner."

"Shh, Jack" says Zephyr, turning her blotchy face to me. I can't see much of her eyes because she always wears dark shades. Each lens is in the shape of a valentine heart, surrounded by a bright pink frame. "Be quiet and listen," she says.

I listen, but I don't hear anything out of the ordinary, just the distant lowing of cattle beneath the shrilling of katydids. Then a new sound begins to swell and overwhelms those other noises. A fluttering, like sheets on a windblown clothesline.

Zephyr clears her throat—a raspy clicking sound, almost like a snicker. "Yes," she says, "they're coming."

Suddenly, a swell of darkness obliterates the setting sun. The darkness rises in the distance like a black mushroom cloud. The fluttering grows more intense, and as I watch, to my amazement, I see that the cloud is not a cloud at all, but a swarm. Tiny dots of darkness fill almost every inch of sky, flitting madly in all directions. They draw closer, and I see the flapping of dark wings.

"Are those . . . birds?" I ask.

Zephyr shakes her head. "No, Jack," she tells me. "They're bats."

In an instant the swarm is over us, turning the twilight to night. I duck—I cover my head, expecting them to dive from the sky, to suck my blood, to tear at my flesh.

But Zephyr only laughs. "They won't bother you, silly," she says. "They're Mexican Free-Tails. They eat bugs."

I dare to turn my eyes upward to see the moving mass of bats, an endless stream of sinewy wings that beat past so powerfully they create a wind. The smell of bat guano is thick in the air, like a hot day at the zoo—but Zephyr takes a deep breath and smiles. "I love their smell," she says. "It's so . . . different."

The bats just keep flowing across the sky. I figure they have to stop eventually, but they don't. "How many more could there be?"

"It will take two or three hours for all of them to leave the roost. They'll feed, then flood the sky again on their way back home, just before dawn."

"There must be millions of them!"

"Twenty million," Zephyr quickly says, "but my momma says there's many, many more—more than anyone could ever count."

"That's impossible," I tell her. Now they have formed a blanket of night above us, as dark as black coal. "Where do they come from?"

Zephyr smiles. "Come back tomorrow," she says, "and I'll show you."

"Stay away from that one," Uncle Weldon says when I tell him about my afternoon with Zephyr. "The girl's touched in the head. So's her mother."

"What's so weird about them?"

Uncle Weldon shovels his peach pie into his mouth,

and takes his time in answering. His thoughts are always well-measured, even if they are opinionated. "They're not right—that's all I'm saying. They got funny ways. The mother's a recluse and never goes out. I think they belong to some kind of cult."

Aunt Marion serves me up another slice of pie. "Just because they got their own way of seeing things doesn't make them a cult," she says, but I can tell she's just saying it for the sake of argument. She looks away from me, and I can tell that she doesn't like Zephyr and her mother either. "The poor thing is so homely," Aunt Marion says. "You gotta have pity on a girl like that."

"I don't have to have pity on no one," grumbles Uncle Weldon.

"Your uncle doesn't have a charitable bone in his body!"

I can see that the two of them are working themselves up into a huff, so I try to change the subject.

"So, what about the bats?"

Uncle Weldon puts down his fork. "So? We got bats, what of it?"

"Do they always come?"

"Yep." says Uncle Weldon. "Every night, spring through fall, before they migrate south."

"They clear out the bugs, that's for sure," adds Aunt Marion. "Don't even need to crop dust the fields. Of course, there is that awful smell."

"Zephyr likes the smell," I tell them.

Uncle Weldon snorts. "I'm not surprised."

"There's nothing wrong with that," says Aunt Marion, again taking whatever side Uncle Weldon isn't on. "When I was a little girl, I liked the smell of cow pies," she says. "In the winter, on the way to school, I would even stick my feet in them to keep warm."

"Oh, gross!" The thought of sticking my feet into a steaming cow pie makes me want to hurl.

"Now look what you've done, Marion, you've gone and made the boy ill!"

As I think about it, I wonder which is weirder: cow pie foot baths or a sky full of bats.

"So," I say, "the bats are a good thing then?"

Once again, Uncle Weldon takes his time in answering, so Aunt Marion answers for him. "Of course they are, Jack . . . but I do wish there weren't so many of them."

Uncle Weldon shakes his head. "More and more every year," he says. "Can't be natural. Can't be natural at all."

Zephyr, heart-shaped sunglasses still fixed on her face, leads me across field after field the following afternoon, until I can no longer see any houses in the distance. There is nothing but cactus and scrub brush around us, and the ever-growing aroma of bat. I begin to sense something strange now—as if Zephyr isn't strange enough—now I sense something in the world around me. It's like a premonition without words or thought, releasing itself on my senses instead of my brain. Gooseflesh rises on my arms and legs, sounds are hollow, and the afternoon light is somehow lessened, like a partial eclipse. The feeling is both disturbing and exciting; *different*—like the smell of the bats.

"We're here," says Zephyr.

We've stopped at the edge of what looks like a meteor crater. In the center is a huge hole, at least twenty feet across.

"That's it," says Zephyr, a grin of anticipation on her face. "That's the entrance to Bracken Cave!" She brushes back her brittle hair and begins to descend toward the sink-hole mouth of the cave, but I hesitate. The mouth is speckled with the droppings of bats. Zephyr turns back and takes my hand. "Don't be afraid," she says. "I come here all the time. There's nothing to worry about as long as you're quiet. The bats sleep during the day."

I have to admit, I'm scared to go anywhere near the cave, and I begin to feel humiliated—I mean, I'm almost thirteen, and here I am afraid to go into a place that a ten-year-old girl isn't even afraid of.

But she's not just any girl, I remind myself. The truth is most other girls—most other *people*—wouldn't go anywhere near that cave. There are "danger" signs posted everywhere, and warnings not to disturb the bats. My brain goes into reverse, but my feet are like tires spinning in the mud—they simply won't move me away. Then Zephyr gets close to me and whispers something in my ear that really should frighten me away, but instead it has the opposite effect.

"I've never brought any other boy here," she whispers to me. *"And I'll never bring anyone else here but you."*

I don't know what it is about her words that get my feet moving toward that hole. Maybe the feeling of being special. Being chosen. Still holding my hand, she leads me toward the gaping mouth. "Come on, I'll show you something amazing," she whispers, and she climbs down into darkness, taking me with her.

We reach the bottom of the cave, where I can see very little beside the fact that the walls are moving. I swallow my revulsion, and focus all of my attention on Zephyr's calmness. If she's calm, then I can be, too.

"They're everywhere," Zephyr whispers. "Five hundred babies in every square foot. Soon the mothers will be nursing." She clears her throat again—that weird cackling noise—then she leads me forward into darkness. I want to resist, but find that my fear, tired of being ignored, has finally slipped out of consciousness, leaving me numb and intoxicated by the acidic smell of bat droppings.

Beneath our feet, something crunches like eggshells.

"They're carnivorous dermistid beetles," she tells me, as if its something every kid should know. "They cover the floor, eating dead bats. If you stood in one place long enough, they'd eat you too, but it might take a while."

She moves sure-footedly though the darkness, so fast that it scares me, but we don't bump into a single wall. There are strange clicking sounds all around me.

"What are those sounds?" I ask.

"The bats are echolocating," she explains. "They make those clicks, and use sonar to 'see' in the dark, just like dolphins do."

Every once in a while I feel a bat brush past my face. It really bothers me at first, but after a while I become desensitized to it. I think about summer camp, and how during the first few days I'm always freaked out by the size of the bugs and spiders—but after a week I couldn't care less. It's funny the things you can get used to.

Again Zephyr clears her throat and changes directions. "This way!"

"Where are we going?"

"You'll see."

We walk for what seems like hours, turning every now and then, and I think about how long the walk back will have to be, with beetles below and bats hanging above. I wonder if my fear will suddenly wake up again and send me off into a berserk screaming frenzy.

Finally I see faint shades of light around us, gray on gray. "Okay. So, where are we?" I ask.

"We're home," she says, then pushes open a wooden door to reveal something I never expected. We step into a farmhouse. *Her* house. We are back on the surface again! First, I breathe an incredible sigh of relief that the ordeal is over. Then, it occurs to me how very odd it is that her house opens up into Bracken Cave.

"The cave leads many places," she says, as if reading my mind. "No one knows how deep it goes. My momma says it has roots that grow out the bottom of the world."

I chuckle nervously. "Your momma says a lot of funny things, doesn't she?"

"Would you like to meet her?"

"Not really."

But Zephyr has already gone to a back room—a dark room. I try to think of an excuse to leave, so I can hightail it across the field to my aunt and uncle's house, only a few hundred yards away. But before I can bolt, I hear a voice from the dark room.

"What is it, Zephyr?" The woman's voice is soothing and musical. Her tone seems to coat me like sticky sap, and I can't move. I have to see who belongs to that voice.

"He's here, Momma," says Zephyr. "I brought him, just like you said."

"Come in, Jack," says the woman.

Again, that sense of unsettled excitement fills me—a curiosity that buries my urge to flee. Slowly, planting one foot in front of the other, I step across the threshold of the dark room.

The room is full of paintings—magnificent canvases, all of the same subject: bats escaping into a twilight sky. In the center of the room, sits a woman as pale as an early frost, and with eyelids half closed.

"Come closer, Jack. I don't bite."

She's dressed like some sort of hippy, or earth mother, or something. Her long brown hair is tied into a tight rope-braid so long it coils on the floor around her like a snake. "My name is Gaia, but you can call me Momma, too. Everyone does." The way she moves her head when she speaks, the way her small eyes don't track, makes it clear to me that she's completely-blind. Yet she holds a brush, painting another black-winged portrait.

"But . . . but how . . . ?"

I don't have to ask the question. She knows what I'm about to ask. "You don't need to see what you paint," she says in that musical voice, "if you know every in and out of it."

She wipes the paint from her fingers with a towel and beckons me closer. I step over the coils of her braid, and she touches my face, moving her fingertips over my nose, cheeks, eyes, and neck. It tickles, but it isn't an unpleasant feeling.

"A strong face," she says. "Good bone structure. A fine man he'll grow to be."

"Uh . . . thanks," I say, not sure what else to say when someone compliments you on your bone structure. "Listen, it's probably getting late. I gotta get back for dinner." Although the last thing I have right now is an appetite.

"Not yet," says the strange woman. "There's something you must first see. Zephyr?" Obediently, Zephyr comes to her. "Show him," the woman says, and Zephyr grabs a chair. Standing on it, she reaches up to the rafters, and pulls down a single free-tailed bat, handing it to her mother. "Here you go, Momma."

I shiver as I look up to see a small cluster of bats clinging to the ceiling. *These people live with the bats!* I tell myself. *Their house opens into Bracken Cave. Uncle Weldon was right. They're weird—worse than weird! I have to get out of here!* I feel the panic welling inside me, but instead of making me run, it locks me in place, like a deer on a highway. I can't escape this now. Whatever horror is bearing down on me, I can only watch it happen.

Gaia gently brushes the bat's fur, then stretches out its wing. "This isn't your ordinary free-tailed bat," she says. "This one comes from the new generation. The generation that will emerge at last tonight!" The skin of its wing is as dark as crude oil.

"Touch it, Jack," Gaia tells me. "Touch his wing."

Her voice is gentle, but it resonates in me like a command I can't ignore. Besides, a part of me wants to touch the bat; a part of me that seems to be growing stronger the more time I spend with Gaia and her ugly daughter.

I move my finger toward the wing. It's so dark, I can't see any texture on the thin membrane. What happens next catches me completely by surprise. I reach for the wing, moving my finger closer, and my finger passes right through it. I gasp, and draw back my finger, thinking that I've punctured the membrane of the wing. But when I look at it, I don't see any hole in the wing. That's when I realize that the wing isn't really a membrane at all. It's not flesh, but rather an absence of flesh. A hole in space, the shape of a wing. I reach forward again, and my whole hand passes through into the darkness of the wing, as if I've reached through a small window into another place. I can feel my fingertips getting cold, and I pull my hand back, shivering.

I peer at the bat, trying to grasp what has happened. All I can see in that wing is obsidian darkness.

I slip to my knees, suddenly dizzy. I'm afraid. I'm confused. "I . . . I don't feel so good."

"Sit with me, then," says Gaia, "and I'll tell you a story."

I sit beside her allowing her to comfort me. She starts to coil her heavy braid around me, and I begin to feel like a baby tightly wrapped in a warm blanket. Gaia rocks me gently.

"Forever and forever ago," she begins, "before time had a memory, a flock of bluebirds burst from a hole in the void and spread their mighty wings across the chaos. They filled the space from yonder to yonder, until nothing remained but the blue of their wings, which became the blue sky above a new world of light."

Then she leans close to me; so close I can smell her breath. It smells like the depths of Bracken Cave, but somehow cleaner, as if the acid were washed away, leaving only a rich, organic aroma behind. "It's time you knew, Jack," she says, "that the time of the bluebird sky is over." That's when she touches my chin, and turns my head to look at Zephyr and for the first time, Zephyr reaches up, pulling off her dark sunglasses . . .

. . . to reveal that she has no eyes.

I gasp, but it comes out as a pained wheeze. I look away, not wanting to see, but Gaia gently turns my head back, forcing me to look at her daughter.

There are only faint indentations where Zephyr's eyes should be, covered by smooth skin. No lids, no lashes. No brow.

"It's all right," Zephyr says brightly. "Don't worry, I can still 'see' just fine." Then she opens her mouth and clears her throat, as she's done so many times before . . . only now I realize that she's not clearing her throat at all. She's sending out little sonar clicks, echolocating like a bat.

For a moment—for a brief instant, I come to my senses, to realize the depth of the trouble I'm in. I am bound in the endless coils of a massive braid, looking at a hideous mutant girl.

All at once I hear the sound outside—sheets flapping on a clothesline. I know that sound. It is the bats! Millions of black winged bats taking to the sky.

I struggle to pull myself free from the braids that tie me.

"It's no use," Gaia tells me, "and it's best you don't see. Stay here, Jack, with me and Zephyr."

I don't even answer her. I fight to free myself from the

cocoon of her hair. At last I uncoil myself, and, tripping over the knot of braid, I race out of the dark room and toward the front door.

"No, Jack!" cries Zephyr, but I don't care what she says anymore. I burst out the door to see the twilight sky disappearing behind a flood of obsidian-black wings. I know if I could reach up and touch each of those wings, that my hand would pass through them as well, into darkness. It's as if they are devouring the sky—and soon I see objects falling from up above. Dead birds. *Bluebirds.* They fall like hail, littering the fields around us.

"No!" I cry, "It can't be! This can't happen!"

Zephyr stands in the doorway behind me. She won't come out. Instead she turns her face up, and clicks to the sky. "It's beautiful," she says.

The light around us is fading beneath the great membrane of a million black wings. And soon the bluebird-covered ground begins to speckle with bat droppings, as lightless as the bats themselves. They are like spots of black paint flung at a canvas, obliterating the world beneath it.

"Don't stand there, Jack," says Gaia from the door. "You must come here. You'll be safe here."

I would run to my aunt and uncle's house—but I know I would never make it. I would be buried under a fall of bluebirds and bat droppings. I can't even see their house in the distance anymore. Maybe it's already washed away. I hurry to the doorway, terrified of being struck by black droplets, for fear they might burn right through me. The three of us watch as the sky disappears into darkness. The ground dissolves and sizzles beneath the rain of black.

"What about my parents? What about my aunt and uncle?"

"Everyone you know will be gone," says Gaia with

sympathy and compassion. "When the bats stretch from yonder to yonder, they will be no more. They will fade peacefully with the world of light." She says it as if it is a wonderful thing. I feel sick to my stomach.

"Why won't it take us?" I ask. "Why are we spared?"

"There must always be a seed for the next world," she tells me. "You are young, but time will help you to understand."

And then her words come back to me. *"Good bone structure . . . a fine man he'll grow to be."* She said it as if Zephyr and I would be together for a long, long time. Me and that ugly, ugly girl with no eyes.

"There are only the two of you now," says Gaia. Earth Mother. Mother Earth. "Only the two of you, and me to pave your way."

Outside, the trees and fenceposts, the grass and hills crumble to nothing, dissolved by rivers of black. Gaia closes the door, closing out that world. She comes closer, dragging her endless braid behind her. I back up until I'm against the wall. There's nowhere for me to run. I can't get away, and if I screamed there would be no one to hear me.

Gaia touches my cheek, feeling my tears. "You are in pain," she says to me. " *'If thine eyes offend thee, pluck them out.'* "

Then both her hands shoot to my temples, I feel my head pressed between the vise-grip of her palms. She presses her thumbs against my eyes and I feel a fiery pain. I am about to scream out, but suddenly the pain is gone, replaced by a different feeling . . . a *draining* feeling, as if my sinuses are clearing. Something opens up deep within my mind. Then she takes her fingers away.

I reach up to feel my eyes, and find that they are gone. No blood, no holes—it's as if I never had eyes at all.

There is only a faint indentation in the bone of my face where my eyes should be—but no sockets beneath that, only solid bone. Like Zephyr.

This can't be happening! I tell myself. *You can't erase a person's eyes with the touch of a finger.* Everything before me now is black . . . no, not black . . . *absent.* Not dark, not light, but simply not there. I have no sense of sight whatsoever, or even a memory of what sight was like!

Overwhelmed by it all, I have a sudden, uncontrollable urge to clear my throat, and when I do, it comes out in a series of hollow clicks. Echolocation! In a flash of echoes, everything around me becomes clear. It is more than sight, more than sound, but a sense that is completely new. I am blasted by a wave of incredible perception!

My terror is extinguished like fire drowned in water. I can "see" Zephyr and Gaia, their shapes formed by the echo. Not just their shape, but the density of their flesh, and the exact dimensions of the room around me. I can "see" things not just in front of me, but all around me!

It is Zephyr's face that catches my attention. I step closer to her, and click again. It's amazing—the way the bones and flesh of her face echo back my signal. It's such a pleasing sensation, I want to echolocate her again and again.

"Zephyr!" I say, "you're beautiful," for she truly is. What was hideous to my sense of sight is glorious to this new sense. I don't think I've ever experienced anything so beautiful—so perfect—as the echo of Zephyr's face.

"I'm happy you think so," she says. I can feel the smile on her face from where I stand.

"All is in tune for a new beginning, then." Gaia puts her hands on our shoulders and slowly moves us toward the wooden door at the back of the house.

Was I frightened a few moments ago? Was I mourning the loss of the world I knew? It's as if when Gaia took away my sight, she also took away all the bad feelings, leaving behind only the excitement, and a feverish desire to go forward into this new unknown. Gaia swings open the door to Bracken Cave. I echolocate through the door, and find a breathtaking expanse of caverns, the shape of their echo as pleasing and satisfying as a colorful landscape, although I can't even recall what color is.

It is now that I realize that there is light here—immense radiance all around me. It's not daylight, but the light of spirit, so much easier to see without the burden of eyes.

I "ping" the caverns once more. The echo shows me winding tunnels that stretch to . . . well . . . the bottom of the world.

I want to go down there! I want to explore, to be a part of it, but I sense that something is missing. I raise my hand and feel the empty space beneath my arm. Yes, there is something missing. I turn to Gaia, and she cups her hand gently against my face, knowing what I'm thinking. "Some things must be earned, Jack." Then she lowers my arm to my side. "In time, both you and Zephyr will earn yours. But for now you must go on without them."

Understanding, I take Zephyr's hand. We send our signals ahead of us into the bottomless depths of Bracken Cave; they resound together in perfect harmony beckoning us downward into this new place. This new world.

Sometimes change catches us off guard. We fight it with fear and denial. We run from it, hide from it, until it envelops us, only to leave us wondering what there was to be afraid of. I'm ready for what comes now—whatever it is. And, so, together Zephyr and I race off into the endless labyrinth, holding our arms out wide as we run, hoping that soon, very soon, we will earn our wings.

Where they came from . . .

I often get asked what planet I was on when I wrote a particular story. Well, rest assured, it was good old Mother Earth . . . at least I think it was. In any case, here are sparks of ideas that led to each of the stories in *Mind-Storms*.

Pacific Rim

I'd always been intrigued by paintings I'd seen of ships falling off the edge of the Earth. Recently, I received a brochure in the mail, advertizing the largest cruise ship in the world—truly magnificent to behold—and it occurred to me that the only thing more bizarre than old sailing ships falling off the edge of the Earth, would be a giant cruise ship suffering the same fate . . . but if you think the story is far-fetched, consider the fact that there are actually people living in our modern society who support the idea of a flat Earth! In fact, in the 1930's a guy by the name of Wilbur Glenn Voliva offered $5000 to anyone who could prove that the world was round. The weird thing is, that he never had to pay out a cent. Talk about truth being stranger than fiction.

I of the Storm

It was the windiest night of the year. Papers flew through the air, trash cans rolled down the street. It was as if the wind had a personality, and was having . . . a tantrum. That thought hit me at about one in the morning, and kept me awake until I finally dragged myself out of bed before dawn and began to write this story.

Opabinia

My son had to give a first-grade report on an animal. Of all things, he chose the weird, extinct Opabinia—something I had never heard of. We went on the Internet to do some research, and were dazzled by the amazing history of the Burgess Shale—and that if the creatures of the Cambrian period didn't die off, we might look very different than we do now. . . .

Dawn Terminator

It occurred to me some time ago, that if the Sun were to start pouring lethal radiation out over the world, the people on the dark side of the Earth wouldn't know until the sun rose. And then it occurred to me that there are places where you could escape from sunlight, if you really had to. . . .

Midnight Michelangelo

I can't take full credit for this one. The concept was originally the "brain-child" of writer Terry Black, before I got my "ten-tacles" on it. We developed the story together as a short film script, because sometimes two brains are better than one, and I liked it so much, I decided to write it as a short story.

Ralphy Sherman's Inside Story

Ralphy's rapidly becoming my favorite character. He makes a cameo appearance in just about all of my novels, and this is the second story that he stars in. He is the master of exaggerations, tall tales, and bald-faced lies, which opens quite a few possibilities for stories, because in Ralphy's world, the more improbable an event, the more likely he is to swear it really happened. As to where I got the idea for this particular story, to be honest, I haven't got a clue. Maybe I blocked it out.

He Opens a Window

When I was in high school, I had this thing about painting windows that open up to other worlds. In fact, when I was in college, I painted a few windows-on-other-worlds murals. But the illustrator came up with the cover for this book without knowing any of that. When I saw the cover sketch, it inspired me to come up with a story, and I began to consider who, more than anyone else, might need to escape through such a window. I only wish such a window could exist, and that there were millions of windows like it.

Clothes Make the Man

I am no stranger to luggage troubles. A certain airline, which shall remain nameless, shattered my laptop computer, and at a different time, shredded a brand-new piece of luggage. Have you ever noticed when you travel, that there's always one or two pieces of luggage left going around the carousel that no one claims. Ever wonder who they might belong to? I do.

The Bob Squad

A few years ago, I saw the movie *Angels in the Outfield.* I remember how, in the end, Christopher Lloyd flies practically out of the screen, turns to the audience, and says, "We're always watching." At that moment, a little kid in the theater behind me began to cry, apparently terrified by the thought of Christopher Lloyd standing behind him, watching him twenty-four hours a day for his entire life. I don't know about you, but it would certainly make me feel paranoid!

The Living Place

Lots of stories begin by superimposing several ideas and coming up with something completely different. In my novel *Scorpion Shards,* I toyed with the idea of a star being a living thing. But what if the Earth was a living thing as well? Then, I recalled an episode of *Seinfeld* where the character Kramer shoots a golf ball into the Atlantic, and manages to kill a whale by clogging its blowhole. Then I began to think about how when someone in your family is dying, it's as if your whole world is dying with them. When you toss those ideas together you get an Earth that's dying because someone's clogged its blowhole—which could be quite silly, but I chose not to go that way. Instead, I wanted to turn it into a metaphor for our own emotions and attitudes toward life and death, when someone in our family has a life-threatening illness.

Ralphy Sherman's Patty Melt on Rye

A friend of mine who used to live in Hawaii challenged me to come up with a story that incorporated the Hawaiian gods. When I began to read up on them, I found the volcano goddess Pele to be the most interesting. My kids and I love lava lamps—we have four of them, a red one, a green one, a blue one, and one that's shaped like an alien's head. Well, I put two and two together, decided to turn Pele into a giant lava lamp—and who better to do it than my favorite recurring character, Ralphy Sherman?

Open House

After watching my own children terrorize dolls and action figures as sweet, innocent toddlers, I began to wonder what life must be like for the dolls themselves. Limbs twisted and chewed, hair mangled, tormented toys forced to have tea parties and play house every day of their lives. If they were alive, they'd think we were monsters! I wanted to tell a story of Ken and Barbie's escape to freedom from the clutches of a little girl. I had considered having them really escape, and find a happy life of plastic bliss . . . but then I figured, naah, they're Ken and Barbie: Torch 'em!

Mail Merge

While I was writing for the *Animorphs* TV show, I developed an online friendship with a number of kids who were *Animorphs* fans. I occasionally joined them in a chat room. There were two kids in particular whose messages were so eerily similar, people began to believe they were the same person. Then I thought—what if they began as two people, but were merged into one by the end of the story? Writing a chat room story was lots of fun, and anyone who's ever been in a chat room probably knows people like each of the chatters in the story.

The Peter Pan Solution

All of my short story collections feature new stories, but for once I decided to take a little trip back in time. *The Pe-*

ter Pan Solution was a story I wrote when I was seven-teen, and although I rewrote it for this collection, I tried to keep its style true to its original draft. I remember sending it off to *Omni* magazine, and I actually got a personalized rejection letter—and they never give out personalized rejection letters to snot-nosed high-school students, so I figured I might actually have a future as a writer. It seems my story sensibilities haven't changed all that much since I was in high school. That's even scarier than the story.

The Body Electric

I was talking to my kids one day, explaining to them all of the things that Thomas Edison invented. The lightbulb, motion pictures, recorded sound—in fact, most of our modern technology can be traced back to either Edison or Bell. It's almost as if the two men were ahead of their time. When I realized the story I wanted to tell, I knew I had to tell it as a mystery in a second-person voice. The character is the reader, slowly uncovering the truth of their own identity, and thus their destiny. Different readers will figure it out at different places in the story, and that's part of the fun!

Bad Fortune at Wong Lee's

I have cousins like the Greenblatts, who are connoisseurs of Chinese food. When I was a kid, we used to let them order for us when we went out to our favorite Chinese restaurant, Richard Yee's. The reading of the fortune cookies was always like some mysterious sacred ritual. When you think about it, fortune cookies in and of themselves are rather absurd, surreal things, aren't they? The secrets of life, wrapped in a pastry shell. To be honest, I came up with the last line, and final image of this story first, and I liked the ending so much, I knew I had to come up with a story that got me there!

Obsidian Sky

There's a famous wood-cut by the artist M. C. Escher—a metamorphosis of a flock of white birds in a black sky into a flock of black birds in a white sky. I've always kind of felt that my stories are like literary Escher pictures. This story began at a Cub Scout meeting, where the den leader brought around a bat for all the kids to look at. I was as fascinated as my kids, and knew I wanted to write a story about bats. Then, a few weeks later, I chanced upon some information on Bracken Cave on the Internet while searching for subterran